Story Overview

Christina has made her own way for as long as she can remember and juggled men for even longer. The love 'em and leave 'em type, she finally said goodbye to Virginia, moved to Maine, and made a fresh start. Or so she thought until her best friends were pulled back in time. Better yet, when a stubborn Claddagh ring on her finger declares she can run but can't hide. Not when it comes to men from medieval Scotland.

First-in-command of MacLomain Castle, Graham MacLomain has more secrets than most and wants nothing to do with a lass from the future. Especially not one who is promised to King Robert the Bruce. Yet the moment he makes contact with Christina before she travels back in time, he is drawn to her. Soon enough, despite his own commitments and a life that can never include her, he's eager to be by her side.

Friends from the start, Graham and Christina devise a plan to pretend true love found them. Now they can discreetly dodge destiny and follow their own paths. The only problem? Destiny is unavoidable. Passion sparks and love ignites. Days before the Battle of Bannockburn, they'll have to face the truth and make a heartbreaking choice. Give in to how they truly feel and destroy all those they care about or turn away, and save Scotland from ultimate ruin.

~Promised to a Highland Laird~

Series Overview

The term *a new beginning* brings to mind many things. Hope and opportunity. A fresh start. For the MacLomains and the rest of Scotland, the year twelve ninety-six meant anything but. Instead, it marked the beginning of a new and oppressed era fraught with two long wars with England. This particular series revolves around the First War of Scottish Independence that took place from twelve ninety-six to thirteen twenty-eight.

Heroes are often lost to time and folklore, especially when magic is involved. *The MacLomain Series: A New Beginning* shares those mystical tales. Stories about Scottish lairds that came to the aid of Sir William Wallace and King Robert the Bruce. Brave warriors and their lasses who single handedly changed the face of history…or so the story goes.

~Promised to a Highland Laird~

Promised to a Highland Laird

The MacLomain Series
A New Beginning
Book Three
By
Sky Purington

~Promised to a Highland Laird~

Edited by *Cathy McElhaney*
Cover Art by *Tara West*

Published in the United States of America

~Promised to a Highland Laird~

Pronunciations

By popular demand, I'll now be including a glossary of pronunciations for Scottish and Viking names and places that run a little trickier to enunciate. The following names are characters you'll run across in this particular book.

Aðísla (*ah*-ue-ee-slah)
Rona (rohn-*ah*)
Fionn Mac Cumhaill (ˈfɪn məˈkul)
Iosbail (ees-*uh*-bel)
Balquhidderock (bælkˈhwɪdərˈrock)

If you come across other names or places you'd like to see included when reading my books, shoot me an email because every tale's pronunciation glossary is a work in progress. I love to hear from readers and consider your feedback valuable. Thanks so much for reading!

Email me anytime at Sky@SkyPurington.com or message me on Facebook.

Dedication

For Deb and Joy.

Virginian women don't come any better than you.

Thanks for all the good times and for making my transition to the South an unforgettable experience!

Love you both.
xoxo

Acknowledgements

A little extra 'Thank you' to Noah as well. Your Southern input kept me chuckling.

Introduction

Still holding down the fort in New Hampshire, Christina is near her wit's end. Most of her friends have traveled back in time, and now it seems she might be next. How else can it be when she not only dreams about Robert the Bruce but he dreams of her too? A fact she learns when she makes contact with Lindsay at Mystery Hill via some sort of time flux. If that isn't enough, she ends up walking straight through a MacLomain Scotsman that makes her head spin in more ways than one. Though they vanished and she remains in the twenty-first century, she's bracing for a whole lot of trouble. And so the story goes…

Chapter One

North Salem, New Hampshire
Autumn 2017

SHE SHOULD JUST move back to Virginia. Life would be *so* much simpler.

Or would it?

Because, Lord above, life had *never* been all that simple down south. But this? What she had been experiencing since Milly vanished? This was just pure batshit crazy.

Christina propped her hip against the side of the barn, not sure which way she wanted to go. Certainly not back into the woods or into the house. Back the way she had come, most specifically, Mystery Hill and what she discovered there, was a bit too much for anyone. And the house? Well, that either had Jim and Blair playing their games or Jessie being a royal pain in the butt.

"Ye look as thrilled to be here as me, lass."

She about jumped out of her skin when a woman with long flaming red hair appeared at the barn door.

Christina frowned. "Who the *heck* are you?"

"Rona MacLomain," she responded as she eyed Christina. "Daughter of Niall and Nicole MacLomain." She perked her brows as though her next words would make it that much clearer. "Sister to *Graham* MacLomain."

"Graham?" Christina shook her head, not overly daunted that a strange woman had appeared out of nowhere dressed in medieval clothing. "You say that like it's supposed to ring some bells, but it doesn't, sweetheart."

Yet she had a feeling where Rona might be going with this, so Christina kept talking. "You've been sent here from medieval Scotland, haven't you?" Oh yeah, she was becoming damn good at taking all of this in stride. "And my bet is, though you look nothing like him, you're talking about the man I just ran into at Mystery Hill."

The larger issue, among many, was that she literally ran *through* him not *into* him, which was half the reason for her fed-up attitude right now. Then there was the astounding news that Milly had traveled back in time and hooked up with some highlander. If that wasn't enough, one of his relatives showed up here a few days ago. Better yet, appeared out of thin air with Jim.

Then let's not forget her dream or what just happened this morning. First, seeing Lindsay in a place that was *clearly* not the stone dwellings at Mystery Hill before sort of merging with a man then shooting out the other side of him.

Way too much. All of it.

Hence her debate about heading south.

"Aye, 'twas my brother ye ran into," Rona said. "And if I heard correctly, ye also ran into Lindsay, and she caught ye up on what was happening."

Right. Lindsay. *Another* friend who had apparently traveled back in time.

"And how is Linds since the last time we spoke?" Christina asked, rather nonplussed about all this though she should be freaking out. "Did she find her one true love like Milly did?"

Say no.

Say this was all some sort of mistake and the ring Christina now wore was part of an elaborate hoax. That the Claddagh ring that had mysteriously appeared on her finger a few days ago was one big joke.

"Aye, Lindsay *did* find her true love," Rona conceded, her eyes never leaving Christina. "My best friend and cousin, Laird Conall Hamilton."

Well, *shit*.

If Lindsay, who swore off men years ago, had hooked up with a man, then that was that.

It wasn't looking good for Christina.

She sighed and shook her head. About the last thing she needed was for any of this to be true but pretty much figured it must be at this point. Now she just had to continue remaining calm like she had all along. More than that? She needed to make sense of her dream.

"*So.*" She tried to sound like she wasn't all that concerned. "Lindsay and Milly have met both William Wallace *and* Robert the Bruce?"

"They have."

Rona kept eying Christina, and it was starting to get on her last nerve. About to say as much, she bit her tongue when Blair appeared at the front door of the house, shaded her eyes from the sun and called out, "Bloody hell, is that ye, Rona?"

"Aye." Rona grinned and headed in her direction. "'Tis good to see ye, Cousin."

Right on time and riding Blair's wake, Jim appeared at the door as Rona and Blair embraced. Christina met his eyes and shook her head before she headed into the barn, content to let him deal with yet another time-traveler.

She should have known better though. The minute she settled in a chair toward the back, ready to pretend to hide in a good book, he joined her. Quiet the whole time, he plunked down on a stool and eyed her in that annoying way he'd adopted over the last few days.

"What?" She frowned and shook her head. "I know what Rona's here for, and I don't need a pep talk."

As it turned out, Jim had already traveled back in time with Milly. That, of course, was where he met Adlin's cousin, Blair. Adlin, naturally, was the *wizard* Milly was in love with now. So in love, she hadn't returned.

"It's not like you to hide away in a corner when yet another interesting character shows up." Jim eyed her e-reader and shook his head. "Not the best prop of avoidance you've ever used either." The corner of his mouth shot up in amusement. "But I suppose Blair and Rona don't know that, eh?"

"That I don't like to read?" She winked. "Nope."

"We both know you like to read." He gestured at her device. "Just not on that thing."

She shrugged, not much in the mood to talk about her reading preferences when there were bigger fish to fry. "So we know why

I'm hiding out here." There was no stopping her grin. "Question is why are *you* hiding?"

Jim didn't bother denying it but leaned back against the stall, crossed his long legs out in front of him and scowled in the direction of the house. "That woman drives me crazy."

That woman being Blair.

Christina shook her head and snorted. "Yeah, in more ways than one."

Jim didn't quite meet her eyes. "Do you blame me?"

"Seeing how I'm not into women, I can't really comment." She rolled her eyes. "One thing's for sure though, you two need to decide if you're in love or hate because listening to you guys is gettin' old fast, honey."

Jim was Milly's ex and best friend and had from time to time crushed on Lindsay and Christina. What sparked between him and Blair, however, was another whole brand of something.

Something annoying mostly.

"I'm just not used to dealing with medieval women," he muttered. "Especially one like her."

"You mean one that knows she can kick a man's butt anytime she pleases?" Christina gave him a pointed look. "Or one who lost her brother and is courageous enough to want to avenge his death?"

Christina might not entirely know what to make of Blair, but she knew one thing. She was her kind of woman.

Jim gave her a look that said all she needed to know.

"Ah, so you weren't referring to any of those things. No, I'd say you were getting at the endless push and pull between you." She shook her head. "Why don't you just sleep together and get it over with already? It'd make life easier for everyone in the immediate vicinity." Her brows shot up. "Namely *me*."

"We're not that bad," he argued.

"You are and need to figure things out one way or another." She set aside her tablet and stood. "Meanwhile, I better get back to watching Jessie seeing how you're in here."

"Blair won't let her go anywhere." He stood and caught her elbow before she got too far. "Hey, what happened this morning anyway?"

Following his example, she didn't quite meet his eyes. "Not sure what you mean."

"The hell you don't." He sighed and tugged at her arm a little until she looked at him. "I've never seen you act so strangely. Out of it. Like you'd seen a ghost or I don't know...something. What happened?" His eyes narrowed. "You've been pretty laid back through everything that's been going on, but you weren't this morning. Care to share?"

"My guess is she was dreaming of a famous Scottish king," Rona said as she leaned against the entrance to the barn yet again, this time facing inward as she raised a brow at Christina. "Or am I wrong?"

Though by now it shouldn't seem bizarre that a perfect stranger knew what she had just shared with Lindsay at Mystery Hill, it was. She might be trying to convince herself otherwise, but there was no getting used to what was happening around here. It was something out of anyone's wildest imagination. Even so, she supposed she better deal with things sooner rather than later.

So she brushed by Rona, saying over her shoulder, "C'mon then, let's go inside, have a drink and talk about why you're really here."

Christina winked at Blair in passing. The Scotswoman nodded as she leaned against the old oak tree out front sharpening a dagger, likely to get a rise out of Jim. He had been telling her since she arrived she didn't need weapons, but she kept them visible and sharp at all times regardless.

As usual, Jessie was sitting in the living room with a small, ancient looking book in her hand as she stared at the fire. A fire that Christina had kept going for nearly five days now. Since the night she, Milly, Lindsay, and Jessie had come together here to celebrate Milly's new home.

A house, it seemed, that had been with Milly for several lifetimes.

"Hey there, sweet pea," she said softly, plastering on her warmest smile as she crouched in front of Jessie. "You need anything? Tea? Something to munch on?"

"No, I'm fine." As always, Jessie's face remained emotion free as her eyes met Christina's. "You heard from Lindsay, didn't you?"

An herbalist recluse from upstate Maine, Jessie was a recently declared empath and one of the strangest people she had ever met. Yet like Christina, she had Broun heritage, and that was the tie that had brought them together online a few years ago. A forum, as it happened, that was created by Cassie, a woman who had already traveled back in time to medieval Scotland and found her one true MacLomain love. Blair, as she recently discovered, was their daughter.

"I *did* hear from Lindsay," Christina acknowledged as she squeezed Jessie's hand. She was more worried about her friend than she would admit. "How'd you know that, honey?"

Jessie gave her the same look she always did. One that hinted at a far more rational mind than she typically displayed. No offense to her but she was remarkably different from most people with her distant nature and voodoo-like way of living.

"My gifts might be quite different than yours," Jessie said softly, her eyes all-knowing as they held Christina's. "But that doesn't mean I don't know when things are happening to you." She squeezed her hand right back. "Intense things that are overwhelming you."

"Not sure what you're talking about," Christina began before Jessie cut her off.

"I'm talking about you dreaming about Robert the Bruce." She cocked her head. "Then running into a man that made your head spin."

That's pretty much how it went too.

Christina hid behind a warm chuckle and shook her head. "You're reading too much into it."

"No," Jessie said calmly. "As you well know, I'm a witch just like you and can see things. Especially things that affect my closest friends."

Christina could deny it all she wanted but why bother? She had known for a long time she was different. When she came here, and a label was finally put on it, she didn't argue. There were worse things to be called in life.

"I'm gonna make you some fresh tea then whip up some comfort food." Christina patted Jessie's hand. "How's that sound?"

She kissed her cheek and headed for the kitchen, pretending like she didn't hear Jessie say, "It sounds like you're avoiding one too many men."

Christina loved Jessie to death, but she would do just about anything to have Milly and Lindsay here right now. They would make sense of everything going on in a way that didn't set her on edge. Yet she suspected if her friends were here, they would be just as blunt. Especially in light of everything happening. Trying to keep that in mind, she set to doing what she did best in times of crisis.

Cooked.

It helped clear her mind.

So she clipped up her hair, washed her hands, and put a cute frilly apron on that she'd dug out of one of Milly's moving boxes. Then she got busy. First off, she pulled up Pandora on her cell and made sure she labored in style to some upbeat music. That meant anything that'd make her hips swing. Next, she poured herself a glass of chilled white wine, be damned the early hour.

Humming along with the music, she pulled spices out of the cabinet, meats, and vegetables out of the refrigerator and put water on to boil. Though slightly frustrated that Rona hadn't followed her in when they had a lot to talk about, she figured it was for the best. At least right now.

She seared stew meat and added it to a crock pot before she started on gravy. Once that was finished, she set it aside and started scrubbing potatoes, all the while mulling over what she had dreamt about last night.

A man.

One heck of a man for that matter.

He called himself Robert the Bruce and shockingly enough, claimed to be promised to her. Or she was promised to him. She couldn't quite remember.

What she *did* recall were his good looks.

Not for the first time, it hit her who he actually *was*. A famous Scottish king from the distant past. A man who seemed to be reaching across the centuries trying to find her. Trying to be with her. She shook her head as she began cutting potatoes a few minutes later. The connection between them had felt so strong. So unavoidable. As if they were always meant to be together and they both knew it.

"You're out of your mind, Christina," she muttered as she set aside the potatoes and started washing carrots. It was obviously just a dream. It *had* to be. It better be. What a dream though. It was so intense that she shot up in bed hours before the sun came up and started researching Robert the Bruce online.

Sure, she had watched the movie *Braveheart* because she loved all things Scottish, but beyond that, she hadn't done nearly as much research about the country as Milly. They all descended from the Scottish Brouns, and that was enough for her.

"Brouns that are meant for medieval MacLomains," she muttered. "Who knew?" She perked her brows at nobody and chopped away. "No MacLomains for me, though." She shook her head. "Nope, I'm too damn busy dreaming about famous Scottish kings I couldn't even *imagine* traveling back in time and meeting." She added the carrots to the potatoes. "But then stranger things have happened. I mean what southern girl in her right mind resorts to making homemade New England beef stew this often?"

She took a few sips of wine and swung her hips as she cut up some onions, tossed all the veggies in with the meat then added the gravy and turned the pot on high. As far as she could see out the window, Blair and Rona had vanished. Good, she supposed. At least for the moment.

She might need answers from Rona, but the truth was she wasn't all that eager to answer any questions the Scotswoman might have for her. Namely, about her brother.

"Graham," she whispered, still dancing as she added a few extra spices to the stew before she covered it. "What were you doing there?"

She had been asking herself that since her run earlier. A run she barely recalled setting out on. But then, like Jim had said, she was pretty out of it. Nevertheless, her dazed sprint brought her to Mystery Hill, Salem's little Stonehenge through the woods. That's where she found, of all people, Lindsay. Not Lindsay in the common sense but more a ghost of her. Bizarrely unfazed by it all, they chatted for a while, and Lindsay caught her up on everything. A truly wild tale from start to finish.

A shiver went through her as she recalled what happened next.

Not a bad shiver by any means. More the sort of shiver a woman might have when remembering a pleasurable sensation. An unanticipated but very welcome intimacy. Christina stared out the window as she recalled darting after Lindsay only to pass right through someone else.

"Now your sister's here," she muttered, talking to the memory of that *someone else* as she made Jessie's tea. "I can't help but find that curious, Graham."

Though she only caught a glimpse of him, he was hard to forget. Those super dark, thickly lashed eyes, chiseled cheekbones, and strong jaw. That rich, black hair, five o'clock shadow, and tanned skin. He had the sort of swarthy good looks that must make women trip over themselves to get near him.

She was so lost in thought about not only his utter hotness but how it felt to pass through him that she was oblivious to anything else. That is until she turned around for a spoon and ran smack into a hard body. For a split second, she thought she was still in her own head as her eyes crawled upward and landed on the very face she was just thinking about.

"My sister *is* here," he rumbled, his brogue thick as hell as he responded to her private mutterings. "But I dinnae think ye find it all that curious, Christina."

"Hot *damn*," she whispered, staggering back a few steps until she bumped into the countertop. "Is it happening again?" Unable to drag her eyes from his handsome face, she patted herself to see if she was really here. "Are we doing that crossover thing again?"

"Nay," he murmured, his voice so deep and sexy she felt it down to places that had been off limits to men for a while. "I am really here, lass. Like my sister, I've traveled through time to find ye."

"Ye," she whispered, so caught up in his wicked eyes that she sounded like a dumbass. "Like me?"

"Aye." He nodded. "Ye."

"So not me but you," she whispered.

"Nay, *ye*." The corner of his mouth curled up, and a dimple appeared on his cheek. "Not me."

Now it was her turn to grin. "I mean *you* when you say *ye*."

"Laughter is not something I embrace," Jessie said softly. "But if I did it would happen now listening to you two."

Startled that her friend had actually left that chair, Christina finally managed to drag her eyes from Graham to look at Jessie. "Hey there, sweetie." She blinked several times, trying to get her thoughts straight. "Your tea's almost ready."

Jessie nodded, her eyes never leaving Graham.

He, in turn, was clearly uncomfortable beneath her intense appraisal. Unlike any woman in her right mind, Jessie wasn't checking him out but almost studying him.

So Christina made introductions to try to break the ice then set the tea on the counter in front of Jessie, all the while overly aware of Graham. "There ya go, honey. Can I get you something else? Hungry?"

"No." Jessie's eyes never left Graham. "He's coming, isn't he?"

Graham's brows edged together. "Who, lass?"

"Tell him not to come." Jessie shook her head. "He's not welcome here."

Christina frowned, baffled more than usual by Jessie's behavior. "*Who's* not welcome here?"

"Everyone knows very well who," Jessie replied softly. "The dragon." Her eyes narrowed on Graham. "You should go."

"Jessie," Christina exclaimed, apologizing to Graham before she ushered her friend out of the kitchen and repositioned her in front of the fire. She crouched in front of her and tilted her head in question. "What's going on? Were you talking about his cousin Bryce? Because we both know he's a dragon shifter."

"But is he the only one?" Her eyes met Christina's, her tone not quite right. "Or is another coming that will destroy all hope for Scotland's history? More so, destroy all hope of any of us surviving?"

Chapter Two

H E SHOULD HAVE stayed in medieval Scotland. Life would be so much simpler.

Or would it?

Since the moment Conall and Lindsay defeated their warlock, and the skirmishes at Earnside and Happrew happened as they should, Graham had been braced for the inevitable. Either he or his cousin Bryce was up next.

That meant they were destined for a lass from the future.

Most specifically, a Broun.

Though he had played along thus far when first Milly traveled back in time then Lindsay, he knew time was running out. Eyes were narrowing on him, curious to see what he would do next considering he had already made contact with Christina. Though he had done his best to navigate around things, who knew a lass would end up running straight through him?

A lass he figured for sure he would be able to get out of his mind.

A lass he could never be with.

Even so, Christina was a Broun. So she *was* meant for one of the MacLomain men, and he needed to figure out which one. Therefore, when Uncle Grant asked Rona to go to the future to help Blair keep an eye on things, he discreetly followed. Had he not, Bryce would have come and who knew what that might have meant for any innocent lass here.

After all, dragons were unpredictable.

Or so he told himself as he watched Christina interact with first Rona then Jim. When she headed inside, he made sure Rona and Blair kept Jim busy so he could finally meet her on his own terms.

What he didn't expect as he used his magic to enter the house undetected and bypassed the lass sitting in front of the fire was to find Christina such as she was.

The moment he stood at the threshold of the kitchen and laid eyes on her, all his magic fizzled away. Her back was to him, and she was clearly enjoying herself. He couldn't stop a small smile as he watched her dance. Her shoulders bobbed,, and her hips swayed as she cut vegetables. If that wasn't entertaining enough, she hummed to music in between endless mutterings.

There was no way to know how long he stood there mesmerized. It was clear she was a happy spirit like him, and she wasn't about to let all this heavy true love connection stuff get her down.

More confident by the moment that she was the lass for him because she was surely too open-minded to commit, he continued enjoying Christina. Her clipped-up sun streaked light brown hair glowed in the sunlight streaming through the window, and she was taller than most lasses. His eyes trailed down her slim back to her tight waist right down to an arse that shot blood straight to his cock.

Bloody hell she was in good shape, wasn't she?

When her mutters started to address him directly—or her prior meeting with him—he knew he should say something. But he was too caught up in her voice, her movements, and most certainly how good she looked from this angle. He had never been more tempted to touch a lass. To wrap his hands around her small waist, bend her forward as she kept swaying, and see what came of it. Because he didn't doubt it would be exceptionally rewarding.

"Now your sister's here," she muttered. "I can't help but find that curious, Graham."

She was still talking to herself.

Yet he found himself responding after she spun and ran right into him.

"My sister *is* here," he rumbled. "But I dinnae think ye find it all that curious, Christina."

In that singular moment, before she stumbled back against the counter, he realized his well-laid plans might not go as smoothly as he hoped. Not when their eyes locked for the first time beyond that ethereal connection they had made before.

He had never seen such a beautiful face or eyes so fetching. Pale smoky green and shimmering, they reminded him of fog curling off the morning loch as sunlight danced over it. She had luminous sun kissed skin that almost seemed to glow. Funny, how everything about her reminded him of the sun. Its warmth and vitality. Because she certainly had plenty of that with her well-toned shapely body

Once they began speaking, he knew he might be in even more trouble. She had a sultry drawl that made him want to keep listening. Even better? It seemed she had a sense of humor or so said their conversation about 'you's' and 'ye's.'

Now she was in the other room seeing to the wee lass named Jessie. A lovely little thing that clearly had no use for men or even dragons. A mythical beastie she seemed all too familiar with. He listened to their conversation with his superior hearing, sure to look distracted when Christina returned.

"Sorry about that," she murmured as she gestured at the door and offered him a charming smile. "Care to take it outside, handsome?"

"Aye." He couldn't help a small grin. There might be no hope for the two of them, but he liked her anyway.

Fortunately, his sister and cousin were still off poking around at the Stonehenge with Jim, so there were no distractions as he followed Christina outside. She tossed him a smile over her shoulder and headed down the drive. "C'mon, this way. Nobody except Jessie ever seems to wanna head out of this place, so we should find some privacy in this direction."

"Ye arenae afraid to go off alone with me?" he asked. "A man ye just met?"

"Not in the least." She eyed him over her shoulder again. "Should I be?"

"Nay." He smiled. "Not at all, lass."

Graham was just fine with privacy if it meant he could continue to admire her. It was only a matter of time before Bryce arrived and he hoped to get to know her a little bit better first. He wasn't all that surprised to see she wore a Claddagh ring to match Milly's and Lindsay's. The gem at the center of its hand held heart was clear whereas it would eventually shine the eye color of her one true love.

That is if an evil warlock didn't get in the way first.

27

He frowned as he joined Christina and watched her out of the corner of his eye. He had known her mere minutes, and already the idea of evil going anywhere near her made his insides twist.

"You look about as happy now as your sister did when I first met her," she commented as they walked. "How come? Because scowlin' doesn't seem natural to you, sweetheart." Her eyes narrowed as she considered him. "Not to say it doesn't hold a certain appeal in a bad boy sort of way."

He liked that she was straightforward and said what she was thinking.

Though he had far more important things to discuss with her, he found himself saying, "So ye like bad boys then?"

A sly grin curled her lips. "I'm surprised you know what that means."

"I have a mother and aunts from the twenty-first century," he reminded, trying to keep his eyes off her sinfully long legs. He wished more lasses from his time dressed like her. What sort of trousers were those anyway? They didn't leave much to the imagination. Not that he was complaining.

"I've had a bad habit of going for the wrong kind of man in the past," Christina continued, well aware he was discreetly admiring her based on the knowing look she shot him. "Or maybe it's the other way around. Not quite sure."

Now *that* got his attention. "So ye were a bad girl?" He couldn't stop a wide smile. "Tell me more."

"Me? Bad?" The corner of her lips hitched, and she winked. "Naw." Then she shrugged. "What I meant was I never stuck around long because men always end up showing signs."

Enthralled, he cocked his head. "Signs?"

"Yeah, signs that they can't handle me," she muttered, then frowned and shook her head as they continued walking. Before he had a chance to ask her what she meant by that, she flashed a smile at him. "Sorry, forget I said that, okay?"

Christina might be smiling, but he recognized the wary glint in her eyes. She had said more than intended. She had secrets, and he well understood that. So he changed the subject.

"What do ye know about everything that's happening in my era, lass?" he asked.

"I've been filled in on a lot of it." She shrugged, clearly relieved they had moved on. "I think the bigger question is how well I actually *understand* it." Her eyes slid his way. "Blair and Jim shared a lot then Lindsay caught me up on what's happened in medieval Scotland since then, but I'll be honest..." Her voice dropped an octave. "It's a whole lotta crazy, and I'm having trouble wrapping my mind around it."

"Aye." He nodded, charmed by her odd accent and the way she phrased things. "I cannae imagine what everything must seem like from yer viewpoint."

"Scary as shit," she said bluntly before muttering something under her breath. "But I'm doing my best to take it in stride."

"What was that?" he asked. "I didnae quite catch what ye said in between."

"What?" She frowned in confusion before she realized what he meant. "Oh." She chuckled. "Old habit. I tend to apologize to my granny when I swear. She wouldn't like it. Bit of a Bible thumper, that one."

He nodded in understanding before resuming their original conversation. "'Tis good that you're taking everything that's happening in stride. I'm glad to hear it." He eyed their surroundings. The riot of colors and the beauty of the forest lining the dirt road they walked along. "Yer not from around here, are ye?"

"Nope." She sighed and met his eyes again. "Do me a favor?"

"Anything." And he meant it.

"Don't dance around information you already have to get my take on it," she said. "Because my bet is before you arrived you already knew I was from the South and moved up here less than a year ago."

"I *did* know that," he conceded. "And yer right, I *did* want yer take on it. I wanted to better understand ye and mayhap yer life." He gave her the sort of mischievous grin that made most lasses swoon. "Can ye blame me for doing my research?"

"No, I suppose not," she replied, a small smile hovering on her lips. "Just so long as we're honest with each other from here on out." Her brows shot up with curiosity. "Can you do that, Graham? Can we skip all the BS I know we're muddling through with the MacLomain, Broun connection and save-Scotland's-history thing and just be honest with each other? Because I sure would like one person in all this that tells it to me straight." She shrugged. "If something's on your mind just say it, don't dance around it."

He couldn't stop a smile if he tried. Where had she been all his life? Clearly not in medieval Scotland.

"Aye, lass." He nodded and kept smiling. "I would verra much like us to be honest with each other."

"So would I." Her eyes lingered on his for a moment, her smile just as wide as she nodded then looked ahead again. "Good, I'm glad we got all that awkward stuff out of the way."

Graham nodded and kept grinning. About the last thing he expected to find when he traveled to the future was a lass like Christina. It almost seemed too good to be true. She was most certainly the one that *should* be meant for him, and he said as much. "So will ye travel back in time with me, lass?" He gestured at the ring. "Will ye agree to be mine so we can ignite the gem's magic, and defeat our warlock?"

Christina stopped short, a hint of amusement in her narrowed eyes. "Are you tryin' to skip all the fun stuff to get to the boring stuff?"

"The fun stuff to get to the boring stuff?" More confused by the moment, he cocked his head. "Shouldn't it be skip the fun stuff to get to the better stuff?"

"Not in my experience." She chuckled, following his meaning. "Though I'll say up front I'm happy that it has been for you." That same smirk still hovered on her lips. "So there's been nothing but flirting, fun, happiness and then great sex with all your women, huh?"

Maybe not now but most certainly at one time. So he kept being honest.

"Aye." He winked. "*Verra* good sex."

"Hmm." She twisted her lips and eyed him up and down with appreciation again. "I really *do* get it."

They met each other's smiles, not a bit of discomfort between them as they discussed things that would be entirely inappropriate with any lass from his time. More than that, anything he would ever talk so casually about with a lass he just met.

"So back to fun stuff not becoming better stuff betwixt us as we move forward together and try to save my country." He considered her. "Are ye up for it, lass?"

She seemed to contemplate it as she continued eying him. "So let me get this straight. You want to skip all the love and sex and see if we can get out of this ring-binding thing while we pretend to be together?"

"More the pity on the sex part but aye," he said. "What about ye? Do ye want to move forward with me and take control of our own destiny rather than have anyone or," he glanced at her ring, "*anything* dictate it for us?"

She crossed her arms over her ample enough chest and tapped her foot as she thought about it. "Y'know what, Graham, I reckon I do." She shook her head. "But can it be done? Can we be together without actually *being* together?"

"I think 'tis best that we give it a try." He nodded, more sure of this quickly hatched plan by the moment. "Just as long as ye realize we cannae truly be together."

"That sounds doable." Yet he saw the curiosity in her eyes. "So what gives? Are you in love with someone your kin has forbidden?" Her eyes rounded in intrigue. "Secretly married?"

"Is it so important to know?" He remained perfectly honest with her. "Because I would rather not share quite yet." Graham issued his most charming smile. "Right now, 'twould be best if, by the time we return to the house, we could say we're smitten and desire one another." He shook his head. "And no one else."

Christina's full, perfectly shaped lips twisted as she considered his offer. "What'll happen if we don't?" Her foot tapped a little faster. "Is Bryce gonna want me?" She cocked her head. "And is he a real dragon?"

"Half dragon," he said, sure to sound grave. "But aye, the MacLeod can easily shift into a ferocious beastie." He shook his head. "One that is frightening to behold."

A little smirk returned to her lips as she listened to him. "You're exaggerating, aren't you?"

"Nay." His brows flew up. "I've seen my cousin embrace his dragon, quite recently in fact, and 'twas terrifying."

Her smile didn't budge, and her bonnie eyes never wavered from his. "You're determined to play this up I see." She stepped a bit closer, her tone that of a co-conspirator as she looked right then left before she met his eyes again. "All right, I'm game." She pointed between them. "You and me. How do we go about it without everyone knowing we're trying to trick 'em?" She held up her hand between them and eyed the ring. "And what about this?"

"I think, for starters, we let my cousins see how intense the attraction is betwixt us already." He nodded. While he had intended to spend more time getting to know her, it really wasn't necessary now. She was on board with deceiving everyone, and that's *exactly* what he needed.

"Wow, glad to see you're decisive," she commented, but he could tell she approved. "Just wondering…won't your kin see right through it? Especially your sister?"

"Nay, they havenae been around me enough to know better," he provided.

"Ah." She gave him a knowing look. "So you really *are* off with lots of women." Her look turned sly. "Or one extra special top secret mystery gal."

"I didnae say that," he denied.

"You didn't have to," she said with approval, eying him over again. "Like I said, it makes sense."

He smiled. "Thank ye."

"You're welcome."

"Yer quite bonnie yerself," he said, comfortable with how frank they were with each other.

She grinned, and said, "Hell if I don't know it," before she promptly apologized to her granny for cursing.

"So we are in agreement then?" he said, still dishing out his most charming smile though he knew he didn't have to. "We were smitten the moment we met, and refuse to be with anyone else."

"That sounds about right." She held out her hand. "Walk back with me authentic-like then?"

"'Twould be my pleasure." He slipped his hand into hers, caught off guard by how soft it felt. "What will we say when we get back? We've only known each other for a verra short time."

"Isn't that all it takes?" Christina gave him a pointed look as she wiggled her ring finger. "From what I've learned, this thing's supposed to declare us together so why don't we let it?"

Intrigued, he murmured, "Go on."

"Well, who says we don't see this gem matching your eyes from the get go?" She peered at it mockingly and squinted. "Not sure what

32

you see, but it's a rich dark brown as far as I can tell." She grinned at him. "The exact same shade as your eyes, I'd say."

Something about her smiling at him made it impossible to do anything but smile in return.

"Aye." He nodded, peering at it. "'Tis verra much the shade of my eyes."

She chuckled and shook her head. "I thought meeting you and facing this whole MacLomain, Broun thing was gonna be a lot harder," she said. "And a whole lot scarier." Relief lit her eyes. "But it's not." Her smile only grew warmer as their eyes held. "Thanks for that, Graham. For making this feel so normal."

"Aye, my thanks to ye as well," he replied, feeling the same way about her. "'Tis no easy thing knowing yer expected to fall in love. 'Tis unnatural in some ways, in my opinion."

"I couldn't agree more," she exclaimed and shook her head. "I still find it hard to believe Mil and Linds fell so hard so fast. Sure, maybe in Mil's case but Linds is a *huge* stretch. She swore up and down she'd never hook up with a guy. Not like that." Her eyes met his as they walked. "You saw it all happen, didn't you? First Mil and Adlin then Linds and Conall?"

"Aye, a good part of it in both cases."

"And?" She watched him closely. "*Did* it seem unnatural?" Her eyes narrowed. "What you saw happen between my friends and your cousins? Were the connections they made somehow against their will?"

"Och, nay." He shook his head. "What I saw betwixt my kin and yer friends was genuine. 'Twas verra real from nearly the moment they met." His eyes stayed with hers. "But such cannae happen with me. 'Tis important ye ken that."

"Ken?"

"Understand," he explained.

"Ah." She nodded. "I *ken* then. Totally get it. No worries."

Based on the look in her eyes, she meant it, and he couldn't be more grateful.

"So what happens next?" she asked.

"After we reconnect with Rona, Blair, and Jim, we travel back in time."

She flinched. "Are you sure there isn't any way we could pull this off from right here in New Hampshire?"

"Nay, Christina." He stopped and made sure her eyes stayed with his, so she understood how serious he was. "Ye face many things, lass. Love being the least of the threats."

"Right." She sighed. "Evil."

"Aye, and 'tis verra real," he said. "That's why 'tis so important to leave and return to Adlin and Grant. They are the strongest of us all and 'tis best to travel alongside them if possible."

"And where is it we'll be traveling again?"

He could tell she was trying to seem unaffected by all this. Trying to put on a brave face.

"First, if all goes as it should, to my home," he replied. "MacLomain Castle."

"Adlin's castle," she said. "Right?"

"Aye." He nodded. "I'm his first-in-command."

"So unlike the rest of your male cousins, you're not a chieftain."

"That's right." He grinned. "'Tis a rather simple life all things considered."

"Somehow I doubt that," she said softly. As her eyes lingered on his, he swore for a moment she saw deeper, that she caught a glimpse of things she should not.

Jim's muffled words drifted through the forest, interrupting the unexpected connection. He and Graham's kin were nearly back.

"Are ye sure yer up for this?" Graham asked her again.

"I am." She nodded. "Just as long as you'll stay by my side no matter what."

He was touched by how much trust she already put in him.

"Aye." He nodded. "I will, to the verra best of my ability. Ye have my word."

She grinned, clearly trying to find humor rather than fear in all she faced. "You mean *you* have my word."

"Nay, I mean *ye* have my word." He chuckled and pulled her after him. "Come, lass. 'Tis nearly time for us to play our parts."

They had almost reached the oak in front of the house when Rona, Blair, and Jim appeared out of the forest. Everyone's eyes immediately fell to Graham and Christina's hands.

It didn't take long for their interest to turn to doubt as they approached.

"I can see that." Blair's eyes narrowed. "How…convenient." Her brows drew together. "Christina's gem still looks clear to me."

"Aye, but it isnae," Graham assured. "'Tis the color of my eyes." He shrugged. "Mayhap ye dinnae see it yet because of the warlocks' influence over its creation." He smiled at Christina. "But my lass and I see it, and that's all that matters."

"Good then." Rona smiled at them, her gaze less doubting and more interested than anything. "The gem's glow can only help things."

He was a little surprised his sister wasn't more doubtful. But then, her attitude, in general, had changed since their last adventure. Though he wouldn't call her chipper she was far less dour. Not only that but she was here in New Hampshire. Truth told, whether it was Grant asking or not, that she had finally left Conall's side in medieval Scotland spoke volumes.

"Aye, 'tis good the gem glows the color of Graham's eyes," Blair murmured, clearly not convinced. "Though I didnae think these MacLomain, Broun connections happened quite that fast."

"Well, we're living proof it can happen that fast," Christina began before Jim appeared at the door, worry in his eyes as he said, "We've got a problem, Christina."

Her eyes whipped his way as if she knew what was coming. "Oh, no, tell me she's still in there…"

"Can't do that. I've checked the whole damn house, and she's gone." He shook his head, upset. "Jessie's nowhere to be found."

Chapter Three

"SONOFABITCH," CHRISTINA MUTTERED as she flew through the house, determined to find Jessie. "I leave for ten damn minutes and she up and vanishes!"

"Her car's still where you parked it down by the ranch," Jim announced as he reentered a short time later.

"I could've told you that because it was sitting there when Graham and I walked that way." She planted her fists on her hips and eyed the untouched tea on the coffee table then Jessie's faithful chair by the fire. "She must've gone for a walk and all the power to her for doing it considering she barely moves from that thing."

Rona and Blair were already out looking, but Graham had stayed by her side, claiming no Broun lass should be left alone. She glanced his way as she pulled on a heavy hoodie and running sneakers. "I'm going out looking for her." Her eyes went to Jim. "Stay here in case she returns."

He nodded and tossed Christina her cell phone. "Keep in touch and be careful. Bad weather's coming in pretty soon."

"You got it." She glanced at Graham as she did some warm up stretches. "You should stay here too. I move fast."

Already at the door, he shook his head. "Not a chance."

She eyed his heavy boots and fur cloak. "You're not dressed for running, darlin'. You'll only slow me down."

Not daunted in the least it seemed, Graham tossed aside his fur and held open the door for her. "After ye, lass."

"All right then." She nodded thanks as she strode past then started jogging before she picked up the pace and let her instincts take over. Her brand of magic.

Jessie had a unique essence about her. One that seemed to magnify everything around her. Scents. Texture. Even the way light worked. That's what Christina focused on now as she sprinted through the darkening woods.

Though she never detected anything that would lead her in that direction her feet carried her to Mystery Hill. It was almost as if she was stuck on autopilot when she ended up in the same exact spot she had run into Graham earlier.

"'Tis far tighter than it seemed when we met here before," Graham commented as he ducked in and crouched rather than remain slumped over.

"I don't understand," she whispered as she moved her cell's flashlight around. "Why did she lead me here?"

"Who?" He frowned as he watched her. "Jessie?"

"Yeah." When she realized what she said, she shook her head. "I mean no."

It was enough to realize she was almost out of the 'witchy' closet never mind flat out admitting it.

"I thought we agreed to be honest with each other, lass," he said softly.

The way he said it made the fine hairs on her arms and neck stand on end. Almost as if there was a unique electrical charge between them. One that made her a little too aware of him. Funny how she could keep Graham and all his hotness in perspective anywhere but here. It had been somewhat easy until now.

Until they were in this spot.

"It's a decoy," she whispered, not sure why she said it or even felt it.

"What do you mean?" he replied, his voice suddenly very serious.

Christina didn't comment on the fact he said 'you' instead of 'ye' but met his eyes through the darkness as she crouched as well. "I don't know." She shook her head. "This just all seems too planned out somehow, don't you think?"

"Planned out?" He frowned. "How do you mean?"

"I'm not sure yet," she murmured. "What I *do* know is that Jessie isn't here." She swallowed hard and ignored the worry and sadness that spiked through her. "And I get the strangest feeling she hasn't been for a while...not really."

Thankfully, Graham didn't question her but nodded his head toward the exit. "Let's go back then, and let the others know."

He had no idea how grateful she was that he didn't question her more right now because there were a lot of confusing emotions ripping through her. Namely, how this place seemed to magnify everything so much more than it did earlier. Even more so than when she came across Lindsay then ran through Graham as they crossed time barriers in broad daylight. Well, as light as it could get in here.

"Are ye okay, Christina?" he said, stopping her as they exited the small stone dwelling.

Overly sensitive from so recently using what her granny called her *lightn'*, she stepped away from him. He was too close. Too *him*. Tracking Jessie and her unique signature was one thing. Graham, however, was a whole lot of something else she needed to be awful careful of. He was all hot male flesh and had a spicy scent that made her want to run her tongue over his hard skin.

He smelled like dessert.

"If everything I've heard is true then Jessie could be in real trouble," she said, putting a little pep in her step as they headed back through the woods. "Because she's not anywhere near here, Graham."

"Aye then." That's all he managed to get out before she bolted, in need of a flat out sprint. She might be racing toward nothing but she needed to get her stress out and the energy affiliated with it.

What she didn't expect was Graham keeping up. She probably shouldn't be all that shocked though based on the cut body she sensed beneath his clothing. Barely winded, his eyes met hers with appreciation when they reached the front door. It seemed he was impressed by her running skills and speed.

"Jessie's not out there," Christina announced as they entered. "She's not anywhere here."

Rona, Blair, and Jim were standing in the kitchen.

"What makes ye say that?" Blair frowned as she looked from Graham to Christina. "Did something happen?"

"No." Christina shook her head, yanked off her hoodie and deflected with a bit more bite than she intended. "Seeing how you're all just standing there doing nothing, I'd say you already figured that out though. Because you sure as shit haven't found my friend, have you?"

Sorry for swearing Granny, she thought to herself and sighed.

In truth, she was just feeling cranky and needed to backtrack from her statement. One that hinted at her special gifts. Though in all honesty, she should probably be sharing them by now.

She shook out her hair, and scowled heavily before she turned toward the fire and muttered, "What I wouldn't do for some moonshine the way Granny used to make it."

"You made some, remember?" Jim handed her a small flask. "At your place in Maine."

"That's right." She nodded thanks, took a small swig then turned an eye to the fire as she absently handed the flask to Graham. "We should keep that going."

"Is it really so important right now?" Rona asked as Christina put a few more pieces of wood on the low flames.

"Storm's coming which means we'll probably lose power soon," she provided. "So yeah, it's important."

It felt like a connection to Jessie somehow. A way to keep her here though she somehow knew it was too late for that.

"We found something." Jim came alongside, eying her with that look he got. The one that said he knew she was *way* off her game right now. "A note beneath her tea cup."

"A *note*?" She frowned and took the tiny scrap of paper he handed her.

"Well, a picture actually."

Christina kept frowning as she eyed it. "It looks like a dragon on fire…"

"Aye," Graham murmured, studying it with the same frown before he looked at her. "Ye dinnae know what this means, do ye, lass?"

"You know I don't," she whispered. Ensnared by his eyes, strange words just kept falling out of her mouth. "You know me better than anyone."

"What are you guys talking about?" Jim said, his words cutting through their odd conversation. One Graham seemed just as confused by as he frowned and tore his eyes away.

"Death comes to those who fly," Rona whispered, her words barely audible from the kitchen. "Death comes to Scotland."

Blair looked from them to Rona, her hand on the hilt of the dagger at her waist. "Nay, it doesnae. We need to get back to the past." Her eyes met Jim's. "And ye need to stay here and keep an eye out for Jessie lest she returns."

"Not on your life." His eyes went to Christina's. "If you go back, I go back."

Done with the endless cat and mouse games he and Blair played together, she shook her head. "Now's not the time, you two."

She stared at the fire, drawn by it more than usual.

They needed to find Jessie.

She was alive somewhere, and it had to do with this fire.

"What makes ye say that?" Graham asked.

"Say what?" she managed, tearing her eyes from the flames to look at him. "About Blair and Jim?"

His eyes held hers for a moment before he nodded. "Aye, about Blair and Jim."

Why did she get the feeling he wasn't talking about them at all but what she had just thought in regards to Jessie?

"Either way, Grant got us all here," Blair said. "So I think we're stuck here until he comes for us." Her eyes went to Christina's ring. "Unless that gets around to doing what Milly's and Lindsay's did." Her brows whipped together. "I never noticed a ring on Jessie's finger. Did ye?"

"No," Christina murmured, her gaze returning to the fire. "But that doesn't mean she didn't have one."

"I'm sort of surprised, all things considered, that none of us noticed or better yet asked her about a ring from the start." Jim frowned and shook his head as he glanced from Blair to Christina. "Doesn't that strike you as odd?"

"Aye," Blair murmured as Christina only nodded in response.

The more she thought about the last few days, not mentioning such an important ring seemed the least bizarre of it all. How often did Jessie *really* leave that chair? Christina swore she had used the bathroom but maybe not. And had she ever changed once? Showered? Her frown deepened as she thought about the endless beef stew she had been cooking because Jessie had requested it. While she assumed Jessie had only picked at her food, now she wondered.

Had she ever eaten anything at all?

"Something's wrong," she whispered and shook her head as her eyes went to Graham.

41

"Aye, lass, but we'll figure it out."

She took unexpected comfort in his eyes as his hand slipped into hers. In how confident he seemed.

"Jessie will be all right," he assured.

As their eyes held, something seemed to shift. At first, she thought it was just the lighting then realized it was far more when Graham suddenly yanked her against him.

"This is our chance to make a good first impression, lass," he whispered in her ear before it felt like the floor dropped out from under them. Her ears popped and colors swirled around her. Yet rather than feeling afraid she was caught by the sensation of being against him. The strength of his body. The pure power she hadn't felt until this moment.

What *was* that?

She inhaled deeply and closed her eyes, not fazed or frightened in the least that she was very likely traveling back in time. Instead, she felt calm in a way she hadn't in a long time. Soothed in a way that was somehow exciting. Not thinking clearly, or maybe thinking clearer than she had in a while, she wrapped her hands in his hair and pulled his lips down to hers.

What she discovered when she did was more than she bargained for.

He tasted even better than he looked and smelled, and that said a whole lot. Both groaned as they didn't take it slow but rushed right into it, their tongues tangling. Sweet Heaven above, the man knew how to use his mouth. Not to mention his hands as he caressed her ass with one hand and used the other to trail his fingers up her spine until he cupped the back of her neck. Gone, caught in a blistering storm of sensations, Christina had no awareness outside of him. Outside of his heat and the material of his shirt as she twisted her fingers in it.

"It seems to be a common thing, aye?" came a distant, amused brogue. "Your friends kissing my cousins when traveling through time?"

"Like I said," Graham whispered between kisses. "This is our chance to make a good first impression. Show them we're together."

"You got it," she whispered back and kept on kissing him. Why not? He was great at it, and she wasn't quite ready to face a scary new reality.

Yet when a woman cleared her throat, something about it made Christina finally pull away. Well, not away but at least no longer kissing as her eyes landed on an attractive older woman with short red hair. Her brows were raised as she assessed Christina. Not in an amused or curious way but more of a who-the-hell-are-you way.

Fondness lit the woman's eyes as they went to Graham and she nodded hello. "Son." Then her less-than-impressed gaze returned to Christina, all warmth gone. "And you are?"

While tempted to say she likely already knew the answer, Granny had raised her with better manners than that. So she pulled away, closed the distance and held out her hand. "Hi, I'm Christina." She glanced sideways at Milly and whispered out of the corner of her mouth, "So glad to see you, sweetie!" before her eyes shot back to Graham's mother. "It's very nice to meet you, ma'am."

The woman frowned, her eyes going from Graham to Christina before they went to Milly and Adlin. "Seriously? This is my son's one true love?"

"Och, Ma," Graham grumbled before an older but just as handsome man stepped forward and took Christina's hand. "Hello, Christina. Welcome to MacLomain Castle. I'm Niall MacLomain." He pulled Graham's mother against his side, the affection obvious in his gaze as he looked at her. "And this is my wife, Nicole."

Christina plastered a warm smile on her face and greeted them both. What was Nicole's deal? Why so hostile? But then she knew there had been a divide in the family for a while. Since Graham's cousin, Fraser had died. Rona had pretty much abandoned her parents to spend all her time at Hamilton Castle with Conall. And Graham? Well, she was beginning to suspect Fraser's death had affected all of his cousins one way or another because Graham clearly wasn't around enough either.

Nicole nodded but offered no real greeting before her eyes floated to Rona who seemed to be the only one to have traveled back in time with them. What happened to Blair and Jim?

"It's been a long time, Daughter." Pain flickered in Nicole's eyes. "We've missed you."

"Aye, Ma." Rona nodded as she closed the distance and wrapped her arms around Nicole. "And for that I'm sorry."

Clearly stunned, Nicole's arms remained limp until she finally returned the hug. Meanwhile, his eyes moist, Niall wrapped his arms around both his wife and daughter. It seemed Christina had arrived in the midst of a family reunion.

"So what do ye think, lass?" Graham whispered in Christina's ear. "Are ye not impressed by the castle?"

"Impressed by what?" she began before she suddenly snapped out of the bubble Graham had somehow sucked her into and finally took in her surroundings. The mind-blowing enormity of everything.

"Well, I'll be," she whispered, staring at the gorgeous castle not two hundred yards out and the loch beyond. Then she just kept looking and looking. From the moats to the drawbridges and portcullises to the people. Oh, but the *people*.

"Just look at 'em," she whispered, wide-eyed as she took in their medieval attire. "I knew…I was told…you and your cousins were dressed like this…but to see *everyone* like this just…"

When she trailed off, Milly grinned. "Pretty amazing, huh?"

"Mil," she managed, incredibly happy to see her friend again even though she couldn't tear her eyes away from everything around her. "I'm so glad you're okay, honey."

"Back at ya," Milly murmured before she gave her a big hug. Christina finally managed to screw her head on straight and hugged her back. "Hey there."

After they pulled apart, Milly introduced her to Adlin.

"Always a pleasure to meet another Broun lass." His eyes twinkled as he smiled at her. "Welcome to medieval Scotland."

"Thanks," she replied. "Nice to meet you as well, Adlin."

"How are you, sweetie?" Milly searched Christina's eyes. "This is an awful lot. Are you okay?"

"Yeah," she managed, somehow able to play her part regardless of how wowed she was. "Despite my new guy's mom hating me on sight."

"Your new…" Milly's eyes widened as it clicked. "Oh…you mean…Graham?"

"Who else would I mean?" She frowned. "Did you not just see that kiss?"

"I did," Milly replied slowly, her eyes going from Graham who was speaking with his family back to Christina. "And while yes, it was pretty hot, that doesn't necessarily mean anything."

"Right." She nodded, knowing exactly where Milly was going with this. "You're talking about Linds and Conall kissing their way through time and…" She frowned. "Wait a sec, they ended up together so what *do* you mean?"

"I don't know," Milly began before she clamped her mouth shut, eyed Christina with uncertainty then shook her head. "No, I do know. This is weird, hon." She gestured at Graham. "You and him." She pursed her lips then cocked her head. "Or maybe not considering you guys ran into each other already in another dimension. What have I missed since then? Did much time go by in the future?"

"No." Christina shook her head, seeing the perfect explanation hidden right in Milly's very own words. "Like you said, we ran into each other." She made a flustered motion with her hand and released a breathy sigh. "That's all it took. We had this instant unavoidable connection. From there, things just took off." She eyed him up and down with appreciation. "I mean, just look at him, Mil. *Damn* fine, am I wrong?"

He really was, wasn't he? Something about seeing him here in his element only seemed to amplify his already drool-worthy good looks. Her mind went back to the feel of that long, hard body against hers. More so, the steely and more than ample bulge between his legs.

"Of course Graham's handsome," Milly said, cutting into her thoughts. "All the MacLomain men are."

"I'm sure," Christina murmured, pretending to still admire him though, in truth, she couldn't tear her eyes away.

"There's another single guy around with MacLomain blood too," Milly commented. "In case you're interested."

"Why would I be?" she said absently, her eyes still on Graham.

"Because he might be meant for you."

"Meant for me?" She held up her ring finger, her eyes still on Graham as she shook her head. She was about say something about her gem glowing a certain color. Instead, the words caught in her throat as a strong hand locked around her wrist and a deep voice said, "Aye, meant for you, lass."

The next thing she knew she was whipped against yet another hard body and another set of lips altogether came down on hers.

Chapter Four

Cowal, Scotland
1312

GRAHAM DIDN'T THINK but acted as he tore Bryce away from Christina. Aye, it made sense that he did such, but he wasn't doing it to put on a show.

He was truly infuriated.

Bryce, it seemed, was just as angry. When his cousin chanted, and fire came roaring at him, Graham chanted right back and doused not only the fire but Bryce and mistakenly, Christina, in dank moat water.

"Enough," his mother bit out as she stepped in front of him and glared up. "You're first-in-command of this castle, Son. Act like it."

"Bloody well straight," Bryce sputtered, dripping wet as he glared at Graham.

Nicole spun and narrowed her eyes at Bryce. "And the last time I checked, you were a damn chieftain so shape up, Laird MacLeod."

Bryce hung his head and sighed. "Aye, Auntie."

Ma's eyes whipped back to him, and she gestured loosely before she spat, "Come with me, Graham. We need to talk."

When Adlin went to speak up, she shook her head sharply.

That, as usual, silenced his cousin.

It always amazed him how everyone fell beneath his mother's wrath lately. His aunts said it was a combination of her being heartbroken over the loss of Fraser, then Rona being gone all the time, as well as Graham. Then there was mention of something called menopause. That, it seemed, was the true root of her power because his father and uncles always backed away and vanished when that plight came upon her.

He and his mother didn't go far and certainly not far enough away from Christina before Ma spun on him with her hands planted on her hips and her eyes a little wild. "What the *hell* are you doing?" She poked him in the chest. "And where the *hell* have you been?" Before he could respond, her eyes welled, and she threw her arms around him, mumbling, "I was so damned worried about you. You have no idea." She sniffled. "I worry every time you run off."

Again, he tried to respond but had no chance to before she pulled back, wiped away tears that barely had a chance to fall and crossed her arms over her chest. Eyes narrowed, she shook her head. "Tell me what's going on because I can already tell I don't like any of it." Her eyes shot to Christina then back to him. "And I'm not sure I like her either."

Not sure was more than he dared hope given his mother's current state. He imagined Christina managed to get that much approval because she was from the twenty-first century.

He knew he had to tell his mother what he would tell everyone else, but he was having trouble finding the words. Though he'd been keeping secrets more often than not lately, he had never lied straight to her face. Maybe he could manipulate his words to say things in such a way that he wasn't *really* lying.

She tapped her foot when he didn't respond right away. "Well?"

"I love her, Ma," he announced, shocked when the words rolled off his tongue. That he *was* truly capable of lying to his mother for the greater good. "She's the one meant for me. My one true love."

"Really?" Her frown wavered a little, as though a smile might be lurking somewhere beneath. "Are you serious?"

"I am." He nodded. "She's the one."

"Oh," his mother said softly, tears welling again as she eyed him. "That's sort of big, Son."

"I know," he said just as softly.

"She's southern," she commented.

"So?"

"I don't know." She shrugged, not quite meeting his eyes. "I guess I'd hoped you might find a nice New England girl like myself."

He just couldn't help himself knowing full well his mother was not as sweet as she pretended. "Really, Ma? You were from Boston's South End, and I've heard the tales of yer youth."

"Watch your tongue, Graham." Yet there was a flicker of humor in her eyes. "So you truly feel that Broun, MacLomain connection with her? That deep love?" She eyed him, clearly not all that convinced. "The sort of love your father and I share?"

"Aye." He nodded. "I do. *We* do."

"And the ring?" she asked, her eyes never leaving his face.

"What about it?"

"Does the gem shine?" She tapped the corner of her eye. "Is it the color of your eyes?"

Graham made to respond but tripped over his words. She didn't need to use her magic to suddenly see the truth. No, she just used her motherly powers to see right through a plan he had barely had a chance to implement.

She flat out knew he was fibbing.

"Please, Ma," he whispered. "Help me do what I need to do, aye?"

"Why should I when I don't think I like her." She narrowed her eyes at Christina again who was chatting with Bryce.

"Because I like her," Graham said. "Verra much."

His mother's eyes returned to his and held for a long moment. "You do, don't you?"

"Aye." He nodded, never more truthful. "I've never enjoyed a lass's company so much." He grinned. "She makes me laugh."

"You're quick to laughter these past few years," she countered. "Oddly enough despite all we've been through."

She *genuinely* makes me laugh though, he nearly said but stopped himself. If he said that it might lead to more questions. Mainly about the chipper false front he put up far too often nowadays. Which might lead to secrets that ran too deep. Even from his mother.

"I care for her, Ma and that's all that should matter right now in light of everything," he said. "More than that, the poor lass just traveled back in time and is about to face some verra frightening things. Do ye not remember what it was like when ye first traveled back and met Da?"

"Oh, I remember," she murmured as she sighed and cupped his cheek. "It just all looks a little different when you're the mother of a highlander meeting his modern day lass. So bear with me, okay?"

He smiled and nodded, always amused by how modern she still sounded after living in medieval Scotland for well over twenty winters. But his mother was stubborn, so he supposed it made sense on some level. She would only adapt so much.

"So what's next?" She pulled her hand away, worry in her eyes. "Is it your turn to go to the next historical battle and face a warlock?"

"Aye, I think mayhap 'tis," he said. "Though it could be Bryce."

"We both know it's not," she said softly as she took his hand. "Just promise me you'll stay safe, Graham. Promise me you won't do anything stupid?"

He frowned. "Stupid?"

"Yeah, stupid." She stood on her tip-toes, kissed his cheek and clenched her jaw. "Like get yourself killed."

"He knows better than that," his father said as he joined them. "Aye, Son?"

"Aye, Da." He embraced his father, always glad to see him. "How have things been here? Have the Sassenach been about?"

"Nay, not for a few weeks," he replied. "It's been…eerily quiet."

He tensed at that. Quiet could be good or very, very bad.

"What of the surrounding clans?" He looked back and forth between his parents. "Any word? I know many were set to seek shelter here."

"Aye and some have," his father reported. "The MacLauchlins any moment now."

He tensed even more, tempted to scan the woodline, better yet lead out scouts. "I will gather men to greet them."

"Adlin's already sent them," his father said, watching him a little too closely. "With any luck, they should be here soon."

"Good." Graham nodded at his parents. "'Tis verra good to see ye both. We'll talk more later, aye?"

Before they had a chance to respond, he headed Adlin's way. It almost seemed his cousin anticipated his words because he spoke before Graham had a chance to.

"I sent twenty of our best warriors, Cousin," Adlin said. "So ye need not worry."

Because the countryside had become so dangerous, Adlin usually only trusted Graham to oversee things like this. That was half the reason he had spent so much time away from the castle the past few years. Not only did he help protect allied clans but often brought many back to seek shelter behind the castle walls.

"I will head out anyway," he said, troubled. "They may need my help."

"And leave yer new lass alone at such a crucial time?" Adlin frowned and shook his head. "Ye'll do no such thing."

"She willnae be alone." Graham met his frown. "All of ye are here right now."

"So ye are not worried about Laird MacLeod then?" Adlin sounded dubious. "When Milly and I came together, the verra last thing I would have been inclined to do was leave her alone with any man so interested in her." He eyed Graham with amusement. "Especially one who just kissed her."

He made a good point.

Graham kept frowning as his eyes drifted to Bryce who was by Christina's side, enjoying her company. She, in turn, seemed to be equally enamored as they walked together over the drawbridge.

"Bloody hell," he muttered and headed in that direction after he nodded to Adlin that he would remain here for now. Christina smiled when he joined her, clearly glad to see him again. But then she seemed to be offering that same charming smile to Bryce as well.

"My apologies for getting ye wet, lass," he said. "'Twas not my intention."

"No worries." She grinned then scrunched her nose. "But a bath is gonna feel good because I'm pretty sure I stink."

Not to him.

"Nay, not at all." He took her hand and narrowed his eyes at his cousin. "Laird MacLeod, however, is another story."

"Och," Bryce muttered. "You're lucky my dragon didnae go after you, Cousin."

"Aye, ye might've had more than just the moat but the whole bloody loch thrown at ye," Graham said. "Though I should have tossed as much at ye anyway for kissing my lass against her will."

Smug, Bryce grinned. "I wouldnae say 'twas against her will."

"Well, it wasn't *voluntary*," she countered but certainly wasn't chastising him as her eyes sparkled with amusement.

Bryce saw hope in that. "But 'twas good, aye?" He shrugged. "It seems to be the thing to do with lasses from the future so I didnae think you would overly mind."

"Actually…" Christina gave him an apologetic look. "Though you seem sweet enough, that can't happen again, Bryce." Her eyes went from him to Graham. "Because I'm already taken."

Though Graham was pleased with her words, he found himself wishing he had waited a moment longer when Bryce first kissed her. *Would* she have kissed him back? *Had* there been a spark there? Because there were far more sparks than anticipated when Graham had kissed her.

He dragged his eyes from her face and tried not to think about how she had felt in his arms. How he had not wanted those kisses to end. They had fit together so perfectly. Not just their mouths but everything else. He could only imagine what it would be like to lie with her. To feel her soft but toned body against his.

She was in exceptionally good shape, and he had seen it first hand when she ran through the forest earlier. Yet he sensed something else as well. Magic. Her magic. It complimented her physical form somehow, giving her more speed and agility than the average human.

"So did Adlin mention if there had been any sign of Jessie?" Her worried eyes met Graham's. "Because I assumed he pulled us back in time, right?"

"Actually, he didn't," Milly said, catching up with them. "It seems you two are mysteriously time-traveling like the rest of us did." Her eyes met Christina's. "Why, what's going on with Jessie?"

Christina explained everything that happened. "It all started getting really strange right before we traveled back. As if, maybe, she might not have been there all that time. Or at least part of it."

"What does that mean?" Bryce frowned. "Was she glamouring herself somehow?"

"Glamouring?"

"Aye." He nodded. "'Tis a form of magic that allows a person to look like another or mayhap be in one spot when they are really in another."

"Ah." Christina shook her head. "I have no idea." She shrugged. "Maybe. Because something definitely wasn't quite right."

Milly tilted her head in question at Bryce. "I thought glamouring was a dragon thing?"

"Aye, it typically is," he said. "But it can sometimes happen otherwise. Our great uncle, Colin MacLomain, could do such a thing and he was no dragon but a wizard who could shape shift."

Christina's eyes widened. "So you're saying Jessie might be a...*shape-shifter?*"

"Aye." A little light entered Bryce's eyes. "Or mayhap half dragon herself."

"*What?*" Milly and Christina exclaimed at the same time.

"Ah, I heard another time-traveler had arrived," Aunt Cassie announced as she and Uncle Logan approached and introduced themselves to Christina. She was clearly relieved they welcomed her a bit better than his mother had. She was also thrilled to meet the woman who had created the forum where she and her friends had met.

He had to give his aunt and uncle credit. Though times had been especially difficult for them since losing Fraser, they remained strong. Unified. Focused on their clan. Perhaps it was because they had led the MacLomains for so long and were determined to keep morale up or maybe it was something more. Maybe deep down they refused to accept their only son was gone.

"You poor thing. We need to get you cleaned up." Aunt Cassie shook her head as she frowned at Graham and Bryce before smiling at Christina. "It's not always easy being caught in the middle of wizards who clearly still have some growing up to do, is it?"

"It seems not," Christina replied, grinning. She was about to say more but suddenly stopped, cocked her head as if listening to something, then whipped around.

Graham and Bryce followed as she sprinted back the way they had come. She moved so fast, they couldn't keep up with her before she barreled right into his mother who had remained beyond the first portcullis talking with Rona.

"What the *hell?*" his ma gasped. For a split second, he and everyone else remained confused until Christina held up an arrow and mumbled, "I think trouble's coming."

Shocked by her unthinkably quick actions, he and Bryce glanced at each other, before Adlin started roaring orders and everyone sprang into action. Christina pulled his mother up, and they ran across the bridge with Da protecting them.

Meanwhile, Adlin went very still, eyed the forest and murmured a chant before he muttered, "I dinnae know who shot that bloody arrow but there's trouble a ways out. Our men escorting Clan MacLauchlin are being attacked."

"Sassenach?" Graham asked. Or something else? Uneasy, he remembered Jessie's cryptic warning to Christina back in New Hampshire. Something he probably should have mentioned by now. So he filled Adlin and Bryce in about what she had said. About another possible dragon coming that might be determined to ruin Scotland.

"Another dragon?" Adlin frowned and shook his head as he resumed giving orders. "Bryce, I need ye to stay and defend my castle. Embrace yer dragon if need be." He spoke to Graham next. "Gather weapons and men. We're riding out."

He nodded and raced for the armory. After he had strapped on as many weapons as he could handle, he found his second-in-command and had him rally a handful of well-trained men. Christina was with Milly in the courtyard, more composed than he imagined she would be.

"Thank ye for saving my ma, lass." He pulled her close as if it were the most natural thing in the world. "Go into the castle with Milly and dinnae come out again until Bryce says it's safe, aye?"

Christina nodded, her eyes skimming over his weapons. "You stay safe too, okay?"

Caught not only by the genuine concern in her eyes but the fear he felt leaving her behind, he kissed her with more passion than intended. When she kissed him just as deeply, he wrapped his arms around her and held on tight.

Pretending with this lass was very easy indeed.

"'Tis time, Cousin," Adlin called out. His words barely got through until Da cleared his throat. "I willnae let anything happen to her, Son. I'll keep her safe."

Graham pulled away, brushed his fingers down her cheek then nodded before he turned away and swung onto his horse. Moments later he raced over the drawbridge, then across the field beyond the castle. When he glanced back, the gates were shutting, and Bryce was standing on the battlement above. He clenched the blade at his side and nodded at Graham in reassurance before they left the castle behind altogether and flew into the forest.

"*Be wary, men,*" Adlin warned, able to enter everyone's mind. "*Someone shot that arrow and though I cannae sense them that doesnae mean they arenae about.*"

As it turned out, they never came across anyone in the darkening forest, dragon or otherwise, but rode hard for some time before Adlin slowed. Graham frowned as he concentrated, trying to sense what his cousin did.

"Many Sassenach still live." Adlin shook his head. "So expect the worst and prepare to fight."

"*We'll not use our magic unless necessary,*" he said into Graham's mind. "*In case a warlock or something else may be about.*"

Based on the concern in Adlin's internal voice, he realized his cousin was more daunted by that mysterious arrow than he let on. Did he think an unknown dragon was involved? Or mayhap a warlock? Perhaps to set a trap such as this or even worse, leave MacLomain Castle more vulnerable?

They left their horses behind and crept through the night until they spied campfires. Evil warlocks and mysterious dragons in mind, it seemed more of a trap based on how few men the Sassenach had guarding the area. Tired men without armor. The rest sat around campfires with many tied up nearby, including several MacLomain and MacLauchlin clansmen.

In any case, trap or not, they needed to save these people.

His heart in his throat, he searched their faces, eager to find one in particular. Where was she? He ground his teeth and clenched the hilt of his sword tightly, awaiting Adlin's orders. Thankfully, he issued them soon after, and they took out the watchmen first. Graham came up behind the Sassenach closest to him and slit his throat before he attacked the small encampment alongside his comrades.

Seconds later, he heard a lass's scream.

"Kenna," he roared as he crossed swords with a soldier before he knocked the blade out of his hand, punched him in the face then kicked him hard in the gut.

He scanned the encampment as he crossed blades with another. They didn't fight long before Graham lopped off his sword hand then sliced his throat open. His heart pounded as he kept eying the area while battling yet another.

There was no sign of her, but he knew she was here.

She must be in one of these tents.

"Kenna," he roared again, unable to find his usual berserker laughter as he fought like a madman.

"Graham," she screamed in reply.

She was close. A few tents over.

He cut down man after man, trying not to panic. Please don't let it be too late. Please don't let her be hurt.

Nothing but pure fury hazed his vision as he opened a tent flap to see a man on top of her. Enraged, not sure if she had been raped or not, Graham yanked him back, drove a blade into the side of his neck, and seethed, "Get off my wife ye bloody Sassenach."

Chapter Five

HAVING BATHED AND changed into a flattering green dress, Christina stood at the window in the room she had been given and stared out into the darkness. While she should be concerned about showing so much of her gift earlier, instead she worried about Graham.

"He'll be all right," came a voice from the doorway. "My son's an excellent warrior."

About the last thing she wanted to do right now was deal with Nicole. Outside of a brief thank you from his mother for saving her life, they had not spoken since. Christina tried not to sigh as she turned and managed her best fake smile. "Good to see you, Nicole."

"Oh, please." Nicole shook her head as she entered. "You don't mean that, and I don't blame you. I was a real bitch earlier."

"You really were," Christina agreed, cursing inwardly. She hadn't meant to be so blunt. "But no worries. You're allowed. You're a mom."

"If only it were that simple." Nicole joined her by the window and handed her a mug. "I brought you something to drink. It was the least I could do."

"Thanks." Christina took a sip. "Whisky?"

Nicole nodded and stared out the window. "I haven't seen Graham like he was today in a long time and I know I have you to thank for that as well."

"What do you mean?" Christina leaned against the sill and shook her head. Though she knew she was supposed to gush about how instant their love was, she didn't. "Because we only just met."

"Like your friend Lindsay apparently is, Graham has become quite the actor." She sighed. "As I'm sure you've heard, Cassie lost her son Fraser a few years ago, and it's been a rough road for all of us since." She pressed her lips together, clearly trying to keep her emotions under control. "Fraser was like another son to me. Hell, I think all of us felt that way. Me, Jackie and Erin. He wasn't just Cassie's but all of ours." She swallowed hard. "But then we're close, so I suppose we feel that way about all of our kids."

Christina nodded, understanding how that might happen.

How it could happen if her, Milly, Lindsay, and Jessie shared the same sort of life here.

"After we lost Fraser, all of our kids suffered one way or another," Nicole continued. "Rona pretty much moved into Hamilton Castle to be near Conall who reminded her of Fraser. And Graham..." Her eyes met Christina's. "Well, he did what he did best and helped people, but it took a toll."

"What sort of toll?" Christina said softly.

"Before Fraser died, Graham was a different sort altogether. More stern and structured." A wistful smile came over her face. "We all knew he would have gladly become Clan MacLomain's chieftain if Adlin wasn't here. Not that he ever held it against the clan for wanting Adlin to lead after Logan. He felt it made sense. Besides, he always had a great deal of respect for Adlin."

Christina remained silent as Nicole continued.

"After Fraser died and his Uncle Darach went missing, Graham decided he needed to save the world...or at least Scotland. Or should I say as much of it as he could reach." Nicole shook her head. "The country's in rough shape, and he's been trying to pick up its broken pieces ever since."

"How so?" Christina said, her whisky forgotten.

"Mainly by putting his life on the line at every given opportunity to protect one clan or another," she replied. "As he did, the face he showed us changed. It became not hardened as you would think but more lighthearted to overcompensate for what he saw out there. We had already lost Fraser, and I don't think he wanted us to see him grow darker because of what he willingly saw happening all around us."

"So his good nature now is, what...fake?" Christina murmured.

"Yes and no," Nicole said. "I think in some ways, it's becoming real. A coping mechanism. Or at least I hope so." She shook her head again. "It's hard to know because there's nothing my son wouldn't do to make sure as many people as possible are happy including his own family. The English have ravaged this land and just about broken its countrymen, so I think Graham is capable of anything at this point. And I think he's capable of becoming anyone we need him to be."

"That sounds so sad," she whispered, again speaking before thinking. "But uplifting in its own way. All things considered, it sounds to me like he's a survivor." She met Nicole's eyes. "And while I'm flattered I somehow affected his behavior since we met, it sounds like he was just embracing who he usually is lately."

"To the common eye," Nicole said. "But not to mine and his father's." She took Christina's hand. "What we saw today was real. Somehow, some way, though he wasn't stern like he used to be, we saw our son again for the first time in years."

"Well, I'm glad," she replied, not sure what else to say. She certainly had no clue what to think of it. "He's pretty amazing."

No lie there. He truly was. Watching him leave earlier, set to fight, was harder than she anticipated. Far too hard considering she had only met him hours before.

"He sure is." Nicole cocked her head, curiosity in her eyes. "Nobody's going to ask about it because they figure you've got to be overwhelmed, but I just can't help myself." Her brows inched up. "How'd you do it? How did you save me earlier without even Adlin, such a powerful wizard, ever sensing that arrow coming?"

"I..." Christina started, wanting to share but unable to push the words past her lips.

Seeing her struggle, Nicole squeezed her hand and shook her head. "No, that's okay, you don't have to share. Not yet and certainly not with me."

"But I want to," she began before a commotion sounded in the great hall.

"They're back," Nicole said softly, catching her unaware when she embraced her, patted her on the back then pulled away. "Now you're going to want to drink a little, sweetheart." She gestured at the mug. "Go on."

When Christina narrowed her eyes, Nicole put the mug back in her hand. "Trust me, okay?"

When she hesitated, Nicole's eyes rounded. "You don't want to upset me again, do you?"

Christina shook her head, took a few hearty swigs and offered Nicole a crooked grin. "Good enough?"

"Probably not but it'll have to do." She looked Christina over and nodded. "You look great. Beautiful actually. The green really picks up your eye color and that figure and face…" She shook her head. "I can see why you turn so many heads."

Christina frowned, curious if Nicole was up to something. "So are you trying to set me up with Graham or push me toward someone else?"

Nicole's eyes narrowed. "Which would you prefer?"

"You know which."

Her eyes narrowed further. "Do I?"

"I'd like to think so," she said carefully, not sure in the least what to make of this conversation.

Soon enough it didn't matter because Milly appeared at the door. "Hey there." Her smile was a little off as she looked from Nicole to Christina. "They're back, and they've brought visitors."

Nicole nodded as they exited the room. Though the conversation with Graham's mom hadn't really been all that bad, Christina winked at Milly in passing and mouthed, "Thanks for saving me."

Milly shook her head, the look on her face odd as Christina joined her and Nicole at the balcony looking down on the great hall. Her eyes flickered over the huge tapestry of a Viking before they fell to the people below.

More so, Graham and the gorgeous woman by his side.

Her stomach flipped as she gripped the banister. They weren't touching or even looking at each other, but she knew they were close. Very close. As if he sensed her standing there, Graham's eyes rose to hers. At first, he seemed startled before a wide smile blossomed on his face, and he waved.

"Come down, lass, and play along, aye?"

Disconcerted by her thoughts, she blinked several times. If she wasn't mistaken, those thoughts, or *words*, had come from him.

"Like I said," Nicole murmured. "You might want to take a few more sips, Christina."

Not one to dismiss good advice, she polished off her mug and followed them downstairs. Though the atmosphere was somewhat somber as more and more clansmen arrived, weary from travel and battle, Graham's smile only widened as Christina joined him.

"Christina, I'd like ye to meet my good friend, Kenna MacLauchlin."

He introduced Kenna to Christina.

Even prettier up close with dark hair and hazel eyes, Kenna offered a small nod and weak smile. Christina had always been taller than most women at just over five foot nine, but standing next to this woman made her feel like a giant. She was even shorter than Jessie. Maybe five foot one if that. Which made Graham at what had to be at least six foot five look larger than life.

"This is the lass I told ye about, Kenna," Graham declared as he wrapped an arm around Christina's back and pulled her to his side. No kiss hello just pure awkwardness. What was going on?

"She's my one true love," he continued, his body tense but his smile easy. "I'm glad ye had the chance to meet her."

"Me too," Kenna said softly, eying Christina curiously. "'Tis not the average lass that can win over Graham MacLomain's heart."

"I...uh..." she stuttered before Graham intercepted.

"It seems I render her speechless, aye?" He grinned at Christina. "Come, lass, we'll find ye another wee dram then mayhap ye'll find yer tongue."

"Hard to know," she whispered as he nodded at Kenna then ushered Christina through the ever-thickening crowd. Instead of heading outside, which she would have almost preferred, they went in the direction of the massive fireplace with intricately carved faces on the mantle.

Graham received two mugs once they reached the fire which he set aside before he pulled her against him. He didn't give her a knee-buckling kiss this time but brushed his lips across hers before simply holding her.

Cheek against his chest, she murmured, "So what's going on, darlin' because I'm not quite sure how much you need me to act the part right now."

"You're doing just fine," he said softly. "This is enough for now."

"Maybe for you," she joked. Or did she? "So who's Kenna for real? Is she why you need me?"

"Aye," he whispered. "She is."

Christina ignored the way her heart skipped before it slammed into her throat. "So what? You're in love? Want to run off together?"

"Married."

Forget heavy heart thumps. Hers pretty much stopped.

"Or soon to be," he continued.

Not helpful. Her heart was still too wonky for her taste.

"Tell me more," she managed. She had agreed to play this part. This was what she wanted. Not a screwy heart. Not over a man she barely knew.

"I care about her and intend to do right by her," he continued, rubbing her back absently. "We've come too far."

"Well, *shoot*," she ground out and frowned up at him. "Did you get her pregnant?"

He frowned. "What?"

"Pregnant."

"Nay." He shook his head. "Why would you think that?"

Not *ye* but *you*. Something he seemed to be doing more and more with her.

"Never mind. Not pregnant," she said. "So just plain ol' love then?"

"You think love's plain?" he murmured.

"Not really the point of my question." She shrugged. "But yeah, it tends to be. At least for me." She gestured in Kenna's direction. "Back on track, handsome. What's up between you two?"

The corner of his mouth curled up, and his eyes softened. "I like when you call me handsome."

"And I like when you say *you* instead of *ye*." She grinned. "It really is easier to follow in the long run."

"I wasnae saying you."

"You were."

"Was I?"

"Yup and you wanna know why?"

He kept grinning. "Aye, I think I do."

"Because you're flirting with me for real, not for fake," she provided.

He chuckled. "For fake?"

"Sure, why not?" She met his chuckle. "It got my point across right?" Then she snorted. "And I *am* operating under the influence of a quickly downed mug of powerful whisky."

"Something tells me you can handle the whisky," he murmured as their eyes held. "Something tells me you can handle anything."

Ah, there, now her heart was back to normal. Sort of. It was downright racing. But at least it was consistent. She frowned and tried to remain focused. Mainly on Kenna. A woman she wished more by the moment didn't exist. Yet she did. As a rule, Christina tried her best to steer clear of cheating bastards, so she needed to get to the bottom of whatever Graham was up to.

"Time to let me in on what you're playing at, sugar," she said. "Because you've got something pressed against my stomach that shouldn't exist if you're really with Kenna."

When she tried to pull away, Graham's arm only tightened around her. "I'm not, lass." He pulled her cheek against his chest again, his voice very soft now in her ear. "I'm promised to marry her so that the MacLauchlin's are protected by the MacLomain's. We were about to marry in secret but then Milly traveled back in time, and the rings and gems started doing what they're doing. That's why I need your help. So that I can bypass whatever's happening and see through my commitment to the MacLauchlin's."

While she should have asked far more logical and pressing questions, instead she murmured, "So you don't...love her?"

"Aye," he replied. "But only as a brother might love a sister."

She hated how relieved she felt by that. Damn it, Christina. "I get most of what you're saying." She met his eyes. "What I don't get is the need to marry, in secret or otherwise. Adlin doesn't strike me as the type to turn away a clan in need. Wouldn't the MacLomain's protect the MacLauchlin's no matter what? Didn't you just do that today?"

"Aye, but doing such a thing might soon be out of our hands," he said sadly. "As it stands now, the MacLauchlin's are beholden to several clans for various reasons and Kenna being the former chieftain's daughter, is a prize above most. Before her da died, he promised her to a number of lads from a few clans unbeknownst to the others. Anything to get what he needed to keep his clan alive."

"That's awful." Christina frowned. "Why didn't her father come to Adlin first and ask for help?"

"Pride amongst other things," he murmured, not quite meeting her eyes.

"What other things?" she said softly, sensing more to all this.

"It doesnae matter anymore."

"It does to me." She cupped his cheek, so his eyes stayed with hers. "Who is she really, Graham?"

"Ye mean, who *was* she," he said softly.

Christina pulled her hand away from his face and looked at him in question.

"She and Fraser once loved each other," he finally relented, his voice pained. "Friends since wee bairns, they swore to marry."

"Oh, God," Christina whispered and finally managed to wriggle free of Graham's arms. She didn't go far but kept a hand on his chest. "I'm so sorry." She shook her head. "What happened outside of the obvious and y'all losing him? Did they ever tell anyone? Because I would think that alone would ensure the MacLomain's protection."

"Her bloody da is what happened," Graham growled. "Then her uncle who refused to see her married to Fraser unless my cousin became chieftain which wasnae going to happen." He shook his head. "Her uncle was a cruel man. An opportunist who thought he might be able to accrue more with allied clans. For years, he used her as a pawn held just out of reach as he continued to entertain the highest bidders. Chieftains who have grown tired of waiting for their prize. Now her uncle's dead too, and she's been left verra vulnerable."

He glanced at Kenna, then the MacLauchlin's meandering about as he continued. "They've verra little left now beyond this lot." His eyes met Christina's again. "So 'tis important that I avoid the MacLomain, Broun connection and see this through with Kenna. That way, she and her clan are given a fighting chance. A chance to be free of the lairds that nearly sunk them and protected from clans that think they have claimed rights to their land and livestock. Most especially Kenna herself."

How awful for poor Kenna. She could certainly see the reasoning behind getting her married to a MacLomain as soon as possible. Though tempted to ask him why he felt the need to take this on himself when there were clearly other MacLomain clansmen around, she refrained. His mother had mentioned his need to save everyone, and it seemed she was right. Not only that but it really wasn't any of Christina's business. So if he felt he needed to do this, she would absolutely support him.

They had made a deal after all.

"I understand." She nodded, more impressed than ever by him. "I'll play along and help any way I can. You know I will."

"You have my thanks, lass," he murmured. "More than you know."

She nodded, wanting to ask more questions. Mainly, what things would be like once they married. Was he hoping they might fall in love as time went by? Because that sort of thing happened, especially under extenuating circumstances.

Friends turned to lovers then far more.

As her eyes held his though, she didn't ask a darn thing. Mainly, because it was not her place. Not to mention, she wasn't really sure she wanted to hear the answer. Here she should be hoping for such a thing considering all Kenna had gone through yet it was hard to want. It was hard hoping Graham, and the little Scotswoman fell in love and lived happily ever after. Which, as a whole, made Christina feel pretty disappointed in herself.

Irritated with her thoughts, she scooped up the mug he had set aside, took a hearty swig and stood with her back to the fire. Graham remained silent, his eyes never leaving hers as the moment stretched. She saw the emotions in his eyes. The things he wanted to say but never could.

It was there.

Something already existed between them.

Something she had agreed to extinguish before it had a chance to ignite.

A flame snuffed out when it had only just been lit.

She frowned at her own musings. Why were they suddenly so fire-related? Ironically enough, considering he was half dragon, Bryce melted out of the crowd with a strange look in his eyes. "What is it, Christina? Why did you call me?"

She shook her head, confused, but didn't feel overly pressured to answer him as her eyes rose to the Viking tapestry. Easily thirty feet tall, it was a work of art and the man depicted in it more so.

Those eyes of his.

The way they fell to hers.

"Death comes to those who fly," he whispered, his words barely audible just like Rona's had been when she said the exact same thing in New Hampshire. "Death comes to Scotland."

Suddenly the ocean behind him came to life, and the wave peaks took on a familiar symbol.

"A dragon on fire," she whispered.

"That's right," came a deep voice from her right. "Prophecy."

"Holy crap," she managed as her eyes turned to a tall, striking dark haired man with steely blue eyes dressed in leather from head to toe. Tattooed with broad shoulders and braided hair, a wry grin curled his lips as he looked over her head at someone. "Found you."

"Loki's balls, I was not hiding," a blond haired woman said from her left.

"Aðísla?" came a distant voice before Graham yanked Christina against him and the floor dropped out from beneath them.

They were traveling through time again.

"Oh, *man*," she muttered against his chest as she squeezed her eyes shut and wrapped her arms around him. "*Really* not crazy about this."

Graham cupped the back of her head, his arm tight around her waist as they seemed suspended in thin air for a moment before the ground bumped against her feet. Legs braced, he kept them from stumbling as the pressure of time travel faded, and they were left in complete darkness.

"Where are we?" she mumbled against his chest, more than happy to stay there until this nightmare ended.

"I dinnae know."

"Is your voice echoing?"

"Aye."

"I'm here too," came a soft feminine voice. "And scared, Graham. What is happening?"

Kenna.

Of course.

Her adventure though time *would* have to include the other woman.

Not the other woman she preached to herself. Because that would mean Christina was the main woman and that was the furthest thing from the truth.

"Bloody hell ye'd think Adlin could help control this better," came Bryce's muffled voice. "Where are we now?"

"I dinnae know any more than ye," Graham grunted, his voice husky as he kept her close. Despite their circumstances, he was aroused and evidently not all that happy about it.

"Well, ye bloody well better figure it out." Bryce kept muttering as he made some sort of shuffling sound. "Seeing how ye've both yer wife and mistress along, aye?"

"Och." Graham set her back a piece but kept a firm hand on her elbow. "Where are ye, Cousin? I dinnae want to use my magic so what does yer dragon sense?"

"Trouble."

"What kind of trouble?"

"The sort we need help to get out of," Bryce groused.

"Any idea how?"

"Mayhap with help from the other one."

"The other one?"

"Him," Christina whispered, already sensing the dark-haired man nearby.

"Him who?" Graham said.

"Him *me*," came that same deep voice before a small orb of fire flickered to life, and his icy eyes met Graham's. "I'm here to help protect you because what you're about to encounter cannot be faced alone. King Robert the Bruce will happen this way soon, and when he does, you must be prepared."

Graham frowned. "Who *are* ye?"

"One of your Viking ancestors," he replied. "Sven Sigdir, Son to King Bjorn Sigdir and Samantha."

Chapter Six

HAND ON THE hilt of the dagger at his side, Graham narrowed his eyes at Sven and debated his next move. Jessie had warned of another dragon, and now one was here. Too coincidental in his opinion. "How do we know ye are who ye say ye are?"

"Ask your cousin." Sven's hard eyes stayed on Graham's blade though he made no move toward his own weapon. "Bryce can sense my inner dragon and knows the truth of it. I have come to ensure your safety."

"Why?"

Sven's eyes met his, his reply straightforward. "Because you are kin."

Graham kept eying him before he called out to Bryce. "Is what he says true, Cousin?"

"Aye," Bryce replied, his voice echoing through the cave. "I sense his dragon. 'Tis related and it doesnae mean us any harm." Before anyone could respond, Christina turned troubled eyes Sven's way and said, "Are you responsible for what I just saw in that tapestry?" Her eyes went to Graham. "A Viking who spoke to me by the way."

"That is King Heidrek," Bryce called out. "What did he say?"

"The same thing Rona said about death coming to those who fly and death to Scotland." Her eyes returned to Sven. "Then you showed up talking about a prophecy."

Graham frowned, his hand still firmly on his dagger as he eyed the Viking. "What prophecy?"

"The one my aunt is trying to save you all from," Sven said. "One interconnected with my own era and my kin. That is all I can share."

Graham could tell by the look in Sven's eyes that they would get very little information out of him. He had a mission and meant to see it through.

"I saw Jessie's picture in that tapestry too," Christina said. "The dragon on fire." Her eyes narrowed slightly at Sven. "Maybe it was just me, but I got the impression you saw it too, and that's why you mentioned a prophecy."

Sven considered her for a moment before he said more than Graham anticipated. "It is connected with Aunt Aðísla's prophecy and must be heeded by my people. It's more related to what's happening in my era than what is happening in Scotland."

Confused, Christina shook her head. "Then why did my friend Jessie draw it?"

"I do not know." Sven shook his head. "But it's my hope that I will find out while I'm here. As it was, that symbol finally helped us locate my aunt. To what end we cannot entirely be sure. Now that I'm here, though, it's clear you need help so I can only hope the symbol is working in our favor."

Graham wasn't sure he liked the sound of this but what could he do? Sven was here and determined to stay.

"I'm surprised you speak English," Kenna remarked softly.

"Because we have often interacted with twenty-first century women over the years, we have made a point of learning it as a second language," Sven said.

"Well, I'll be damned," Christina murmured. "You Vikings hook up with time travelers too?"

"Och, will someone bloody well help me out of here?" Bryce grumbled.

"I dinnae know." Graham shook his head as he and Sven located Bryce. "Because of ye, I doused my lass in moat water."

"Just help Sven get me out," he muttered, wedged at an unfortunate angle between two rocks that seemed to bottom out in an endless crevice. "This is bloody uncomfortable."

"I would imagine," Graham commented, smirking as Christina shook her head and frowned at him as she and Kenna joined them.

"What?" He shrugged. "I will help."

"Ye better." Kenna frowned and rounded her eyes at him. "That's yer blood right there ye bastard."

"I agree," Christina added, peering into what little they could see of the crevice. "I can understand why Bryce would be uncomfortable down there."

"They're kind hearted lasses," Bryce called up as Sven tossed aside his weapons, leapt over the side and began shimmying down. "Too good for the likes of ye, Graham." His random mutterings kept echoing off the rock. "Gets to travel through time with both his lasses. 'Tis not right!"

So Bryce was convinced Christina was his? Good.

He set aside the fact his cousin was under the impression he and Kenna were together when that was supposed to be a secret.

"Och," Graham muttered, tossing aside his weapons before he followed. "Leave it to ye to land here of all places when time traveling, Cousin."

"Do ye think I had a choice in the matter?" Bryce growled.

It was no easy task getting to where he was, never mind helping a man Bryce's size out of such a tight spot. While Sven was easily his size and Graham close enough, Bryce was over six foot seven inches of solid muscle and moody dragon countenance. A foul mood he suspected had more to do with looking so foolish in front of the lasses.

To make matters worse, he was wounded enough that they had to somewhat drag him up.

By the time they all flopped down on the ground, safe, Graham realized how poorly this would have gone had Sven not been here. Even with magic, he wasn't sure he would have been able to pull his cousin to safety.

He nodded at Sven in thanks before he frowned at Bryce. "Have ye a broken bone then?"

"Nay." Bryce frowned and shook his head as he sat back against a rock. "Just bad sprains here and there."

"Why is it so damp?" Christina asked, trying to peer beyond the small torch Sven had somehow manifested, and Kenna now held. "I don't sense water all that close...I don't think."

When Graham and Bryce glanced at her, interested in her odd wording, she clarified. "I meant *hear* not *sense*."

There *was* water much deeper down than where they were now. But how did she know that?

Graham looked at Bryce again, trying to hide his concern over their circumstances. "Why not heal yourself with dragon magic?"

"'Tis unwise to use magic with a possible warlock around and well you know it." Bryce's eyes went to Sven. "You probably should not use yours anymore either."

"After they leave, I will use just enough to help you heal slowly," he replied. "No warlock will sense my magic when used so sparingly."

"After we leave?" Graham frowned. "Nay." He shook his head. "I willnae go without my cousin. He will not be left behind."

More than that, he would *not* lose another cousin.

"You have no choice," Sven replied. "Though it's nearly summer, it will only get colder down here. We are dragon so it will not bother us as much." His eyes met Graham's in warning. "It would be best if Bryce did not appear weakened to those you will be facing."

Graham frowned and glanced at Bryce, not happy with the idea of leaving him alone with a stranger. One who was dragon no less. "I willnae leave ye, Cousin."

"Aye, you will." Bryce frowned at Graham. "The lasses cannae stay down here. 'Tis too dangerous. As soon as I'm recovered, I'll find you. Dinnae worry."

Unsure, and not happy about this, Graham eyed his cousin before Bryce scowled. "You need to go. I'll be safe with our ancestor. My dragon would know otherwise."

Graham sighed and nodded as he clasped Bryce's shoulder. "I will see ye again soon enough, Cousin. Heal well." His eyes narrowed on Sven in warning before he stood, paid close attention to the slight draft then looked at Christina and Kenna. "I'll lead the way. Do yer best to follow my every step and walk with care, aye?"

Both nodded, clearly nervous but remaining strong.

"'Twill be all right," he assured, looking from Kenna to Christina as he took the torch. "I'll go slowly so that you can make your way carefully, aye?"

"Take these." Sven handed him a few more daggers to add to the weapons he already had. Luckily, he still had several on him from battling the Sassenach earlier.

He nodded, his eyes flickering from Bryce to Sven. "Have ye enough left to defend yerselves?"

Sven nodded. "Yes, we will be fine."

"Aye, then," Graham muttered and started up a narrow tunnel in the direction from which he felt the draft. He could not imagine a worse position to be in right now than the sole protector of two lasses. Especially two who had little experience fighting. Kenna knew some but not much and certainly not enough to fight the likes of seasoned warriors. And Christina? None.

Or so he assumed.

His mind went back to how she had saved his mother. Her lightning fast reflexes. They clearly had something to do with her magic. What sort of magic though? Milly could astral-project, and Lindsay enchanted. So what could Christina do? Beyond what appeared to be supernatural senses and notable strength and speed.

Then again, that was more than enough.

When "*I would think so,*" floated through his mind, he smiled then felt a bit more than that. The sound of Christina's voice in his mind was bloody arousing despite their unfortunate circumstances. Though tempted to respond, she didn't know she had spoken to him telepathically, and that was for the best. He should not allow their connection to become too authentic.

As he took a left then a sharp right before continuing, he conveniently set aside what their speaking within the mind might mean. While he would not be opposed in the least being destined for a lass like Christina, it was just not possible. He would not let Kenna and her people down.

The way wasn't as bad as it could have been and they made it to an exit within the hour. Based on the position of the moon, he would say it was just past midnight. Now what? Luckily, it was warmer than he expected so at least they didn't have to worry about lighting a fire. Still, he had no way of knowing precisely where they were located or which direction to go in.

A moment later, bless the gods, much welcomed company appeared out of the forest.

"Linds?" Christina exclaimed softly before she closed the distance and embraced her friend.

Graham smiled in relief as Conall and Uncle Grant appeared as well. He embraced them both, muttering, "'Tis about bloody time ye showed up."

"Aye." Uncle Grant shook his head. "And 'twas no fault of mine. One moment we were at Hamilton Castle, the next here." He looked beyond them. "Did you travel alone with the lasses then?"

"Nay." Graham shared everything that had happened including Sven's apparent role.

"Sven?" Grant mused, not overly concerned with his revelations it seemed. "It's been many winters since I last saw him. How fares the boy?"

So they had met? Why did that not surprise him?

"Oh, he's no boy." Christina chuckled and winked at Lindsay. "The furthest thing from it actually."

Lindsay's brows shot up in curiosity before she embraced Graham. "Good to see you again, darling." She tossed a knowing look from him to Christina. "And you're here with Christina. What a shocker." Then her eyes landed on Kenna. "Well, hello there." She sauntered Kenna's way, with a look in her eyes he knew all too well. "And you are? More so, your intentions toward Graham are *what* exactly?"

"Och, nay, lass." Conall redirected her away from Kenna. "You'll not be enchanting the lass into giving truths she may not want to give."

"I was doing no such thing," Lindsay murmured softly, eying Conall flirtatiously. "Now let me just go ask her…"

"My name is Kenna MacLauchlin," Kenna provided, looking at Graham with affection. "Graham is a longtime dear friend and saved my life this verra night."

"Is that so?" Lindsay's eyes widened on Kenna then Graham. "And where was Christina when you were off saving Kenna?"

"At MacLomain Castle getting to know the family so retract your claws, honey." Christina chuckled as she slid her hand into Graham's and looked at him with adoration. "I look forward to spending more time with them…and Graham." She wiggled her ring finger then placed her hand on his chest. "Especially seeing how we're destined to be together."

This time surprise lit not just Lindsay's face but Conall's and Grant's.

"Seriously?" Lindsay exclaimed. "You two hooked up already?" She frowned. "What did I miss? Have you already been on your adventure?" She cocked her head at Grant. "I thought you said we arrived here mere days *before* the Battle of Bannockburn?"

"We did. We *have*." Grant nodded, eying Graham and Christina with a mixture of amusement and mayhap disbelief. "So 'tis a love connection betwixt you already then?" His wise eyes fell to her ring. "The gem shines the color of Graham's eyes?"

"It does," Graham and Christina said at the same time as he dropped a kiss on her cheek and pulled her against his side.

"It happened verra quickly," he explained. "Within minutes of meeting her."

"In New Hampshire," she added, pressing against him. "It surprised us both, but we're not complaining." Her eyes met his. "Are we, handsome?"

"Nay," he murmured, enjoying their pretend exchange tremendously. "Yer a bonnie lass, ye are."

"Well, thank you darlin'," she said softly, batting her lashes.

"Anytime, lass," he whispered, caught by the sparkle in her eyes that seemed to exist solely for him. He was so caught up in looking at her, he didn't snap out of it until Grant cleared his throat.

"Though I'm glad to hear you two made a connection," he said. "I worry that it might have been faster than usual so 'tis best that you both remain vigilant to the threat facing you."

When Graham finally tore his eyes from Christina and met Grant's skeptical gaze he knew his uncle had figured them out. Which, no doubt, meant Adlin likely had as well. Nonetheless, he intended to keep putting on a show until he knew otherwise.

"We will be vigilant," Graham assured as his eyes met Christina's again.

"Very," she agreed, grinning even though they were talking about danger. Something that should have them frightened, not smiling into each other's eyes.

"I see this is going to be an interesting adventure indeed," Conall remarked under his breath.

"Looks like it," Lindsay said with amusement.

"So where do we go next?" Kenna asked. "And where are we exactly?"

"Och, ye poor thing caught up in all this." Grant put a comforting arm around her shoulders. "I know this might be hard to believe, but ye've traveled through time a wee bit," he explained. "Not far. Only two or so years into yer future."

Her eyes rounded with curiosity rather than fear. "My future?"

"Aye." Grant nodded, eying her with interest. "This is not the first ye've heard of time travel, is it, lassie?"

When Kenna remained silent, Grant patted her on the back and stepped away. "'Tis all right, lass. Ye dinnae need to share until yer ready."

As Graham considered Kenna, the truth became clear. Fraser had shared the Broun, MacLomain connection with her. But then that wasn't surprising he supposed. Fraser's mother was from the twenty-first century as well as his aunts and great-aunts. Fraser and Kenna had loved each other so it made sense that his cousin might have confided such a thing to her. That he might have warned her just in case a Broun headed his way someday.

"I found a place we can seek shelter for the night," Grant said. "'Tis best that we find King Robert the Bruce on the morn."

"King Robert the Bruce." Kenna's eyes widened. "Is he not in hiding? Mayhap even killed?"

Kenna was going off the reality they had just come from. A Scotland going downhill far faster than it should. A Scotland where Robert the Bruce was barely holding his own. Unless that is, Graham and his cousins ensured that all went as it should at the Battle of Bannockburn.

"Not here, lass," Grant said softly as he ushered Kenna along. "Not yet."

"So I take it you haven't seen Milly or Adlin here?" Christina asked Lindsay as the two of them walked ahead of Graham and Conall.

"No," Lindsay responded before they continued their conversation softly.

Meanwhile, Graham spoke to Conall within the mind lest the lasses hear them and grow concerned. *"Have ye scouted the area? Have ye located the Bruce and his kin?"*

If history proved correct, Robert the Bruce should be leading a sizable retinue of Scottish warriors alongside his brother, Edward Bruce, Earl of Carrick and his nephew, Commander Thomas Randolph, 1st Earl of Moray. Not—though it got bloody confusing—of the same lot as Andrew Moray who fought alongside William Wallace at the Battle of Stirling Bridge.

"*We've had little time,*" Conall replied. "*We arrived here shortly before ye, and Grandda felt it best to find safety for the night knowing we'd have lasses to protect.*"

Graham nodded, grateful yet still concerned. "*So ye've come across no Sassenach? No tracks?*"

"*Nay but we both know that doesnae mean anything.*" He glanced at Graham. "*Ye play a dangerous game if yer lying about Christina's gem, Cousin.*"

He had always been close to Conall so shared more than intended. "*Christina and I are doing what we must.*"

"*Ye do remember what Adlin and Milly dealt with when it came to their warlock, aye?*" A heavy frown settled on Conall's face. "*Then Lindsay and me?*" He shook his head. "*Ye cannae go up against these beasties without the power of the ring, Cousin. Without finding true love with yer lass.*"

"*Aye, but 'twill be all right,*" he replied, surprisingly convinced by his words. "*I dinnae doubt it.*"

"*'Tis fine enough that ye dinnae doubt it,*" Conall replied, glancing at him. "*But remember, whatever game ye play, 'tis not only yer life on the line but yer kin, Scotland's history and most especially, Christina's life. If ye go up against this warlock with lies on yer tongue and a faulty ring then 'twill be a truly terrifying death for her, will it not? Because these warlocks are nothing if not brutal.*"

Discomforted by his cousin's astute assessment and blunt advice, Graham gave no response. He had been so busy trying to save the MacLauchlin's, he had given little thought to the bigger picture. Yet all aside, true love could not be forced. It did not just conveniently happen.

His eyes flickered between Conall and Lindsay. It might have been a bit of a slippery slope, but it had happened rather quickly for them, hadn't it? And though Milly and Adlin had been fated, their love was damn instant as well.

"*There is another Broun lass,*" Graham remarked, not really sure why he said it. "*Jessie.*"

"*Aye,*" Conall replied, humor in his internal voice. "*Fated, it seems, to be with a dragon.*"

"*Or me,*" Graham countered.

Conall chuckled and shook his head. It might be good to see his cousin returned to a bit of his old humor but still.

"*Why do ye laugh?*"

"*Because 'tis good to see ye dealing with denial now, as I get to nudge ye in a direction ye dinnae see so clearly,*" he said. "*When 'twas so verra recently ye took great pleasure in doing the same to me.*"

"*Och, nay, 'twas never like that.*" Though it was. "*Ye and Lindsay were obviously smitten.*"

"*Aye,*" Conall agreed. "*So said ye and I'm grateful for it.*" Mischievousness colored his words. "*Might I readily return the favor.*"

Graham narrowed his eyes, not missing what his cousin meant by that. Conall offered no further comment just a small smile as they arrived at a clearing surrounded by dense shrubs and trees. Grass and pine needles were to be their bedding.

"'Twill not be a comfortable night for any of us," Grant said as he sat. "I wouldnae recommend a fire or even hunting right now. Not until we're able to get a better lay of the land in the light of day."

"Aw, we can handle this, can't we?" Lindsay smiled reassuringly at Grant as she removed her cloak and handed it to him. "You, however, are going to at least use this, okay?"

It was clear Grant knew better than to argue with her as he nodded. "I'll only accept this because I know my grandson will keep you warm."

"That's right," Lindsay said as she sat down beside Conall.

Graham, in the meantime, found himself in a rather awkward position. It made sense based on their pretense of being together that he lay beside Christina, but what about Kenna? She knew that they were pretending, but regardless, it seemed strange. Uncomfortable. While love didn't exist between them, she would soon be his wife.

Conall, true to his word, seemed to be enjoying himself immensely as his eyes went from Graham to Kenna and then to Christina as they all stood there trying to figure out their next move. In fact, it appeared he intended to become as ruthless as Bryce.

"It seems you're tasked to warm two lasses this eve, Cousin." Conall's tone was comically dire. "Mayhap if you just lie down, they will too."

"Conall," Lindsay chastised, though there was a grin in her voice as they curled up together. "Be nice. That's my friend you're talking about and goodness, sharing her man would be above and beyond what's asked of most of us time traveling gals."

"Actually." Christina stretched, flinched and looked at Graham. "My back's been off since the whole random-arrow-almost-hit-your-mother thing." She shook her head, woeful. "So I'm gonna need to sleep a certain way I'm afraid." She sat carefully, as though wounded, with her back to a tree and her legs crossed in front of her as she gestured at Conall and Kenna. "Please, keep each other warm."

She yawned, rested her head back against the tree, closed her eyes and never said another word. It seemed Lindsay wasn't the only actress around here. Technically, if this farce was working he should be beside Christina, no questions asked.

Instead, he would be joining the lass he was actually with.

Things were backward. Or were they? How had his cousin managed to turn this all around? Because he had. Based on his muffled chuckle, Conall clearly followed his thoughts. Graham scowled and ignored him.

Though it was truly an unseasonably nice night, he was troubled by Christina being alone as he sat and urged Kenna to join him. They did not touch but lay down beside each other. It wasn't the first time they had done such a thing. She was his friend. A good friend at that.

Yet he felt guilty and wasn't entirely sure why. Christina never opened her eyes that he knew of. But then he dozed off faster than anticipated. Almost as if it were out of his hands. The next thing he knew dawn teased his eyelids and his magic alerted him to trouble.

Something was terribly off.

So off that his eyes shot open and locked on Christina.

More so, the man leaning over her.

Blade in hand, Graham roared with rage as he ripped the man away, slammed him back against another tree and pressed a dagger against his windpipe. It only took ten or so swords pointed directly at his head and the stern words, "Unhand the King or be hanged for treason," to finally get through.

What he saw as his infuriated haze cleared was fairly damning.

It appeared he was moments away from killing none other than King Robert the Bruce.

Chapter Seven

20 June 1314
Bannockburn, Scotland

CHRISTINA WASN'T SURE what caught her more by surprise. Waking up to a strange man leaning over her or seeing Graham with so many swords aimed at him.

"No," she managed to croak as she stumbled to her feet. "Don't. Please." She shook her head. "He was just trying to defend me. I swear." When her eyes met the man whose neck was threatened by Graham's dagger all she could manage was a breathy, "Please."

She *knew* him. Better yet, she had dreamt about him less than forty-eight hours ago. He was older now but just as handsome. Battle hardened in a surprisingly alluring way. Seconds later, his identity was confirmed. When it was, she leaned back against the tree, not so sure her legs were going to hold her up.

He was Robert the Bruce, the infamous King of Scotland.

Yet he was more.

"Stand down men," Robert eventually said softly, his eyes never leaving Christina. "Graham MacLomain is a friend, not foe."

The blades pulled away as Graham removed his dagger, fell to a knee and lowered his head. "My apologies, King Robert. I was caught unaware from the depth of slumber. I didnae realize who ye were."

Robert's eyes lingered on Christina's for another moment before he rubbed his neck and gestured for Graham to stand. "All's well. Get up, lad." His eyes went to Grant, and he nodded before they landed on Lindsay, and the corner of his mouth inched up. "Och, lass, ye dinnae look like ye've aged a day. Yer as bonnie as ever."

"Well, that's because it's only been a few days for me." She closed the distance and embraced him. "It's so good to see you again, m'dear."

Christina remained stunned and dumbfounded as she tried to process everything. As the past few days, including her dreams and what happened at Mystery Hill, seemed to manifest right in front of her.

Where in her dream he wore simple trousers and a tunic, now he also had on chainmail, a cloak and carried a fair amount of weapons.

Lindsay finally pulled back and held Robert at arm's length as she looked him over. "I must say, you've aged astonishingly well." She flashed a wide smile. "Ten extra years looks *fabulous* on you, darling."

Christina might be all sorts of shocked, but she couldn't stop a small grin. Leave it to Lindsay to make an uncomfortable, awkward moment feel like a cozy family reunion.

"It really *has* only been a few days for ye, hasn't it?" Robert said, amazed as he touched Lindsay's cheek then his eyes went to Conall and Grant. "Look at all of ye. Just as I last remember ye." Then his eyes returned to Christina as he pulled away from Lindsay. "And ye…Christina, aye?"

"That's right," she whispered, nodding before she managed to find her voice. "Nice to finally meet you in person, honey."

Oh, God *save* her. Had she just called Robert the Bruce *honey*?

A grin tugged at his lips as he stopped in front of her, his eyes never leaving hers. "Nice to finally meet ye as well, Christina. I have been waiting a long time."

Christina wasn't sure what to make of this. Him. More than that, her reaction to him. Because it was strong. Not quite lust but definite interest. She wanted to get to know him better…right?

She blinked against the odd sensation of confusion.

Moments later it vanished as he offered his elbow. "Walk with me, lass?"

She glanced at everyone else, who like her, seemed a little mystified by the whole situation. All except Graham who frowned yet nodded for her to go. Strangely comforted by his approval, she slipped her arm through Robert's. She was safe enough, and they would all be right behind them. As she and Robert walked, they didn't say anything at first, just sort of watched each other out of the corner of their eyes.

"This is very bizarre, isn't it?" she said softly, hoping his men wouldn't hear them. Men who remained close on all sides. "Surreal almost."

"Aye." He nodded. "'Tis almost dreamlike, is it not?"

"My thoughts exactly." Christina warmed beneath his easy regard. "While one part of me knows I should be super nervous because you are who you are..." She shrugged. "Another part feels like I've known you my whole life. Like everything that's happened led me to this very moment."

"I couldnae agree more, lass," he replied. "'Tis uncanny, aye? As if we were meant to be."

"Yeah," she whispered, then caught herself and shook her head. "I mean, it's definitely intense though I can't really speak to anything being meant to be...us that is."

Robert nodded. "I dinnae blame ye for being apprehensive." He shook his head. "The way we first met was strange enough now this..." He made a loose gesture at the woodland around them. "Days before battling. 'Tis not the best time to woo a lass, never mind one the likes of ye."

"Well, thanks." Christina couldn't stop a small grin. "But again, you don't have to..." She shook her head, searching for the right words. "What I mean is wooing isn't necessary because I'm not really in the market for a man."

"Nay?" A mischievous glint lit his eyes. "Why do I get the feeling ye dinnae truly believe yer own words?"

Christina shrugged, bereft of a witty comeback. What she needed to do was remember to play her part, so she shook her head. "It seems I'm meant for another, sweetie."

He frowned. "Another sweetie?"

"No." She chuckled. "I mean yes. I'm meant for another sweetie, but I had been calling *you* sweetie not him."

"Why would ye call me that if yer meant for another?" His curious blue eyes stayed with hers. "Because is sweetie not a term of endearment?"

Way to be technical. She smiled to herself. And savvy.

"You know Grant and his clan. Even Lindsay and Milly. You have history with all of them." She cocked her head. "Which means you must also know about the infamous MacLomain, Broun connection, right?"

"Right," he confirmed, not batting a lash, his gaze undaunted and tender.

"Well, what you might not know is that I'm a Broun," she informed.

"I figured ye must be." He considered her. "So yer determined to be with a MacLomain then, aye?" The corner of his mouth curled up, and a twinkle lit his eyes in direct contradiction to his next words. "Do ye mean to tell me there isnae hope for us? That the connection we made meant nothing?"

"I didn't quite say that." Though she pretty much had. Yet as she eyed him she realized she didn't entirely mean it. "I value the connection we made, Robert." Did she ever. So much so words kept rolling out of her mouth. Strange words a smidge stronger than she actually felt. Words that were supposed to have stayed between her and Graham. "As I'm meant to, I've got to be with Graham…" She leaned closer and whispered, "As far as everyone knows that is."

She clenched her teeth, not sure why she said that. It almost felt like she was cheating on Graham which she wasn't. Not at all. He would be marrying someone else. They were just putting on a show. That's it. Nothing more.

"So we are to court in private then?" Robert considered that and shrugged. "'Tis probably for the best with all my soldiers about."

Christina nodded because that seemed like the logical thing to do. The fact she had seemingly just agreed to have a private affair with Robert the Bruce had not really computed yet. Something else did though.

"You know I did a bit of research on you back home," she led out, cursing how callous that might sound considering he was long dead when she did the research.

"And?" he prompted with a grin when she trailed off. "What did ye discover?"

All things considered, she appreciated his lighthearted manner. It kept her at ease and her tongue loose. "As you can imagine, a lot of things." She winked. "You're pretty famous in these parts, sweetheart." Then she pointed out the rhetorical elephant in the room. "You're also pretty married and have been for some time." She arched her brows. "Since before we first met, actually."

His eyebrows slammed together in confusion. "Nay, ye are mistaken, lass."

"Is she?" Grant asked as he joined them. "Because I have been wondering."

"Wondering what?" Robert looked at him. "If I was *married* when last we met?" He gestured at Christina, his eyes never leaving Grant's. "Do ye think I would have been so determined to be with her had I been?"

"We both know you were under the influence of a warlock at the time," Grant reminded. "So your behavior could not be judged correctly."

"Och, judged!" Robert shook his head. "Something ye clearly did nevertheless, aye, old friend?"

Grant stood up a little straighter but did not back down. "According to history, you're married, King Robert and have been since our Lord's year, thirteen hundred and two."

Robert stopped short and turned wide eyes Grant's way. "So yer saying I've been married for *twelve* winters?" He shook his head. "'Tis impossible. I have only ever been married to Isabella of Mar, daughter of Domhnall I, Earl of Mar and Elena, daughter of Llywelyn ap Gruffudd." He clenched his jaw. "Isabella died before I was crowned." He kept shaking his head. "There hasnae been another since her."

"But there *has* been," Grant said softly. "And 'tis verra concerning that it hasnae happened as it should have."

Robert crossed his arms over his chest and narrowed his eyes. "Who do ye think I married then?"

"Does it really matter if ye have no knowledge of it anyway?" Grant countered.

"Aye," Robert said. "I would like to know who should have become my wife."

Grant sighed. "Her name is Elizabeth de Burgh."

"Elizabeth de Burgh?" Robert's eyes narrowed further. "'Twas talk of a connection betwixt us years ago. She would have been a fitting match at the time."

"Aye," Grant agreed. "Considering she's the daughter of such a powerful Irish noble. Richard Óg de Burgh, Second Earl of Ulster." His brows edged up. "A close friend and ally, I believe, to Edward I of England at one time." Disgust flashed in his eyes. "May

Longshanks forever rot in hell where he belongs. 'Tis good Scotland has been rid of him for seven winters now."

"Aye, now we've got to deal with Edward of Caernarfon," Robert muttered. "'Twill be good to cut down his garrison soon."

Christina frowned. "Who's Edward of Caernarfon?"

"Longshank's fourth son, Edward II," Grant said absently, still eying Robert, his expression hard to pinpoint. A mix of curiosity and concern. "He still holds your daughter, Princess Marjorie captive, aye? Isabella's daughter?"

"Aye," Robert confirmed. "'Twas rumored Longshanks was going to confine her to a cage in the Tower of London but instead sent her to a convent at Watton in Yorkshire." He scowled fiercely. "The poor wee lassie."

"That's awful. I'm so sorry." Christina frowned. "How long has she been gone for?"

"She was taken at nine winters old," he murmured. "So neigh on eight winters now."

"Dear Lord," Christina said softly, unable to imagine what the poor child had gone through.

"If all goes as planned during this battle," he said. "I will be able to take some verra important people hostage to barter for her safe return."

"'Tis a sound plan," Grant murmured, a heavy frown on his face.

Robert eyed Grant with curiosity. "Is it then?"

Grant shook his head. "Ye'll not get anything out of me about the upcoming battle, so dinnae bother asking."

Robert only chuckled, the look on his face confident that he would eventually find out all he needed to know.

It wasn't long before a vast encampment appeared through the trees. Christina slowed then stopped, her eyes wide as she took it all in. From the blue and white Scottish flags blowing in the wind to the endless men, horses, tents, and campfires not to mention weapons. Lots and lots of those.

Robert and Grant stopped as well, then everyone else. They must have realized that this was all *finally* hitting her. Where she was and what was happening.

"Darling, why don't you sit," Lindsay said softly, "and take a moment to gather yourself."

"No, it's okay," Christina murmured, staring at everything for a stretch before she shook her head. "I'm okay."

"Aye?" Graham asked. "'Tis a lot. 'Twould be understandable if ye need to take some time."

"Time?" She snorted. "I think taking time or swoonin' at the sight of so many warriors is the last thing I should be doing." Christina forced a chuckle and tried to look calmer than she felt as she met Graham's eyes. "I'm all right, sugar. Don't you worry."

When he grinned, she couldn't help but grin right back. The man knew how to lighten her mood, didn't he?

"Please, come to my tent and break yer fast with me," Robert said. "All of ye. I insist."

Nothing was more comforting than Graham taking her hand as they continued. Men far and wide stopped what they were doing as they passed, their eyes trained on either her, Lindsay, or Kenna. Some stared at them from around fires as they ate or while they sharpened their weapons. Some stopped mid-swing of their blade as they prepared for battle.

Robert nodded at many but did not stop to introduce them. Why would he? This wasn't a social visit, now was it? And she and Lindsay could not be more out of place if they tried.

Like Conall was doing with Lindsay, Graham made it more than clear that Christina was with him as he kept her close. Now that she was over her initial shock of walking into a medieval war party and truly realizing how dangerous a time she had traveled to, she was starting to take things in. The battle-hardened state of the men. The determination in their eyes. Even the pungent aroma of roasting meat and sweat that filled the air.

Robert led them to a massive tent near the center of the encampment. Two men stood on either side of the entrance, one of which he murmured something to before they entered. Two more men sat inside and stood the moment they realized Robert wasn't alone. Both were bearded and relatively tall, around Robert's height. The darker haired one was Robert's younger brother, Edward Bruce, Earl of Carrick. The lighter haired one who looked closer to Robert's age was apparently Robert's nephew and military commander, Thomas Randolph.

"Please sit." Robert urged everyone to sit at a large round table as a young man came in with mugs and started pouring what she assumed was ale. She didn't miss that Robert sat her beside him. Graham, thankfully, sat on her other side, never once letting go of her hand.

After that, conversations mostly revolved around the upcoming battle and naturally, who Lindsay and Christina really were. They might be dressed the part, but their accent was remarkably different.

Christina was surprised how honest Robert was with his family about them and where they came from. It seemed Grant was as well based on his guarded expression as Edward looked dubiously at the women. "So yer from the future?" His eyes flickered over Lindsay then landed squarely on Christina, his interest apparent. "The twenty-first century? Truly?"

"Aye, she is and my lass as well," Graham responded, his brow furrowed as he casually rested an arm on the back of her chair and wrapped his fingers with hers. A gesture that caused an unexpected roll of heat in her stomach, then lower.

"Aye," Robert agreed, his eyes narrowed at his brother. "And ye best well remember it."

Edward's eyes held Robert's for a moment before he nodded. "Aye then, Brother. As ye wish."

When Christina's eyes met Robert's, he nodded once in reassurance. Yet there was a little something else in that look too. A bit of possessiveness if she didn't know better. It seemed based on the way Graham cleared his throat, he had seen it too.

Grant cut into the awkward moment as he eyed the maps strewn across the table. "So ye intend to take advantage of the soft, boggy ground in the area as well as both the Bannock and Pelstream burns to trap the Sassenach?"

"Nay, we'll be fighting further south and trap them here two days from now," Thomas replied as he pointed at a different area, his steady eyes rarely going to the women but watching Grant, Conall and Graham closely. "'Tis a sound plan. Dinnae ye agree?"

"Aye," Grant replied, remaining vague. "As sound as any."

Yet Christina got the distinct impression that was *not* how things were supposed to go.

Thomas's jaw tightened, but he said no more as food was brought in. Hungrier than expected and impressed by the seasoning, she dug right in. Graham grinned and gave her some of his when she polished off her plate in record time. Meanwhile, Lindsay just shook her head and offered Christina a wry smile. She imagined if they were alone, she'd say something along the lines of being amazed Christina's hearty eating habits didn't catch up with her waistline.

Edward and Thomas, however, seemed a bit taken aback that she had such a healthy appetite. Or so said the odd, not-so-impressed looks they tossed her. Eventually, she called them on it as she polished off her last bite, sat back and grinned at them. "Haven't you ever seen a woman enjoy her food?"

"Not with as much relish," Edward said bluntly, a hint of humor in his eyes. "They tend to be less...ambitious."

"Less *ambitious*?" She chuckled, truly amused. "What does that even mean, darlin'?" She arched a brow. "If I were to guess, I'd say they don't eat as heartily as you men because they might be called just that. *Ambitious*." She kept grinning. "Like it's some kind of crime."

"I, for one, like how ye eat," Graham spoke up, his chuckle matching hers. "'Tis refreshing to see a lass truly enjoy her food."

"Heck yeah." She grinned at him. "One of these days, you're gonna have to let me cook for you."

"I would like that verra much." He met her grin and winked, evidently recalling their first meeting in the kitchen back home. "Especially if ye dance whilst doing so."

"I think I can manage that," she replied, her response more throaty than she planned. But flirting with him felt so natural. "Just as long as you dance along with me, handsome."

"'Twould be my pleasure." He squeezed her hand, still smiling. "Verra much so."

She had to give him credit. He acted very well.

This time, Robert cleared his throat and pulled her eyes his way. She almost felt guilty that she had been focused on Graham when Robert was *right* here.

So close.

So desirable.

She frowned, confused by the overwhelming pull she suddenly felt for Robert when she was definitely feeling the same way or more so for Graham.

She tried to convince herself that it was no big deal. That it's perfectly normal to be attracted to two men at once. Yet something felt off, and she couldn't quite put her finger on it. Maybe it was because she was in medieval Scotland and things were just downright crazy.

Or maybe it was something more.

She took a swig of ale, wishing it were water. She wished even more that she could lie down and rest for a few hours. Last night she had been too wired to sleep though she desperately needed it. Back at MacLomain Castle, she had used a particular sort of energy to save Graham's mother and her body needed rest to recharge.

Especially now that she had eaten.

She'd refueled and her muscles needed to heal. There had been no stretching earlier, no preparing before she saved Nicole. It had been a one, two sucker punch of magic on muscles not nearly prepared for the strain.

She didn't realize she was yawning until Graham said, "King Robert, might Christina and I find shelter in yer camp for a wee bit? As ye can imagine it's been a trying time for her with all the time-traveling."

"Aye…" Robert's eyes met hers, hopeful that she might say otherwise. "If ye truly need the rest."

"Actually I do," she replied. "Thank you."

And thank the good Lord that Graham seemed to sense it.

Her eyes went to Lindsay and then Kenna by affiliation she supposed. Girls needed to stick together. Especially in this day and age. "Will you two be okay without me?"

"Of course, sweetness." Lindsay smiled and nodded. "Go get some rest." Her eyes went from Kenna back to Christina. "I won't let anything happen to our new friend." Then she looked at Graham. "Promise."

When Graham's eyes met Kenna's and lingered, the little Scotswoman nodded and offered a small smile. "I'll be just fine. Go get some rest, Graham."

Robert's eyes were a little too knowing as they flickered from Kenna to Graham before he urged them to follow him.

"Though ye have our thanks ye didnae need to escort us yerself, King Robert," Graham said. "One of yer men could have seen to it."

"Nay, I dinnae think so," Robert said softly as he ducked into a rather spacious tent not all that far from his own. It had a table, two chairs, a small fire pit and two cots. As soon as the flaps shut behind the three of them, he wrapped an arm around her lower back and pulled her close. He brought the back of her hand to his lips and murmured, "This is where it all begins, my lass."

Christina swallowed hard, caught in the rich blue of his eyes and the way his lips felt against her skin while at the same time overly aware of Graham watching. She had never felt such a harsh push and pull of emotions.

Lust.

"I…" she began, her words trailing off as Robert peppered kisses along the tender flesh of her inner wrist then up her forearm as his eyes held hers.

"Ye what, lass?" he murmured against her skin.

"My thoughts exactly," Graham grumbled from somewhere nearby. "Ye *what*?"

Good question because she had no idea what she was about to say. So she inhaled deeply, rallied all the strength she could muster and managed to gracefully pull away from Robert. While she most certainly enjoyed what he was doing, a part of her would have liked it to have been Graham instead.

She closed her eyes and shook her head.

What was the *matter* with her?

It was an age old habit to fall for a guy and then bail out of necessity. What she had never, *ever* done was fall for two guys at once. Never mind that one was a famous king and the other a damn wizard.

"I really need to rest," she said a smidge breathlessly for effect as she pulled a 'Lindsay' and batted her lashes at Robert. "I'm sure you understand, sweetie…I mean Robert."

"Nay, ye meant sweetie," he said softly as he reeled her close again, brushed his lips across hers, then let her go but not before he said, "And 'tis good." His eyes flickered from Graham to Christina. "I prefer being yer sweetie, lass."

Then his eyes landed firmly on Graham. "I know of this game ye play with Christina for yer kin and 'tis well enough I suppose." He gestured at the back of the tent. "I will have men posted outside so ye can leave to be with yer lass when 'tis appropriate." His eyes narrowed a fraction. "I expect that to be often, as I'd like to visit Christina with equal discretion."

A flicker of surprise lit Graham's eyes as they went between Christina and Bruce. "Aye?"

"Aye," Robert confirmed, far more presumptuous than she ever imagined. "After all, Christina *is* promised to me and *will* be my wife."

Chapter Eight

GRAHAM HAD NEVER experienced such a riot of emotions. Where logic told him Christina's feelings toward Robert the Bruce were none of his concern, everything inside him rallied against it. Truth told, he had been a breath away from drawing his blade on the Bruce when he pulled her into his arms. Then he had envisioned running it across his neck when he kissed her.

Now, *this*.

"He intends to *marry* ye?" he muttered after Robert left. "Bloody hell!"

"Well, I don't intend to marry him." She plunked down on one of the cots, clearly feeling out of sorts. Her thoughts brushed his. Fuzzy thoughts that moments before had seemed so clear. Almost as if she had been enchanted or cast beneath a spell. "I just really need some shut-eye. I'm wiped."

He knew she was and had felt it from the moment she polished off her food earlier. It was as if something had settled over her. Something that urged her to rest and regain her strength. That in mind, he sat down beside her, took her hand and met her eyes. "Are you all right, lass? Are you feeling well?"

"You said you, not ye. Thanks." A small but tired smile curled her lovely lips as her eyes stayed with his. "Honestly, I feel way off." She rested her head on his shoulder. "Maybe even a little too wiped out all things considered."

Touched that she felt comfortable enough to rest against him, he cupped her hands between his to warm them. "'Tis perfectly normal. You've been through a lot."

"You have no idea," she whispered.

"Nay, I dinnae," he murmured. "But I would like to, Christina. Are we not friends? Do friends not share?"

"They do," she said softly. "Or at least they're supposed to."

"Then share," he murmured. "Not now but mayhap after you rest."

"I don't want you to leave," she whispered. "I don't care what Robert says. I don't want to be alone, and everyone thinks we're together, so it makes sense that you stay and watch over me."

"Aye, then." He had no intention of leaving anyway. "As promised, I will remain by your side."

When she didn't respond, he realized she had drifted off to sleep already, so he lay her down gently. Though she appeared to be sound asleep, when he pulled away, she clasped his wrist and mumbled, "Don't go."

Though it probably wasn't the best idea to stay on this cot, he would not refuse her, so he rested beside her. With so little room he had to pull her back against his front. Unfortunately, the position was bound to test him. Had he ever been so aware of a lass? Had one ever fit so perfectly beside him?

She made no further comment, and her breathing evened. In the meantime, he made do with an uncomfortable erection and closed his eyes. While he had no intention of sleeping, he must have been more tired than he realized. Or more content. Either way, when he woke, she had turned and was propped up on her elbow eying him. He met her slow smile, not daunted in the least that she had been watching him sleep. Rather he found it…enticing somehow.

"Hey there, handsome," she murmured. "You've been sleeping for a while."

He glanced at the sliver of dim light filtering through the tent opening only to realize it was growing dark. "So it seems."

She fiddled absently with the front of his tunic as she considered him. "Thanks for stickin' around. I thought I might wake up to find you'd snuck off."

"Och, nay, the thought never crossed my mind." He grinned. "Not to mention I fell asleep."

"So you did."

"So I did."

As their eyes held, and heat simmered between them, he realized she had woken up in a very particular mood. The same sort he had remained in based on his arousal. When her hand left his tunic, and her fingers trailed along his jaw he knew they were heading for trouble.

"It's never been this strong afterward," she whispered, fingering one of the small braids in his hair as her leg inched up his.

"What's that?" he managed hoarsely, knowing bloody well he should pull away. Yet he was too caught by the curious, lustful look in her eyes. By the way she licked her lower lip then rubbed her lips together, spreading the moisture.

"After...well..."

When she hesitated, he prompted her to continue. "What lass?"

"After using what Granny called my *lightn'*," she said so softly he barely caught it.

"*Lightn'*?" He looked at her curiously. "What is that?"

Unsure, Christina eyed him before she finally sighed. "Well, I'm gonna have to tell someone sooner or later, and I'd prefer you to be the first so here goes." She pressed her lips together again as if rallying her courage then came out with it. "The *lightn'* is my brand of magic, for lack of a better word. I seem to have animal-like instincts and quite often, superhuman strength."

"Hence you catching that arrow before it hit Ma," he murmured.

She nodded. "Hence that."

"Why did your granny call it your *lightn'*?"

A small smile curved her lips and maybe even a bit of relief that she had finally got it off her chest. "She always thought I was lighting up when I used my magic, so she called it my *lightn'* which is really *lighting*." She shrugged and offered a lopsided grin. "We southerners don't make the 'ing' sound too much in case you hadn't noticed."

"I verra much like the way you sound," he murmured. "'Tis easy on the ears."

"Is it?" Her brows shot up, and she chuckled. "Can't say I'm told that too often."

"Well, it is." He slipped his hand into hers. "Now tell me more about this gift. And why your granny thought it lit you up."

Interesting considering he had thought Christina was so sunny when he first met her. Almost as if she glowed. And he had thought that every moment since. His cousins hadn't commented on it, so he assumed it was just part of the way he looked at her. Now he wondered if mayhap it was more than that.

"There's not a lot to say about it except that it comes in handy for a variety of things," she said. "As to Granny thinking it lit me up, she always said it was a combination of how the sun seemed to shine down on me when I used it and then, of course, the charity runs and how happy they made me." She grinned. "She said I lit up on both the inside and outside."

A chill ran through him. So her granny had seen the same thing he did when she looked at Christina. Except he saw it all the time.

While he should probably get up and put some space between them, he enjoyed being near her too much. "Tell me more about these charity runs." He grinned. "We're friends after all, aye? And friends share."

"That they do." Yet he could tell she was hesitant. That she wasn't all that comfortable talking about herself. "Well, like it sounds, I run to raise money for various charities." Her cheeks reddened slightly. "And I often use my magic when I do." She shook her head. "Never money for me but whatever cause I think needs it most at the time."

"That's verra admirable," he said softly, threading his fingers with hers. "Yet you sound guilty."

"Sometimes I feel that way," she admitted. "But I can't help myself. I've got this gift, and a lot of people need help."

"You've nothing to feel guilty about," he replied, more impressed by her than ever. "Not if you use your gift to help others. Is that not the verra definition of a gift? To give something good to others?" He kept his eyes on hers, offering the praise she so richly deserved. "I'm verra proud of you, lass. You are a rare sort."

"Not really," she murmured. "You'd be amazed how many people try to help others. Sometimes I'm truly astounded because so many of them barely have money of their own." She shook her head. "But they have two feet and put them to good use."

"When did you first learn of your gift?" he said, already wondering how it might work alongside his to defeat a warlock...if that is, they were to fight one together.

"Oh, I was little," she said absently.

That, it seemed, was the question that finally drove her off the cot.

"'Twill be verra important for me to know," he persisted as he followed her. "'Twas what eventually helped Conall and Lindsay defeat their warlock."

"There really wasn't any defining moment." She shrugged and didn't meet his eyes. "I think it was a culmination of mini-events that made up my childhood."

Graham was about to ask her more when Lindsay called out from the tent entrance, "Anyone awake in there?"

Before they had a chance to respond, she ducked in followed by Conall.

"Hello, darlings." Lindsay's eyes flickered curiously over the tousled bedding on one cot before she smiled at them. "How are you feeling? Did you rest?"

"I think I'm gonna let you keep guessing." Christina winked then gestured at the ale. "We only have two cups, but we're more than willing to share if you're thirsty."

"Nay, we're fine but thank you." Conall's eyes flickered from the cot to them as well. "Kenna is safe with Grant who wanted us to come speak with you before you joined the others."

"Sit on down then." Christina gestured at the chairs, grabbed a mug of ale then perched on the edge of the cot. "So what's going on? Everything okay?"

"So far, aye." Conall frowned. "But Grant is concerned about a few things. Mainly, the timeline and location of the battle. Not only is the area wrong, but the first day of the battle is supposed to happen on the twenty-third whereas right now they're planning to attack the Sassenach on the twenty-second. Though he's not sure how it's all related yet, Grant's of the mind that the Bruce's marital status or lack thereof is somehow part of the problem." His eyes settled on Christina. "And that, he's guessing, must have something to do with the connection you two have made." He tilted his head. "'Tis unusually strong, aye?"

"Um…" Her eyes shot to Graham then back to Conall before she nodded. "Strong enough I suppose."

Lindsay narrowed her eyes. "Since when are you not direct to a fault?"

Christina frowned. "I'm not sure what you're getting at."

"*Please*." Lindsay rolled her eyes. "Rare is the day I hear *um* on your lips. Even rarer is when you don't tell me exactly how you feel about a man or anything for that matter."

Christina buried a grumble in her mug before taking a few sips.

"So it's as strong as Grant suspects for both you and Robert then," Lindsay murmured as her eyes went to Graham. "And obviously pretty strong for Graham too."

"Very strong for Graham," she replied dutifully, staying in part. "As to Robert, it's…there."

Graham ignored a flash of irritation. How *there* was it exactly? How much did she desire Robert the Bruce?

"Be that as it may, Christina," Lindsay replied. "Grant's beginning to think the draw between you and Robert and the fact that he doesn't think he's married might very well be due to your warlock."

"My warlock?" Christina mouthed before taking another swig of ale.

"Both of yours. The warlock that is." A flicker of amusement lit Lindsay's eyes as they met Graham's. "Seeing how you're fated to be together and all."

"At least the gem already glows the color of Graham's eyes," Conall remarked dryly. "So they are well-prepared."

"Right, there is that." Lindsay sat next to Christina, took her hand and eyed the ring. "You're so lucky that it worked its magic right away, dear."

"Don't I know it." Christina cocked a grin at her. "Love at first sight."

"So it seems." Lindsay eyed the tousled cot again. "Even so, we must remain focused. And that focus, I'm afraid, is on how monumentally wrong things will go if you end up with Robert the Bruce."

"Why?" Christina said. "What's the big deal?"

Graham frowned not only at her words but her thoughts swirling through his mind. She couldn't stop herself when she responded to Lindsay. It was almost as if she was compelled. Or did she actually feel that strongly about Robert? More than anything, she was confused, and Graham felt how unnatural that was. Usually, she had a clear mind and knew what she wanted.

"What's the big deal?" Lindsay said in response to Christina, her eyes wide. "The big deal is even if he doesn't remember, Robert the Bruce has been married for twelve years." Her eyes went wider still. "Not only that but his wife, Elizabeth de Burgh, was taken alongside his daughter nearly eight years ago. She's one of the people he's supposed to barter for after all this is said and done."

Lindsay shook her head then continued. "And while many say they were man and wife in name only, Grant suspects it might have been more than that. He thinks getting her back was Robert's driving force in the upcoming battle."

"Uh huh." Christina bit the corner of her lips, nodded and narrowed her eyes. "So just to be clear. Robert and me having the hots for each other is what…the warlock's doing? Because if we end up together, it's going to somehow ruin Scotland's history?"

"Aye," Conall confirmed. "'Tis not the way things are supposed to go." His eyes went from Graham back to her. "You are meant to be with a MacLomain, lass, and no other."

"That's the plan." She grinned at Graham, her smile not quite reaching her eyes this time. "Right, darlin'?"

"Aye." He again warred with an onslaught of emotions. The ever growing desire to keep her close and the promise he had made to Kenna. "We are together well and true, so the warlock willnae use us to accomplish his goals."

Yet he worried. Was he putting his promise to a lass and her clan before the safety of his country? Would such a thing not destroy Kenna and her kin just as readily? His eyes met Christina's again, and he ground his jaw. He had never felt more conflicted.

"Good then." Lindsay nodded and looked between Graham and Christina. "Just as long as you two are together and nothing happens between Robert and Christina, we *should* be just fine."

"But if you are *not* truly together," Conall gave Graham a pointed look, "then I highly suggest you get busy changing that."

"I couldn't agree more." Lindsay stood, patted Christina on the shoulder then took Conall's hand. "But what are we worrying about?" She tossed a grin at the cot. "Because they're *clearly* together."

"*These two are killin' me.*" Christina's words floated through Graham's mind without her knowing. "*Could they be any more obvious?*"

"The Bruce has requested that everyone join him at the fire outside his tent," Conall said. "Before you do, I suggest you two have a talk and make bloody well sure the Bruce knows where your hearts lie when you join us."

Before they had a chance to respond, Conall and Lindsay left.

"Bloody hell," Graham muttered as he plunked down at the table and took a deep swig of ale. "We havenae got them fooled in the least, lass." He shook his head. "I dinnae think we have any of my kin fooled for that matter."

"Then we'll just have to keep working at it, sweetie," she replied optimistically, downing a good swig of her own ale as well.

"And here I thought Robert was your sweetie," he muttered under his breath.

"Well, I'll *be*." She set aside her mug, planted her hands on her hips and eyeballed him with a little grin. "Are you jealous, Graham MacLomain? For real?"

"Versus for fake?" He snorted but couldn't help a small grin to match hers. "So what if I am a wee bit? 'Twould only help our cause and make things appear more believable betwixt us, aye?"

"That it would," she agreed, still eying him with amusement as she sat across from him. "You're not starting to develop feelings for me, are you?"

"Nay," he replied a little too quickly. "What about you?"

"What about me?"

He kept grinning. "Are you developing feelings for me?"

"Lord, no." She shook her head. "That just happens after I use my *lightn'*."

Confused, he looked at her in question.

"Oh, I thought you might be referring to my interest in you when you first woke up," she explained.

Now, this could be fun. "Your interest?"

"Heck, yeah." She chuckled and was so blunt he had to smile. "The sort of sexual interest to match the ragin' erection you had."

"'Tis normal when sleeping next to a bonnie lass," he enlightened, so bloody charmed by her he felt like he had tunnel vision every time he looked at her.

"Sure thing, honey, whatever you wanna tell yourself."

Seemingly restless, she stood and began stretching.

"'Tis hard for you to sit still for too long, aye?" he said. "You like to stay active."

"Sure do." When she wrapped her hands together and stretched her arms over her head, her breasts pressed against the front of her dress. So much so that he had trouble looking elsewhere.

"That's how you stay so slender despite your appetite," he murmured as she began doing things that accentuated her in all the right ways and made his brogue thicken. "Ye burn off food as fast as ye eat it."

"Pretty much," she commented. "Using my *lightn'* creates an incredibly strong need for nourishment, rest and oftentimes sex. A whole lot of sex." She bent over and grabbed her ankles, muttering, "What I wouldn't do for some yoga pants right now. Or even running pants."

Eyes glued to cleavage begging to be released, his words were hoarse. "I ken the food and rest but why sex?"

"I don't know. It just evens me out somehow. Like cravin' an icy cold sweet tea after a mid-summer's nap. You just gotta have it. Lots of it." Her sparkling eyes met his, and the corner of her mouth shot up. "It refreshes like nothing you've ever felt."

He had never viewed sex as particularly refreshing, but he would certainly take her word for it.

"Oooh, and hell if I don't get all sorts of crazy energy," she continued, watching him with the devil in her eyes as she dutifully apologized to her granny for swearing again. "*Nothing* is more wild and untamed than post *lightn'* sex." She blew her hair out of her eyes and fanned her face. "I just wish it could be that way more often."

It can. I could see to that. As often as possible, he thought.

"Aye," he whispered, too dumbfounded to manage anything more coherent or dashing than that. Good thing too considering he was set to marry another woman.

"We should..." He cleared his throat a few times. "Return to the cot."

Her brows slammed together, and she smirked. "Return to the cot?"

"I mean fix the cot." He downed his ale. "So that Robert doesnae come in and think..."

He trailed off, frustrated that he cared. But he did. He *had* to. Right? Truthfully, he was all turned around. They *should* leave the cot in disarray so that Robert knew they were definitely together, but he felt guilty because of Kenna.

Yet as his eyes lingered on Christina, his desire for her only grew stronger. He had never wanted to return to bed as much as he did right now.

"There we go," she announced, not spending much time on the blankets before she turned and grinned. She knew full well where his mind was, yet she had a way of making him feel all right about it. As if it was the most natural thing in the world. She gestured at the tent entrance. "Are you ready to go play our parts then?"

Graham nodded, opened the tent flap and gestured for her to go first. As she passed, she did the last thing he expected. She came close, murmured, "Thanks for being such a gentleman. Now let's get a bit more practice in for all to see," and pulled his lips down to hers.

It was probably a good thing they were more outside the tent than inside because he would have had her back on that cot in no time. She tasted of ale and lass, and he wanted to sample far more of her as their tongues met and danced. The way she kissed him made every muscle lock up in sweet anticipation.

He wanted her beneath him, over him, wherever she bloody well pleased just as long as they were without clothes. He wanted to run his hands all over her while she spent her *lightn'* energy down to the very last drop in his arms.

They were both so lost in the kiss that neither heard Robert approach.

"Och, laddie, ye've put in yer time, aye?"

While tempted to pull her closer, deepen their kiss and show Robert the Bruce just how much *time* he was willing to devote to Christina, he gently ended the kiss instead. Her eyes lingered on Graham's, her body trembling against his in need, as he cupped her cheek. "Are ye well, lass?"

He knew she was. That she was from the moment they kissed. The problem was the deepening connection between them. The very real desire they thought would be easy to control.

"I'm good, Graham," Christina finally responded before she nodded. "So much better than I thought I would be...ever expected to be."

"Aye," he said softly, unable to tear his eyes from hers.

"As I said," Robert came alongside, "ye've put in yer time, aye?" He looked between them. "Both of ye."

"We have," she whispered, her eyes still with Graham's until they drifted to Robert's. What he saw at that moment was alarming. The 'walking on a cloud' place she had been with Graham became something else when she looked at Robert. More so, it was instant.

Adoration. Desire. Flat out lust. But too much too fast. Unnatural.

Dark magic.

He didn't doubt it for a moment.

Or at least influenced by dark magic as Grant suspected.

Robert held out his elbow to her. "Walk with me, lass?"

"It would be my pleasure," she said softly and with more flirtation than usual. "Where are we off to?"

"Not far." Robert shot Graham a smug look before they headed back toward the Bruce's tent. "We're enjoying freshly caught venison and good company before a busy day on the morrow."

"Doing what?" she asked.

"Ye'll have to wait and see." He grinned. "'Tis hard to know if ye'll be interested but I hope so."

She met his smile. "Why not just tell me?"

"And ruin the anticipation?"

Christina's smile lit up her face, managing to make Graham's groin tighten despite his growing concern and aggravation. Though he remained close even as they joined the others, it felt like she was worlds away. Never once did she glance his way.

Eventually, he joined Kenna to see how she was doing.

"I've never seen ye look at a lass like ye do her," she remarked softly. "'Twas how I once looked at Fraser."

"Och, nay," he tried to deny, but Kenna gave him a knowing look then shook her head and murmured, "I dinnae want to take that sort of happiness away from ye, friend. 'Tis not right. Ye deserve true love more than most."

"No more than any other." He frowned at her. "And I dinnae deserve it so much that I'd sacrifice the safety of yer clan for it, lass."

"Ye mean my safety," she said even softer. "Because of Fraser. Because ye feel ye owe it to him."

"Nay." He frowned heavily and shook his head. "Dinnae ever speak like that, lass. Are we not friends then? Have we not been for a verra long time?"

"We have," she conceded as her eyes dropped. "And well ye know it, Graham MacLomain." Her eyes rose to his. "And nearly more at one time if I recall correctly."

"Aye," he whispered. There had been a time before Kenna and Fraser fell in love that something nearly ignited betwixt them. But it had been brief and never acted upon. Now he realized as their eyes held she hoped mayhap they would find it again. That the long years in between had not dulled the embers entirely.

As their eyes continued to hold, he realized that would be a hard line to cross. In truth, at that moment he realized despite his intentions to marry her, loving her would feel like a betrayal to Fraser's memory. That, he thought as his eyes flickered back to Christina, was half of it anyway.

"She is verra bonnie," Kenna said, following his line of sight. "And verra kind too I think."

"Aye, kinder than most," he agreed. And far more bonnie. But he did not voice that. "And braver."

"'Tis good," she remarked. "Because there is nothing but danger here."

He nodded. He knew.

"Yet she has the protection of the Bruce," he reminded.

"Aye, if that's what ye'd call it." Her eyes narrowed slightly at Robert and Christina. "I'd say there's just as much danger there as anywhere else."

Kenna possessed no magic but had always displayed a remarkable sixth sense.

"Aye then?" he said.

She nodded and murmured, "There's nothing but trouble ahead if those two find love."

Graham clenched his jaw and frowned as he tore his eyes from Christina and focused on the fire. Again, he felt incredibly conflicted.

His eyes went to Kenna's when she rested her hand on his arm.

"Yer making this more difficult than it needs to be," she whispered. "Because ye should only ever follow yer heart."

"My heart's torn," he said softly.

"Aye, betwixt yer obligations to me and yer desire for Christina." She shook her head, her eyes pained. "Just trust yer heart to lead ye in the right direction, and my guess is there willnae be a divide in the least. That all will work out as it should."

"Ye have more faith than most," he murmured. "When life hasnae been all that kind to ye."

"Kind enough since ye and yer kin came into it," she reminded, a flicker of sadness in her eyes. "Kind enough that I *did* find love in the end, no matter how short lived."

He nodded, squeezed her hand and was about to say more when Bryce's words floated through his mind. *"We're close, Cousin, but we've run into trouble."*

"What kind of trouble?"

"The kind that happens when men the size of Sven and I cross paths with what have to be Robert the Bruce's smallest soldiers."

Moments later, a man raced through the encampment and cried out, "Trouble afoot! Danger!" He shook his head. "But at least we've already downed one!"

Chapter Nine

"THEY'VE BEEN GONE too long, haven't they?" Christina muttered as she pulled back the tent flap and peeked out. "And who do you think they downed? Sven or Bryce?" She shook her head. "It's hard to imagine either of them."

"Staring out there isn't going to make them return any faster," Lindsay said. "Sit and drink some whisky with us. They'll be just fine."

Graham, Conall, and Grant had gone off with Robert and several of his men to see what all the commotion was about. That seemed like ages ago. Meanwhile, she and the girls were tucked away in Robert's tent with several men guarding the entrance, including his brother, Edward who tossed her a lustful look before she closed the flap.

"How do you know they're fine for sure?" Christina asked as she joined Lindsay and Kenna by the fire.

"I just know," Lindsay assured. "Once you finally see them fight you'll understand. It's breathtaking."

Christina chuckled and perked her brows. "*Breathtaking?*"

"Definitely. You'll see."

"That fighting is breathtaking?" She shook her head. "I highly doubt that."

"Aye, 'tis most impressive," Kenna agreed. "Graham and his kin are verra talented."

Christina couldn't help but wonder if there was a double innuendo there but when her eyes went to Kenna, she dispelled the notion. The Scotswoman was both sweet and strong to a fault. Not the sneaky sort who secretly had designs on Graham and was trying to swindle him into marriage by claiming her clan's well-being was on the line. Because the thought *had* crossed Christina's mind when she watched them together earlier. She didn't mean for it to, but it had.

They made a cute couple. A very attractive one actually. As a matter of fact, they looked so good together on occasion it was enough to draw her eyes from Robert. Enough to cause an annoying itch of jealousy to flare and never let go. If she knew what was good for her, she would support the whole thing and be happy for Graham. Instead, she found herself imagining inappropriate things.

First, that Fraser appeared out of nowhere on a white horse, arisen from the dead as he swept Kenna into his arm's, leaving a crestfallen Graham in his wake. One who quickly turned secretly thankful eyes Christina's way. Then in another scenario, she envisioned Graham lurching to his feet, closing the distance between them before growling, "I cannae be without ye anymore, Christina. I *refuse* to!" Then he would yank her close and kiss her hard.

"Did you hear me, darling?"

Or maybe it would happen all at once. Kenna and Graham would be gazing at each other one second then see the truth clear as day. They would shake their heads and stand at the same time, declaring simultaneously, "This is all wrong! What were we thinking? We're not meant to be together."

"Christina," Lindsay cut into her thoughts. "Did you hear me?"

"What?" She blinked several times and looked at Lindsay. "Can't say I did, sweetheart. Mind repeating?"

Lindsay's eyebrows perked. "I was just wondering if you were going to acknowledge that Kenna just refreshed your drink."

"Oh." She looked from her full mug to Kenna and plastered on the warmest smile she could manage. One she suspected didn't quite reach her eyes seeing how this woman would be sharing Graham's bed the rest of her damned life. "Well, bless your heart, darlin'. Thank you."

"My pleasure." Kenna eyed Christina, her words soft. "I know well of the connections betwixt MacLomains and Brouns. The fated love that exists."

Lindsay tossed Christina a look as Kenna continued. "'Twas something Fraser vowed would not happen to him. He had seen it."

Lindsay narrowed her eyes. "Fraser had *seen* it?"

"Aye." She nodded. "He had the gift of foresight and knew 'twas not part of his fate. Nay." She shook her head. "He was fated for something else entirely."

"Death," Christina whispered.

"Nay, actually." Wisdom lit Kenna's eyes. "Not when he was so young anyway."

"I'm sorry his gift didn't help save him then," Lindsay said softly, respect in her voice.

"So we all think," Kenna whispered. "But 'tis hard to know."

Christina and Lindsay frowned.

"But we *do* know," Lindsay said more bluntly than she likely intended. "He died."

"Did he then?" Kenna's eyes leveled with hers. "How can ye be so sure?"

"Because I've been inside Conall's mind and I saw his last moments," Lindsay said gently as she took Kenna's hand. "He's gone, sweetness. He really is." She shook her head. "And I'm so very sorry."

"Sometimes things arenae as they seem," Kenna replied, not defiant in the least but rather matter-of-fact. "Sometimes there is more going on than meets the eye."

Christina took a deep swig of ale. She couldn't help but wonder why they were having this conversation right now. Why Kenna would not have talked to Graham or any of his family about it first.

"Have you mentioned your thoughts to any of the MacLomains?" Lindsay's lips turned down in concern. "Adlin? Grant? Moreover, Fraser's parents, Cassie and Logan?"

"Nay, nor will I ever," Kenna said softly. "'Tis not my place. They have been through enough, and I willnae dredge up something they are only just healing from."

"Fair enough." Lindsay kept frowning. "But what if he's trapped where Conall's father Darach was? In another dimension created by a warlock?" She shook her head. "If that's the case, we might be able to save him."

"'Tis not like that." Kenna's eyes were haunted. "Where he lives, *how* he lives, may verra well be beyond the scope of saving."

Well, what the hell did she mean by that? Christina was about to ask when a harsh chill swept over her.

Something was wrong.

She barely had time to process what was happening when a dagger whipped in from the backside of the tent and pinned Lindsay's hand to the table. Before she had a chance to turn her head and enchant, three men rushed in. One put a burlap bag over Lindsay's head and muffled her screams not only with a hand over her mouth but with a dagger to her neck as his eyes met Christina's and he shook his head.

She knew what that meant.

Make a sound and Lindsay died.

Though more than tempted to use her magic, nothing said she could take these men down before that blade sliced Lindsay's neck. And that was a risk she wasn't willing to take. Terribly shaken but not about to show it, she stood and prayed her legs kept working as she met Kenna's eyes and nodded. Thankfully, the Scotswoman kept her mouth shut and stood as well. Moments later, she and Kenna were tossed over the men's shoulders and taken.

Though frightened, all she could think about was Lindsay because she was fairly certain her friend had been left behind. If so, had she been killed? She bit back tears as she realized the truth. Why would they let her live when they clearly knew what kind of threat she was? Or so said the fact they covered her eyes and hair, two features very much intertwined with her ability to enchant.

Knowing better than to make a sound, she fell back on what she had been told about the MacLomain, Broun connections. That if she had a true love, they should be able to hear her telepathically. So she took no chances and screamed into her mind, *"Graham, Bryce, help! Lindsay's in trouble! Someone's trying to kill her!"*

She said those words over and over, praying one of them would hear.

What she never expected was a response. *"We're heading back now, lass. What's happening?"*

Bryce?

He might sound different within her mind, but there was no mistaking him.

"We're...they've..." she stuttered in her head, so thrown off he wasn't Graham she could barely make sense of what he was saying.

"Try to remain calm and think clearly no matter how difficult," Bryce responded. *"Once you've gathered yourself share everything with me, aye? Are you safe? Where are you?"*

He was right. She needed to remain focused and calm the hell down. So what if Graham didn't respond. That should be the least of her concerns right now. With that firmly in mind, she managed to tell him what happened.

Afterward, there was silence until he finally said, "*I need you to try to think and communicate more clearly, lass. All you said was the same word over and over again.*"

She had? "*What word?*"

"*Earrach.*"

"*What does that mean?*"

"*Spring.*"

She frowned and flinched against the pain of being jostled on someone's shoulder. "*Sorry, I might know the word spring but not that other word. So I definitely didn't say it.*" Lord above, she wanted to beat the crap out of the man carrying her. "*Why do you suppose I would say that?*"

"*I dinnae know.*" She heard the frown in his internal voice. "*But 'tis uncanny considering today is the last day of spring.*"

That *was* a little strange, wasn't it?

Apparently, Milly and Lindsay had also said seasonal words in Gaelic. Milly, autumn and Lindsay, winter. So it appeared they were going in order. The reason for the words still remained a mystery. If nothing else, they seemed to align with the time of year each one experienced their adventures. The general consensus was that it was a good thing to hear or say the word. It meant they were on the right path.

This didn't quite feel like the right path though.

But then what did she know about destiny and fate?

"*Have you gotten back to Linds yet?*" she asked. Worry, above all, likely clouded her thinking and that's why he wasn't getting her message. "*Is she okay?*"

"*Lindsay will be all right,*" he responded. "*But you must continue on as if you dinnae know that, lass. Do you ken?*"

"*Yes,*" she replied, understanding full well the less her captors knew, the better.

"*Keep reporting back to me, Christina, and stay strong,*" Bryce continued. "*We will come for you. Dinnae doubt it for a moment.*"

She grunted in pain as a creaky door opened and the man started up stairs. The air was musty and cold, all of which she shared with

Bryce. *"It sounds like he's walking on stone. We're definitely in a building of some sort."*

"You're coming across clearly now," he responded. *"Just keep talking to me, aye, lass?"*

"You got it." He might not be Graham but he was a soothing presence, and she was grateful he was there. *"How is everyone else doing, Bryce? Sven and yourself? We were told one of you were hurt."* And because she couldn't help herself. *"And how's Graham?"*

"All's well enough," he replied. *"Nobody was hurt. 'Twas a decoy so that you lasses would be more readily accessible."*

"Oh damn." That made sense.

"As to Graham..." There was a hesitation. *"He isnae verra happy."*

"I imagine not considering Kenna was taken," she remarked. *"And Lindsay was nearly killed."*

Bryce didn't respond to that, but she sensed he wanted to. That there was more to it. *"What is it, Bryce?"*

"'Tis nothing. You need to keep focused on your surroundings," he continued before she cut him off.

"Just tell me, Bryce."

"'Tis you he frets over, lass," he murmured. Silence stretched before he continued, his brogue evident with his emotions. *"And whilst the two of ye claim to be together, 'tis now clear yer meant for me. It cannae be any other way because 'tis me who heard yer call and 'tis me speaking within yer mind."*

Christina wasn't quite sure how to respond to that, so she said nothing. She barely knew Bryce. But then she barely knew Graham. Yet her mind fought the idea of her being meant for anyone besides Graham...or maybe even Robert.

A mind that wasn't supposed to want a man, to begin with.

She cursed under her breath when she was plunked down on a hard stone floor. Then she heard a door slam shut and a key latch lock. She blinked, trying to adjust to the pitch black room but it was slow going.

"Kenna?" she whispered. "Are you here, honey?"

"Aye," came a soft voice.

Relief washed over her. They were both alive, and she reported as much to Bryce.

"*Is there a window?*" he asked. "*Mayhap you can look out and get a better lay of the land?*"

"*Maybe but it's hellishly dark.*"

When she heard scuffling, she frowned. "Kenna, is that you?"

"Aye," she replied, apparently on the same wavelength as Bryce. "I think I see a window. I'm going to look."

Christina nodded and felt her way along the cold, rough wall.

"I can see out the window," Kenna said softly. "We're up high...a castle I think."

When Christina said as much to Bryce, he replied. "*It can only be Stirling Castle.*"

Stirling Castle? She had heard about this castle. "*Really?*"

"*Aye,*" he said. "*'Tis currently occupied by the Sassenach but under siege by the Scots. That means there's a way in and we'll find it.*" He paused. "*It sounds like they put you in a tower. Get as many details as you can from Kenna.*"

So she did, and it was pretty much confirmed.

They were imprisoned in one of the most famous castles in Scotland.

She had just found her way to a corner and was closer to Kenna based on the sound of her voice when a harsh chill raced over her skin. Moments later, it felt like she was sitting in a walk-in freezer. She was suddenly so frightened that breathing became nearly impossible. "*Bryce, I think something's wrong.*"

No response.

"Kenna?" she whispered, straining to see in the darkness.

Unlike Lindsay, she wasn't a big fan of the dark. Mainly because it meant the power had been shut off when she was a kid. There was no money to pay the bills again. Not Granny's fault, not really, just a kind heart unable to say no. A kind heart who had a habit of not putting the scant few dollars they had in the right place.

The electric company.

So Christina would light a candle and read a good book, often to Granny to help ease her guilt. And often the Bible because it was one of the few books they had. Back when books were paper not digital. Good thing, because Lord knows they would never have been able to afford an e-reader.

"What is that?" Kenna's voice was a hoarse squeak in an echoing chamber. "Do ye feel that, lass? The unnatural cold?"

"Yeah." She scrambled toward Kenna's voice until she finally bumped into her. "Sweet Jesus, there you are."

"Aye." Kenna's hand slipped into hers, and she whispered, "I dinnae think we are alone, Christina."

That's when she sensed it. Something dark, foreboding, and towering. Rather than squint into the darkness, she tucked Kenna behind her, closed her eyes and focused. To hell with not using magic. If something was coming for them, she intended to fight it for all she was worth.

At first, there was nothing, then most certainly something. It was tall, slender and clothed from head to toe in black. It stood mere feet away, its soulless eyes watching her closely, its curiosity in her gift obvious.

She remained perfectly still, anticipating the worst.

What was it going to do? How painful was this going to be? Though she should be terrified, she felt rather detached. Ready. More than that? Angry as all get out. This thing was going to hurt Kenna over her dead body.

"Who are you?" she ground out, shifting so that Kenna was better protected. While she should probably stop talking she was far too confrontational for that. "Stop being a coward and give it to me straight."

"Good, yer remaining strong, Christina," it said, his voice raspy and grating. "I had so hoped ye would." He flashed a creepy grin. "The wee witch so hoped ye would."

"What wee witch?" she asked.

"Ye will know soon enough," he responded, his voice like sandpaper on metal.

She opened her mouth to respond, but he was gone. Snuffed out. Just like that, in the blink of an eye, he had vanished and his harsh chill with him.

"'Twas true evil, aye?" Kenna whispered, trembling behind Christina as the moment stretched on.

Was it gone for good? Would it come back?

"Hell yeah that was evil," Christina agreed when she finally found her voice. "Up one side and down the other." As her body caught up with delayed terror, her legs turned to jelly, and she sank down the wall until she was sitting. She tugged at Kenna with a shaky hand. "Join me, sugar." Then her voice grew as shaky as her hands. "I sure could use the company. Conversation. Anything to get my mind off of...*that*."

Kenna slid down beside her and squeezed her hand. "Thank ye for protecting me, Christina. 'Twas verra brave."

"Probably more foolish than anything." She released a nervous chuckle that sounded forced even to her own ears. "I don't think I could've stopped that thing so I'm not so sure you should be thanking me."

"Whether ye could or not, 'twas that ye intended to," Kenna said softly. "And that is more admirable than ye know...especially considering 'twas me ye defended."

She frowned though Kenna couldn't see it in the darkness. "Well, what do you mean by that?"

"'Tis clear ye love Graham," she replied. "And 'tis also clear yer a wee bit jealous of me."

"Hush your mouth," she chastised far too quickly and definitely too lightly. "I'm no such thing."

"What?" She heard a small smile in Kenna's voice. "In love with Graham or jealous of me?"

"Both."

"He feels the same ye know," Kenna commented. "'Tis all over his face every time he looks at ye."

Bull. Yet an annoying little thrill whipped through her.

"Why are you telling me this?" Christina murmured. "When you two are to be married."

"Because we arenae," she whispered. "And I should have already told him as much."

"What do you mean?" Christina swallowed, not sure what to make of this turn of events. "Why not?" She shook her head. "Don't you have to in order to keep your clan safe?"

"Aye," she said softly. "But I will find another way. 'Twill not be like this."

"Like what?"

"I willnae take true happiness away from a friend who is finally so close to getting what he has long deserved."

"And you think that's me," Christina said.

"I know it is." She could almost feel Kenna's eyes turn her way as her voice became whisper soft. "Yer a verra lucky lass, Christina."

Based on the emotion in Kenna's voice, it didn't take Christina long to figure things out.

"Aw, *shoot*," she whispered, seeing it all too clearly now. "How long have you loved him?"

"Long enough," Kenna murmured.

"Before or after Fraser?"

When she didn't answer right away, Christina sighed and leaned her head back against the wall. Kenna had loved Graham all along. "Did Fraser know? Graham?"

"I think Graham only really started to figure it out this eve," she murmured, her voice distant as if caught in memories. "Fraser knew at the end." Her emotional swallow was loud enough to hear. "He learned of it right before he went off to battle that last time…before he left us all."

"God, that sucks," Christina whispered. "For all of you but mostly poor Fraser." She frowned, defending a man she never knew. "Did you *ever* love him?"

"Aye," Kenna said. "Just not as much as he deserved."

Christina thought about that, mulling over what Kenna was willing to do. "Now, when he's determined to marry you, you're willing to just let Graham ride off into the sunset with another woman?"

"Ride off into the sunset?" Kenna asked.

"Up and run off with another woman," Christina rephrased.

"Run off?"

"*Love* another woman."

"Aye," Kenna replied, her voice soft again. Firm. "Because I love him, I want what's best for him…even if that isnae me."

"That's noble of you," Christina replied, more dryly than intended. "But a little unbelievable if you don't mind my honesty."

"Once ye get to know Graham better ye'll ken my actions," Kenna murmured. "He's got such a kind heart and willing way."

Christina tensed. Had they already slept together? "Willing way?"

"Aye," Kenna responded. "There isnae anything he wouldnae do to help those in need."

"Any specifics?" she asked, still fishing for a possible roll in the hay not being discussed.

Silence settled for a moment as Kenna evidently hashed out what to say. Thankfully, it was not what she figured was coming.

"There were many admirable moments that stand out," she murmured. "But I suppose the one I remember best was the time he stood up to my uncle. Da and Fraser were off to battle, but Graham had been ordered to stay behind to watch over MacLomain Castle and its surrounding lands which he readily did." Christina sensed Kenna shaking her head. "He was only fifteen winters but he didnae back down when my uncle came at me."

"How'd he come at you, darlin'," Christina said gently, almost afraid to ask.

"It doesnae matter," she murmured. "What *did* matter is Graham was there and fought the bastard. He protected me the best he could until he was a bloody mess."

"Graham or your uncle?"

"Graham, I'm afraid," she said. "Though I know of his magic, many dinnae in these changin' times including most of my clan. So Graham, not nearly the size he is today, fought him hand to fist. Ye'd have to see the size of my uncle to truly appreciate Graham's courage."

"So he defended your honor," Christina said. "That's great. It is. And I can see that." She cocked her head. "But wouldn't Fraser have too if he'd been there?"

"Aye, Fraser would have," she said. "But 'twould have been a much different story because he is a much different man than Graham. And 'twas not just the one time but many times Graham fought on my behalf. Too often by far."

Dear Lord, what kind of life had this woman endured?

"How would Fraser have been so different than Graham?" Christina asked, truly curious. "Defending honor seems pretty cut and dry to me."

"But it isnae," she replied softly. "Some men can do it and walk away mostly unscathed but 'twould not have been the case with Fraser. He had a rage inside him that when provoked, didnae allow him to stop when fury took him."

Christina contemplated that. "He would've downright killed your uncle, huh?"

"Aye," she said, "and that would have created more trouble for my clan than they already had. Because the MacLomains would have sided with Fraser and strife with such a mighty allied clan would lead to worse things indeed." Her voice wobbled slightly. "Things that would have led to pointless battling and more bloodshed. More loss and heartache."

Moment by moment, she was getting a much clearer picture of Graham. The forward-thinking kind-hearted honorable man he truly was. Something she never doubted but liked to better understand.

Fraser, however, she was starting to wonder about.

"So I take it Fraser had a bad temper," she said, dreading her next question. "Did he ever hit you, Kenna?"

"Fraser? Och, nay, never," Kenna replied, her voice a little lighter. "He would never hit a lass. He was just more intense than most. He took things to heart and often believed battling was a better means to an end than diplomacy. We were wee bairns together, all of us, and his temperament just led him in a certain direction. Battling was always his favorite pastime and plotting the Sassenach's ruin wasnae far behind that."

"What about love?" Christina asked softly, getting a much clearer picture for sure. "Not at the top of his list, eh?"

"He was a true warrior," Kenna whispered, emotion evident in her voice. "And I fear that was all he would ever be. All he truly cared about."

Everything made perfect sense now. Kenna might have loved Fraser if he didn't have what sounded like a hardened heart. And damn, if a man the likes of Graham defended her honor that much, how could she *not* fall head over heels for him?

"Yet Fraser loved you, so he had a softer side," Christina said. "Right?"

"Aye," Kenna murmured, her voice suddenly a bit whimsical. "When he chose to be charming, 'twas verra difficult to refuse him. Impossible really."

"And so you didn't."

"And so I didnae," she whispered.

If Christina didn't know better, she would say Kenna was in love with both Fraser and Graham but decided to leave it alone. She understood things a lot better now and was grateful for the chat. Actually, she was grateful for the time alone with Kenna, no matter how dank their surroundings.

"I'm not lookin' for a man, Kenna," she said for no other reason than she liked Kenna and wanted to come clean. "So you don't have to worry about Graham and me."

Kenna chuckled, squeezed her hand and rested her head on Christina's shoulder without saying a word. Just fine with that, ready for some quiet time to contemplate, she rested her head against Kenna's and closed her eyes.

Big mistake because she must have dozed off.

The next thing she knew, pre-dawn light filled the chamber, and she was being dragged across the floor by her hair. Ever the scrapper, she kicked and screamed, fighting like hell and ready to embrace her magic, but it was too late.

A heavy fist came down hard, and everything went black.

Chapter Ten

"'TIS THAT TOWER then?" Graham growled, eying one of many. "Are ye bloody well sure, Cousin?"

"Aye." Bryce nodded from his perch beside Graham. "Based on Christina's description, that should be the one."

Graham continued to scowl, as he had been doing since the moment Christina and Kenna had been taken. More so, since he learned that Bryce and Christina were speaking within the mind.

"I'll bloody well kill every last Sassenach in there," Conall vowed, on Graham's other side as they crouched behind bushes. "They will pay for what they did to Lindsay."

"Aye," Graham and Bryce agreed. The poor lass's hand had been ruined but was seen to with hopes Aðísla might eventually appear and assist with the healing process. It seemed Sven couldn't help either as his ability to heal only applied to fellow dragons. Lindsay, meanwhile, cared little about the state of her hand and more about the fate of Christina.

"It is just a hand, darling," she had said bravely to Conall earlier as he fussed over it, cursing the whole time. "I have another." Then she gave him a pointed look. "Now go save my friend. Now, *please*." Her pained eyes raked over all of them. "Go on. Now. Right away!"

So here they were, nearly half a day later because they could not head this way any sooner. Not until Robert had a full understanding of what had happened and how he might utilize Grant and the rest of them in getting her back.

Ironically, he had begun devising another battle strategy altogether since Christina's abduction. One that put them closer to the castle than before. A plan that, interestingly enough, if they played things right, might just help history unfold correctly. The battle might just take place exactly where it was supposed to.

They just needed to keep Robert convinced that Christina was still locked away in Stirling Castle. At least for now. So as far as he knew they were out scouting the land looking for a way they might save her. Which was true. Robert just didn't need to know that it would take them hours not days.

Once they figured out how.

"So we're to do this without an ounce of magic, aye?" Conall muttered. "I dinnae like it. There are far too many Scots guarding the outside of the castle." He shook his head. "And we've got to get in and out without them ever knowing we're here."

"Then we bypass them," Bryce said, his eyes locked on the window high above. "The Sassenach got out then back in without being detected, so there's got to be a way."

Likely, because they had a warlock assisting them. He tried not to dwell on that too much, though. They had far bigger things to worry about. Namely an enormous castle.

"The castle is on a bloody cliff with nothing but sheer wall surrounding it," Graham pointed out. But like his cousins, he was already trying to figure out how they might make it up. Better yet, how they might get the lasses back down.

"Nothing's ever as sheer as it looks," Bryce murmured. "Not for a dragon."

"A dragon that cannae use his magic," Conall reminded as they moved forward, staying low beneath the tree cover until they were beside the cliff beneath the castle. It was a mighty long way up.

"Psst." They all spun, weapons drawn, at the whispered sound behind them before a small, cloaked figure appeared alongside Sven.

"Lindsay!" Conall closed the distance between them and pulled her into his arms. "What is it, lass? Are you well?" He shook his head and frowned at Sven before his eyes met hers. "You shouldnae be out here."

"Any more than you guys should." She brushed her lips across his and reassured, "I'm just fine so no worries, all right? My wound has been seen to by the camp healer who is rather good considering the era." She gestured at Sven and smiled. "And I'm fairly certain I have the biggest badass bodyguard around."

Conall frowned at Sven. "A bodyguard who never should have let you come here."

"Your woman has a mind of her own and lets no man stop her," Sven stated. "You should be proud."

"Besides," Lindsay said. "I think it was for the best that we got out of there. Sven especially. He makes everyone nervous."

Graham could well understand that. Sven was as big as Bryce but more intense.

Conall frowned along with the rest of them at the small blossom of blood on the bandage wrapped around her hand. She had to be in a great deal of pain. "Yer gravely wounded, lass and should be resting."

"Oh, goodness, *gravely*?" She rolled her eyes, side-stepped him and stared up at the castle, shaking her head. "Just as I suspected. Impossible."

"Och, nay." Bryce peered up, determined. "I can make it."

"Then what?" She cocked a look at him. "You kindly escort the women down?"

Bryce sighed and crossed his arms over his chest. "I can at least get up there then figure out something once I do."

"*Not* a good plan," she stated, eying the castle. "I have a *much* better one."

Conall scowled and shook his head. "Nay, lass."

"We all know my gift of enchantment seems to go under warlock radar, so it makes perfect sense," she declared. "We'll figure out a way in, and I'll enchant whoever I can along the way." She shrugged. "Those that I can't, you cut down. The English that is. Not the Scots."

"'Tis too dangerous for ye, lass," Graham said. He might be desperate to get to Christina and of course, save Kenna, but he loved Lindsay as well.

"I dinnae like it," Conall added.

"I didn't expect you to." Her eyes met his. "Any more than I like when you run off and put your life on the line." She arched a brow. "But we do what we must for friends and family. That's why we love each other so much, right?"

"One of the *many* reasons," he said, clearly charmed by her faster than ever lately as the two only grew closer. Though he released a hearty displeased sigh, she won the battle. "As you wish then, my lass."

Sven wore a tentative look as he eyed the castle. "Now we just need to figure out how to get in and out without the Scots being the wiser." His eyes met Lindsay's. "How many people can you enchant at once?"

"Quite a few as long as we can get them all in front of me," she replied. "Do that, and I'll keep them distracted while you guys sneak in and save the girls."

"Aye." Graham nodded. "But I dinnae think ye need to distract that many, lass." He shook his head. "Just a few should do."

He gestured for them to follow him to a section of the northwest side of the castle heavily blanketed by trees. As he suspected there were more men than usual posted in that area but not so many that Lindsay couldn't handle them.

"They're guarding that." He pointed at a specific part of the castle as they crouched behind some dense shrubs. "'Tis our best way in without causing too much of a stir."

Bryce eyed the low wall in front of a higher wall in front of a tower and shook his head. "I dinnae ken."

"There's a drop between the two walls that is hard to see, but the Scots know it's there," Graham explained. "'Tis the most accessible area of the castle but can also be the most dangerous."

Sven nodded, eying the widows above. "People think they have found a vulnerable spot and entrance to the backside of the castle, but it is a trap. Once you cross the first wall, you're trapped as arrows or blades rain down."

"That's right." Graham nodded. "But nobody is there right now."

"How could you possibly know that?" Bryce asked.

"I dinnae know," he murmured because he didn't. "I just feel it somehow."

"You *feel* it?" Lindsay glanced at Graham "Is that part of your magic?" She frowned. "I thought you controlled the element of water."

"I do," he said absently, not quite sure where the feeling was coming from, just that this was their best route.

Conall frowned at Graham. "And how do you know about this part of the castle anyway, Cousin?"

"I dinnae sit still well." He shrugged. "And did some exploring when we traveled to the Battle of Stirling Bridge."

Everyone except Sven looked at him in amazement.

"This was behind enemy lines at the time," Bryce said.

"Aye." Graham winked. "'Twas half the fun of it, I suppose."

Conall shook his head and patted Graham's shoulder, clearly pleased despite how foolhardy some might have considered his actions at the time.

"So you work your magic, Lindsay, and we'll sneak in." Conall's eyes met Sven's. "I trusted you to keep her at the encampment, yet here she is. Can I trust you to protect her now?"

"Conall!" Lindsay shook her head and looked at Sven. "Sorry, darling. He's just in a mood because of my hand."

"I will protect her with my life," Sven vowed, evidently not offended or simply not interested in arguing. "Go save your women."

Graham nodded. "Aye." His eyes met Lindsay. "Are ye ready lass?"

"Yes. Absolutely." She nodded and squeezed his hand. "Get her back safely. Don't let me down."

"I wouldnae dream of it," he assured. "I'll get her out, lass. Ye've my word ten times over."

She nodded. "I know I do."

Conall's hand landed on her shoulder and drew her attention his way.

"Be verra careful lass." His eyes held hers, his love obvious. "Please."

"You know I will be." She leaned over, brushed her lips across his, held his eyes for another moment then headed for the nearby Scots.

"Well, hello there," she purred with a very believable brogue as their eyes turned her way. "I was out for a stroll, and the castle drew my attention then I saw ye standing here so gallantly and just *had* to come over and meet ye."

Within moments every last one of them was staring at her with adoration.

"'Tis always bloody amazing watching her do that," Conall muttered, clearly impressed despite his concern.

"Naturally, I'm not alone," Lindsay murmured to her devoted followers as she leaned against a tree seductively and batted her lashes. "What lass would be?" Her smile was blinding as she eyed them all. "My friends are just behind ye now, but they willnae bother ye at all." She cocked her head, demure. "Ye'll just let them climb that wall and be on their way, aye?"

A wall they clearly had no idea was so undefended.

"Aye," the men responded, nodding avidly as they stared at her.

This was their opportunity.

"Remember, lads," Conall commented as they secured their weapons, rushed forward and began climbing. "If we have to fight, keep it quiet. We dinnae want this heard overly much."

If it were, Lindsay would spin a tale to her men about what the sounds must be, and they would, in turn, spread the rumor. Even so, Conall was right. The sound of too much warfare might very well travel too far to be controlled.

They didn't have to climb very far before they dropped over the wall onto a narrow dirt pathway that led alongside the second wall. A wall built so close to the castle it provided easy access to several windows. As expected, the pathway was a dead end in either direction. A means to lure the enemy so they could be slaughtered.

"*You're right, Graham,*" Bryce said, speaking within the mind as he peered up. "*There isnae anyone standing guard there.*" He shook his head. "*'Tis bloody strange.*"

"*But most welcome,*" Conall said as he began climbing and they followed.

As speculated, neither climb was all that far. When they sidled through a window then dropped into a dark stone corridor, Graham was struck anew by its emptiness. What was going on?

"*It just keeps getting stranger and stranger, aye?*" Bryce said into their minds.

"*Aye,*" both he and Conall responded as they slowly made their way down the corridor. As far as they could tell, nothing in this part of the castle was guarded.

"*How far to where the lasses are kept?*" Conall asked.

"*Fortunately, not all that far,*" Bryce responded. "*Though we'll have to pass by the courtyard and main gate.*"

Graham nodded, more than ready. That direction might take them past the bulk of the Sassenach but so be it. A bit of the enemy's blood on his blade would do him good. As it turned out, they found even more Sassenach than anticipated. Some of which were sleeping with their hands on their blades.

"Is it me, or does it look like a battle already took place here?" Graham started before images started flashing though his mind. First, of Christina being dragged by her hair down the very stairs he looked upon.

He ground his teeth and clenched his blade when he realized she was barely coherent. More so, when he saw the raw, purple bruise on her cheek. Far more men than what stood in the courtyard now, hooted and hollered as she was dragged to the center.

"Bloody hell," Graham growled as the man dragging her forced her to her knees in front of him, grabbed his crotch and yelled to his men, *"Now we'll show these Scots a real man, eh lads?"*

They roared with approval as he worked at the strings on his breeches. Enraged, Graham felt Bryce grab him when he nearly barreled down to rescue her from something that had clearly already taken place. Based on the heavy frowns on his cousins' faces they saw the same images.

What had she endured?

What horror did they put her through?

Suddenly, so fast the eye barely caught it, she grabbed the man's ball sac, twisted and dropped him to his knees. Then she narrowed her eyes and roared, "Anybody move and I'll *rip* them right off!"

The man whose balls she held was now flaming red in the face as he managed to squeak, "Listen to her," and shook his head.

Her eyes scanned the numerous men around her. If he were to guess, she was appraising them as though getting ready to go into battle. Did she know how to fight?

Seconds later that question was answered as she grabbed the man's blade, kneed him hard in the balls then one by one went after the others. Though the images continued to come as flashes, two things were very clear. She knew how to fight, and her superhuman strength certainly gave her an advantage.

"Bloody hell," Bryce murmured. *"Have ye ever seen a lass fight like her? Anyone for that matter?"*

Graham and Conall shook their heads as she spun and kicked and punched, using just about every part of her body in creative ways. All the while, she held onto the blade and even grabbed another, using them sparingly. Just enough to slow the men down.

Not only did her fighting take many to the ground but clearly spooked others as they fell back, making the sign of the cross over their chest. How else could it be considering one moment she fought in eerie silence and the next with vicious roars.

Her heart and soul and most definitely her magic were wrapped up in the stunning grace in which she annihilated anyone who got in her way. Nobody stood a chance, and they bloody well knew it. She had a way of looking at her target before taking them down. More than that, he got the feeling she was pre-planning her every move. That she knew just how to wound the man she would be fighting five men later.

"*She glows, aye?*" Conall said. "*And 'tis frightening her enemies.*"

"*Aye,*" Graham and Bryce said. Because she was and it seemed mortals alike knew it.

It made perfect sense why her granny saw her gift as lighting. While he saw her glow to a degree all the time, she was much brighter right now. So one had to wonder...did the Sassenach think she was evil or some sort of warrior for God?

Rather than heading for the gate, she seemed to be working her way back upstairs before the images faded. Graham shook his head as he realized why so many men were here now, what had to be sometime later. They were guarding the door to the tower, likely terrified to go any further.

He was somewhat amazed they hadn't already surrendered to the Scots to flee her wrath.

"*She made her way back to the tower chamber.*" Bryce's eyes met Graham's. "*Back to Kenna.*"

Graham nodded. "*And still no word from her, aye?*"

Bryce shook his head. "*Not since they were first taken to the tower.*"

"*She's still here,*" Graham said, praying his senses were right. "*I can feel her.*"

"*How the bloody hell are we going to get by so many men without causing a stir?*" Conall muttered.

"*Ye two will have to distract them whilst I go up the stairs and save the lasses,*" Bryce said.

"*Why ye?*" Graham narrowed his eyes. "*Those are my lasses up there.*"

"*One of them anyway,*" Bryce replied.

"*I've heard Christina in my mind too,*" Graham growled.

"*But has she heard ye?*" Bryce retaliated. "*I dinnae think so.*" He shrugged. "*Besides, ye and Conall fight better together.*"

"*When we can utilize our magic,*" Graham reminded. "*Which we cannae right now.*"

"*Enough.*" Conall frowned at Bryce. "*Ye bloody well know Graham should go. That 'twill be him both lasses want to see.*"

Bryce scowled and was about to respond, but Conall cut him off. "*We willnae debate this anymore. Not whilst every moment that passes Lindsay risks her life waiting for us to return.*"

Bryce and Graham stared each other down for another moment before Bryce finally nodded and relented. "*Aye, then.*"

Decision made, they wished each other well then Conall and Bryce headed in another direction entirely. As far away from the gates and the bulk of Scots on the other side as they could to keep the sound of battling down. Hopefully, this would allow Graham to escape more easily with the lasses.

When Conall called out a few minutes later, men went running. As he figured would be the case a few stayed behind but not too many. Wasting no time, Graham headed into the courtyard, kept his berserker laughter to a minimum and began fighting like a madman.

He fought to avenge Christina's poor treatment, no matter how brief it had been.

There were only ten soldiers, all of which he was eager to end. He cut two down with a blade across their necks before they barely saw him coming then whipped a dagger into another's gut, finishing him off as well. He punched the fourth so hard in his windpipe, he staggered back and wasn't much use afterward.

That left six.

He side-kicked one in the stomach before crossing swords with two more as he whipped a dagger so that it nicked another's jugular vein. The second the men he battled glanced at the vast amount of blood spewing from their comrade, he tore them both open with a wide swipe of his blade.

That left three.

He swiftly finished off the one he had side-kicked then faced off with the last two.

They were so shaken by that point, that he was able to punch one out cold then parry with the last one for a few minutes before he ended him altogether. Not about to let one bloody Sassenach live, he sliced open the throat of the man he had knocked out.

After that, he headed for the tower. The door had been shut, and not surprisingly, no warriors were posted along the stairwell. It seemed they were so terrified of Christina that nobody stood guard at the top of the tower either.

Relief rushed through him when he spied the lasses alive and well. Kenna, who seemed to have been tucked behind Christina, rushed into his arms when she saw him.

"Thank goodness yer here." She stepped away from him and looked at Christina with worry. "She's been standing guard over me all this time." Kenna shook her head. "She is so exhausted she can barely stand." She kept shaking her head. "I dinnae think she's all that coherent anymore."

Graham headed Christina's way as she leaned back against the wall, shaky. "You have no idea how glad I am to see you, darlin'."

"About as glad as I am to see you, lass." Though tempted to pull her into his arms, they needed to keep moving. "Can you find just a wee bit more strength to get out of here? I can carry you if not but 'tis best that I'm free to fight."

"I'll be okay." She nodded, pulling herself upright with determination as she gripped her blade tighter. "Let's get out of here."

Graham eyed her for another moment, impressed with her drive despite how exhausted she was. He knew being awake that long could be difficult never mind that she had battled hard and used her magic.

"Aye then," he said. "I'll lead the way."

Christina and Kenna nodded and followed him down. Not surprisingly a few men were racing up. He kicked the first into the one behind him then raced down and slit their throats before they had a chance to gather themselves.

After he peeked out the door to find the courtyard empty, he gestured that the lasses follow him. They kept to the shadows and moved fast. Not fast enough though. Three Sassenach were heading in their direction.

Graham whipped his blade into one man's neck, drove his sword into the next one's gut then punched the third. Before the third had a chance to respond, he snapped his neck then pulled his blades free from the others. After that, they started up another set of stairs then down the hallway he and his cousins traveled before.

"I've nearly got them out," Graham said into their minds.

"Good," Bryce responded. *"Once yer clear of the castle let us know, and we'll follow."*

When a Sassenach appeared ahead, Graham raced at him and swiped his sword across his midsection before the man had a chance to utter a word. No more appeared after that. Once they got to the window, he turned to the lasses. "I'll go first then you will jump into my arms, aye?"

Both nodded.

"Kenna first," Christina said. "Then I'll follow."

"No, ye should go," Kenna urged. "I know how to use a blade and yer far too tired, my friend."

"Not so tired that I can't defend us if I have to," she said. "And no offense, but we both know I'm the better choice."

Kenna sighed but didn't argue the point.

Though he hated leaving Christina undefended, she was clearly the better fighter. He could only pray she was not too tired to do so if need be.

"Aye, then." This time he couldn't help but pull her into his arms, unable to stop his thickening brogue as he murmured, "If ye have to fight, then fight with everything ye have, aye? I'll be back to help in no time."

"Don't worry about me," she whispered before she met his eyes then stepped back. "Just go. Now. I wanna get out of here and never look back."

That's when he realized as their eyes held, how bad it had really been. That she had likely killed someone for the first time within these castle walls. He cupped her cheek and gave her a look of reassurance before he pulled away. After one final glance down the corridor, he crawled out the window and scaled down the first wall quickly.

"Come, lass," he called out to Kenna once he reached the bottom. "Jump."

Kenna did just that, landing easily in his arms.

He looked up. "Now you, Christina."

She nodded and was about to crawl out when someone yanked her back.

"Bloody hell," he growled then looked at Kenna. "Crouch down and stay to the shadows. I'll be right back."

"Aye." She nodded, her eyes suddenly moist. "Dinnae let her die, Graham. She saved my life."

"I willnae," he assured as he swiftly climbed back up the wall, doing his best to set aside the stark fear he felt. If she was dead, he would make it his mission to murder every last Sassenach in this castle before the night was through.

When he reached the top, it was to find her on the hallway floor with a man's hands wrapped around her throat. Enraged, Graham yanked him off her and smashed the Sassenach's head against the wall. Meanwhile, Christina gasped and scrambled back, holding her neck. His fury getting the better of him, he slammed the man's head against the opposite wall then started punching him again and again. A blade would be too swift a death.

"*Cousin, ye need to release yer rage, focus and get them out of here*," Conall said into his mind. "*We're running out of time.*"

Graham knew he was right, but all he could see was this man strangling the life out of Christina, so he kept beating him.

"Graham," Christina said hoarsely. "It's all right. Just end it already…please…I'm not gonna last much longer."

That got through.

Her distress.

So he sliced his blade, and finished it, then went to her.

"Just go," she gasped, leaning against the wall. "I'm right behind you."

He nodded and moved fast, rejoining Kenna in record time and ready to catch Christina when she all but rolled out the window, slid over the wall and fell into his arms. Getting her over the next wall was going to be impossible without his cousins' help. She was too far gone, and this wasn't the sort of wall one could climb with someone over their shoulder.

So he let his cousins know what was happening as he rested Christina on the ground against a wall and helped Kenna first. Lindsay was still leaning against a tree with an ever-growing circle of adoring men around her.

Graham made sure Kenna was safely with Sven then rushed back. By the time he rejoined Christina, she was out cold, and his cousins were making their way down. They became a three man team as Bryce hoisted her up the wall to Conall who dropped her down into Graham's waiting arms. She never stirred. Not once.

"Well, lads," Lindsay declared to her adoring fans once everyone was safely away. "'Tis time for me to retire. I'm sure ye ken." Every last man looked crestfallen as she smiled lovingly and winked. "And dinnae forget, I was never here nor my friends, aye?"

They all nodded avidly, one speaking up. "Might ye stay a wee bit longer, lassie? 'Twould mean so much."

"I cannae," she said with regret. "In fact, whilst my friends and I leave, I need ye to keep a close eye on those windows above the wall and shoot an arrow at anyone who might appear, aye?"

They nodded and said, "Aye!"

"Good then." She smiled, blew a kiss and sauntered away, joining Conall at last.

"I dinnae think you needed to swing your hips all that way," he muttered before he pulled her into his arms and kissed her soundly.

"There ye are," came a soft murmur before Grant appeared out of the darkness.

"'Tis bloody good to see ye, Grandda," Conall managed around kisses.

"Aye, I see you're all torn up from missing me," Grant mocked, but there was a pleased smile on his face as his eyes flickered over Conall and Lindsay then landed on the others. "I dinnae yet ken the reason behind their abduction, but I do know that it might verra well push this battle not only to its proper timeline but possibly even the location." His eyes swept over everyone. "We willnae return to Robert's encampment until the day after next. Until then, we will split into two groups to lessen the odds of being discovered."

Graham nodded. That made sense just as long as he remained with Christina and Kenna.

"Sven, Conall, Lindsay, and Kenna, you will travel northwest together," Grant continued. "Graham, Bryce and Christina will travel northeast with me."

"Nay, Kenna should stay with me," he began before Kenna shook her head and looked at Bryce. "Might ye hold Christina a moment so I can speak with Graham alone?"

"Aye," Bryce said, more than willing to take Christina out of Graham's arms before he and Kenna walked a short distance away.

"Ye should stay with me, lass," he started to say before she shook her head and put a finger to his lips.

"I am going with the others, Graham," she said softly, her eyes with his as she pulled her hand away. "And I am releasing ye from this marriage pact."

"Och." He shook his head. "I'll not hear of it—"

"Ye'll hear of it because 'tis done," she said bluntly. "I am verra sorry, but I willnae marry ye, Graham MacLomain."

Saddened by what this might mean for her, he shook his head and was about to speak, but she spoke first. "Yer doing the noble thing and that has always meant so much my friend, but we both know our feelings for each other arenae the same." She touched his cheek. "'Tis all right, Graham. I'll be just fine as will my clan." She shook her head. "I willnae let ye sacrifice yerself."

"'Twould not have been a sacrifice," he whispered. "Ye are my friend, Kenna."

"Aye," she whispered, her eyes soft. "And that isnae the way I want to start my marriage."

"Marriages have been started on far less," he argued, "and found far more."

"Aye," she agreed. "But not ours. Not now."

"Because of Christina," he murmured.

"Aye," she replied and nodded. "Because of ye both and what I wish for ye."

He was about to reply, but arrows started to rain down. Moments later, Bryce raced by with Christina and yelled, "We're under attack!"

Chapter Eleven

"I JUST NEED to make it up these stairs," Christina whispered over and over to herself. "Up these stairs, back into the chamber with Kenna and it'll be all right. Everything's gonna be just fine."

Yet she should have known that would be too easy. That she was lucky to have fought so many and not killed anyone. She had nearly reached the top when an Englishman appeared at the top of the stairs. Clearly realizing the havoc she had caused below, he vanished only to take the coward's way out and head for Kenna.

Christina didn't give him a chance to get far before she raced at him, drove her fist into his kidney and watched him fall. Half a breath later, her head was yanked back by another man, and cool steel met her throat. She didn't hesitate but drove her dagger straight back into whatever she could hit. That, as she soon found out, was a jugular vein.

She turned and met his eyes as he fell to his knees.

"Tell him yer next," he rasped, sounding just like the warlock. "Tell Graham yer both next."

Seconds later, her eyes shot open.

"Kenna?" she whispered, unable to stop shaking as she took her hand. "Are you okay, sweetheart?"

"'Tis me, lass," Graham said softly as his hand seemed to replace Kenna's. "You're not in the castle anymore. You're safe now."

She blinked several times, trying to acclimate. A small fire crackled nearby, and she lay on some sort of bedding wrapped in blankets. By the looks of it, the sun was setting, and they were in a very dense area of woodland.

"What happened, Graham?" she whispered. "Is Kenna all right?"

"Aye." He was crouched in front of her, his touch gentle as he brushed hair back from her forehead. "She's safe thanks to you, lass. You did verra well."

"Aye," came Bryce's voice from somewhere beyond him. "You are a bloody good fighter, lass and verra brave."

Christina frowned as she sat up with Graham's assistance. "Why would you say that?"

"Because they saw you." Grant tapped his temple. "Within their minds."

Her eyes darted between Bryce and Graham. "Both of you?"

"Aye, and Conall as well," Bryce informed as Graham sat beside her and wrapped the blanket over her shoulders. "And Grant too through our minds."

Imagine that. She supposed she was officially out of the 'witchy' closet now.

"Where are we? What happened?" She looked around. "I don't remember much after being strangled." Her eyes met Graham's, and she shook her head. "I'm so sorry I couldn't hold my own at that point, honey. I was just so damn tired."

"Och," he muttered and wrapped his arm around her shoulders. "We had a few arrows fly at us at the end, but we got away. Before that, you did bloody well, lass. I've never been so proud."

"Proud?" she murmured. "What for?"

"For protecting Kenna as valiantly as you did." A frown tugged at his lips as he eyed what she suspected had to be a pretty good shiner. "I had no idea you could fight like that."

"Aye, 'twas most impressive." Bryce scowled at Graham before he turned a warm smile her way. "Where did you learn to fight in such a way, lass?"

Christina shrugged, not sure she was quite ready to go down this road. To share so much. "You wouldn't believe me if I told you."

"You might be surprised," Grant said, kindness in his eyes as he handed her a skin of whisky. "Then, mayhap, I can provide you with some information that will surprise you even more."

As her eyes stayed with Grant's, warmth spread through her veins. Comfort. "Are you doing that?" she whispered without thinking. "Comforting me like that?"

Grant shrugged, winked then urged her to tell them more about her fighting abilities.

"Well, I picked them up off of television." She felt a little sheepish. "We didn't have enough money when I was a kid to put me into karate and rarely had enough to keep a TV going, so I'd sneak through the woods and watch television through our neighbor's window." She shrugged one shoulder. "As it turned out, he watched nothing but old kung fu movies and westerns, so I learned a bit of both types of fighting...minus the gun-shootin' that is."

She could tell by the somewhat stunned looks on their faces that they had not seen that explanation coming.

"So you learned how to fight from watching *television?*" Grant asked, clearly amazed.

"Sure did." She took a deep swig of what she thought was whisky only to find it was water. "Well, thank the good Lord for small favors," she murmured before she tilted her head back and chugged it down to the last drop.

When she finished, it was to find Graham and Bryce watching her with amused, almost charmed expressions. "What?" She couldn't stop a small grin. "Don't tell me you boys are as squeamish as Robert's kin about a girl who enjoys food...or drink in this case." She tossed a look at Graham. "Speakin' of drink..."

She no sooner got the words out before he handed her another skin and grinned. "I wouldnae recommend drinking this one quite so fast."

"Noted," she said before she took a solid swig of whisky then focused on Grant. "Okay, you heard how I learned to fight. What was your big surprise?"

This, it seemed, was something Graham and Bryce were also interested in based on the way they looked at Grant.

"Well, 'tis directly related to your magic and your amazing strength, instincts, and ability to fight," Grant said. "Though distant and no longer godly, your magic is of Celtic origin and pulls forth the power of Fionn Mac Cumhaill, a great warrior god."

All Christina could do was stare at him and mumble, "Say what?"

"'Tis no surprise really as Fionn has a long history with both the Brouns and MacLomains," Grant explained. "And you, my lass, are verra much related to him." Pride lit his eyes. "You are *every* inch a great warrior, and like him, I would imagine a great protector of those you consider innocent."

Speechless and suddenly very thirsty for the strong stuff, she took another swig of whisky then shook her head. "So I'm related to a god, but I'm not a god."

"Aye." Grant kept grinning. "You're a witch with god-like powers. 'Tis bloody spectacular in my opinion."

"Well, it *has* come in handy over the years," she relented. "At least being able to run like I do."

Grant nodded, pleased it seemed that she was taking the news in stride and wasn't confused like some people might be. The truth was, she was happy to finally put an explanation to her gift. To understand it a little bit better.

Right on time, her stomach growled, reminding her that she needed food.

Badly.

"Here, lass." Clearly anticipating her need to refuel, Graham handed her a stick with meat on it. "Plenty more where that came from."

"Thank you." She grinned before she dug in. "I can't remember the last time I was so hungry."

Between going without food and using her magic, it was a wonder she was functioning at all.

"Current circumstances aside, it stands to reason you would always have a hearty appetite," Grant said. "You might not be overly muscular, but your magic will always cause your body to need extra food. It has the needs of a warrior's physique, therefore requires extra nourishment."

"Hmm," Christina managed as she chomped along, not all that concerned. Unlike most women, she had never worried about weight mainly because there was never enough food growing up. To her way of thinking, if she put on a little extra now, so be it. Men could take it or leave it for all she cared. Curvy was just as sexy in her book.

Based on the way Graham and Bryce were eying her, she didn't think she had all that much to worry about.

"Your mind, body, and magic will always work in accord," Grant continued, amusement in his eyes as he watched her eat with gusto. "As such, you will only ever eat what your body needs."

She frowned and swallowed her last bite, not so sure about that last bit. "Why does that almost sound like I don't get to enjoy food much beyond the full feelin'?"

"'Twill be as your magic dictates, lass," Grant said kindly. "But if you continue to run a lot and even battle, my thought is you can eat to your heart's content and remain verra fit."

She shrugged as she polished off her first stick of meat and started on another.

After that, they talked about other things and caught her up on what was happening including Kenna's whereabouts. She, in turn, caught them up on the warlock.

"He's scary as shit," she said softly, apologizing under her breath to Granny for swearing before she took another swig of whisky. "But he didn't hurt us, and I don't get that." Her eyes went to Grant's. "Do you?"

"Nay." He shook his head. "I dinnae ken why it didnae hurt Lindsay either. Beyond her hand that is. Because it could have taken her life after you were abducted." His eyes were both troubled and contemplative. "Nor do I ken its reasoning for bringing you to Stirling Castle. 'Twas an action that could verra well set history back on track which is the opposite of what these warlocks want."

"And what about the mention of a wee witch?" She frowned. "Lindsay told me y'all thought that might be a reference to Jessie." She tilted her head. "Do you still feel that way?"

"I dinnae know, lass." Grant shook his head, his eyes compassionate as they stayed with hers. "'Tis all verra much a mystery still. That this warlock didnae hurt you and seems to have set the battle back to where it needs to be is verra odd indeed."

"Right, because he could've just killed me right then and there." She shivered. "And I'll be damned if for a moment or two it didn't feel like he wanted to. That he was about to..."

"Yet it didnae," Grant murmured. "So you saw it as more of a man than a creature then?"

Christina shrugged. Until this moment she hadn't given it much thought. "Yeah, I suppose, though I really didn't see him all that well. It was too dark."

"'Tis strange," Bryce agreed, his brow furrowing as his eyes went from Graham to Christina then to Grant. "As is the fact 'tis me and only me that Christina hears within the mind."

"Och," Graham started before Grant interrupted.

"'Tis strange," Grant said. "But certainly not enough to separate Graham and Christina if they wish to be together."

"A Broun can only hear her one true love within her mind," Bryce argued. "It has been that way from the verra beginning has it not?"

"Aye." Grant's steady eyes met Bryce's. "But 'tis also true she can hear his kin *after* she had truly connected with her one true love."

What was this?

She chose not to mention that she may have already heard Graham in her mind. Mainly because that might sound like she wanted him to be her one true love.

"So why is it then that I can't hear Graham?" she asked, not realizing she just did what she had been trying to avoid. Implying that she thought he might be her true love. Chalk it up to a rough few days and a tired mind.

"Another mystery," Grant conceded. "But one I suspect has everything to do with you being close to the warlock." He shrugged. "Considering Graham has heard you within his mind from the moment you met."

"Say *what*?" Her eyes shot to Graham. "You have?"

"Aye, lass." He sighed and slid his hand into hers. "I'm sorry. I should have told you sooner."

"Yeah you should've," she muttered but couldn't quite be mad at him as their eyes held. Those dark-as-night eyes she could lose herself in. "What have you heard?"

He shrugged. "Nothing too personal."

The way he said it and the sparkle in his eyes made her lips curl up. "Why do I get the feeling you're lying?"

"Because you feel vulnerable." That sparkle just seemed to be getting bigger and wrapping around them both. "Because 'tis not the easiest thing to know I might be aware of your innermost secrets."

She grinned because she just couldn't help it.

He grinned as well.

Then they just sort of got lost in one another.

Somewhere along the line, she heard Grant bid them goodnight, saying there was a cave nearby that would suit his old bones better. Though Grant could clearly take care of himself, she was fairly certain he asked Bryce to join him for protection. And somewhere in there as her and Graham's eyes held she heard Bryce grumble about how wrong it was to leave his potential true love behind.

Though they waved them off, she really only ever saw Graham as they settled back next to each other as if they'd been doing it all their lives. They had a sturdy tree at their back and a warm fire at their front as they continued to hold hands.

"What happened with Kenna?" she said softly because as far as she was concerned, that's all that really mattered. "I know she's being detoured with Conall, Lindsay, and Sven but…" she squeezed his hand, needing to get to the bottom of things. "How'd she feel about going in a different direction than you?"

He slanted a look at her. "Why does it sound like you already know the answer to that?"

So she told him. Every last word Kenna had shared because she didn't want secrets between them. Not if they were truly friends.

"I'm not sure what she meant about Fraser," she said softly, delicately. "But I thought you should know she's got some ideas when it comes to…well, you know…"

"His death," Graham murmured, troubled. "I dinnae ken why she never shared this with me…"

"Well, it sounds like a complicated situation, sugar." She squeezed his hand again. "She loved you…" She didn't want to tell him what Kenna had told her but knew she had to. "She still does."

"Aye," he said softly, pausing a moment as he appeared to contemplate how to phrase things. "But 'tis not like that betwixt us, at least not for me. It never has been." He shook his head. "I intended to marry her to help her clan and to keep her out of the hands of a husband who would likely be twice her age and treat her poorly. That was all." His eyes met hers, pained. "I never intended to betray Fraser's memory."

She thought about the things Kenna had said. How he had so valiantly fought for her. "Did you ever love her, Graham? Even for a moment?" She tilted her head in question, trying to be as gentle as possible. "Because I can't imagine you not loving her at some point if y'all were so close."

"I tried." His eyes never left hers. "I wanted to."

What to make of that? "What stopped you? Fraser?"

"Nay." He shook his head. "Kenna and I could have been together before them. There was enough of a bond but not..." He paused as his eyes turned to the fire and his voice grew softer. "I didnae see her with the passion a lad should see a lass. 'Twas just a deep friendship. We grew up together."

"Oh," she replied, not expecting such a simple, straightforward answer. So the chemistry just wasn't there. At least not on his part it seemed. "I'm sorry to hear that." Though, in all 'shame on her' honesty, she really wasn't. She genuinely liked Kenna though which made her feel guilty as sin at her own thoughts. "I really am sorry."

His eyes slid her way. "*Why* are you sorry?"

"Well, because." She rounded her eyes at him. "You've got a history with her. A past. Memories." She shook her head. "Where I come from that means somethin' I guess." She bit her tongue and frowned, well aware she was about to ramble before she even opened her mouth. "Not to say I don't think what y'all shared meant somethin'. I suppose, in the end, the heart just wants what it wants, eh? Or in this case not so much."

What the *hell* was coming out of her mouth? What she wouldn't do to just erase this whole conversation. Just make it go away. Because she felt like a fool. Not only that, she felt like she was letting Kenna down somehow when she knew full well she wasn't.

"Aye," he agreed, watching her with amusement and something else. "The heart *does* want what it wants, lass."

Though she almost expected him to pull her close and kiss her, he just kept watching her, his dark eyes reaching into places she barely recognized anymore. She pressed her lips together and tried to ignore the feelings blossoming between them. More so, the lusty way she felt after using her *lightn'*. It might have been a few hours back, but it was still there, stronger than ever and damned if he didn't know it.

"If I kiss ye this time, I willnae stop," he said softly, his brogue thickening as well as the promise in his eyes. "'Tis entirely yer choice, lass."

"I think we both know it stopped being my choice a while back," she murmured. "What I won't do, is kiss you for real or more than that if you're engaged or even if you think you're not but she still thinks you are." She shook her head. "I just won't go there."

"Kenna ended it, lass," he replied. "We arenae to be married anymore."

Well, way to crawl into the bed of the next woman who comes along she nearly said but knew better. Graham wasn't that sort of guy, and this wasn't that sort of situation.

"I heard a rumor you slept with a prostitute the night before the Battle of Stirling Bridge," she remarked, trying to ignore the way heat spread like wildfire over her body at the look in his eyes.

"Aye." He winked. "'Twas a good front, aye?"

So he hadn't but wanted his kin to think otherwise. That made sense.

Oh, to *hell* with this. If they were going to pretend to be together, then they might as well enjoy the benefits. That in mind, she decided to grab the bull by the horns and make the first move. So she straddled him, rested her hands on either side of his strong neck, ignored her thundering heart and murmured, "How's this feel, darlin'?"

His eyes trailed down her torso to the juncture between her legs before they languidly roamed back up as though he had never seen anything more tempting. The way he touched her, as though measuring and worshiping every last bit, made blazing heat fire between her legs. Heat he seemed all too aware of as he gripped her hips and thrust up to remind her of what she was already aware of.

He was aroused and had a whole helluva lot to offer.

"Hot *damn*," she whispered without meaning to as she pressed forward and ground her hips.

Graham seemed wholeheartedly enchanted by her as he didn't bother ripping her clothes off just yet but wrapped a strong arm around her lower back and pulled her close. Both were breathing heavy as he held her like that, inches apart, their lips itching to touch each other's as they enjoyed the feel of their bodies so close.

"Ye feel bloody good, lass," he whispered in answer to her previous question as one hand cupped her cheek and neck. "But are ye sure…because we both know this isnae—"

She didn't let him get another word out before she closed her lips over his. Yes, she was sure. More sure than she had ever been about anything. Especially when it came to a man. After all, she had never been with a man who knew about her gift...knew that she wasn't quite right. More than that, she rarely let things get sexual because she wasn't sure what would happen.

Gift or no gift, she was strong.

Powerful in a way she worried might hurt someone.

Graham though, he was a different sort altogether. He not only understood her but she bet he could handle her as well. Or get handled well she should say. Because she had feared pretty much her whole life that she would break a man in the sack which made her hold back. That meant orgasms weren't something she often enjoyed. That is, unless the guy was tough as nails, or had impressive endurance. So all and all, she couldn't count them on half a hand.

Yet as her and Graham's kiss deepened, she knew he would be up to the task. Though she tried to keep that as her reasoning, that she deserved good sex, deep down she knew it was more than that as their tongues wrapped and their kissing intensified.

She wanted him more than she had ever wanted a guy.

And that suddenly scared the heck out of her.

She pulled her lips away abruptly, breathing heavily and shook her head, worried this was all too much. That it was unstoppable. Breathing just as heavily, his eyes held hers, and he nodded once. Just enough that she knew he felt the same.

That should have been it.

She probably should have crawled off him and kept a nice, decent friendship intact.

But looking into his dark, sexy eyes and feeling his steely length between her thighs had nothing to do with decency...or friendship. Not the least bit concerned about anyone seeing them she ran her forefinger along his lower lip then pressed it into his mouth as she ground her hips again.

All the while, thoroughly enjoying the way he twirled his tongue around her finger and nibbled it, she yanked up her dress. Just as lost in her eyes and clearly enjoying the taste of her finger then her palm, then the heel of her palm, then further up, Graham accommodated. Sweet anticipation built as he pulled at the string on his breeches, not about to waste any more time on removing clothing than she was.

She had never been so eager, so needy, as when his lips met hers again. Their kiss deepened, desperate, both so hungry for what the other had to offer that when she sank down, and he finally began filling her, the world beyond them snuffed right out.

She saw nothing but him.

Her lips fell open, and air whooshed out of her as he gripped her hips beneath her skirts and eased his way in. She dug her hands into the material at his shoulders and bit her lower lip hard to keep from groaning too loud.

Hell, he felt good.

So good she pressed her teeth together hard and sped up a process that was going way too slow. Hands still wrapped tight in his tunic, she pressed down until they were fully together.

"Och, lass," he groaned as his head fell back, his eyes half-mast but still with hers. There were more words to be said. By her. Him. But neither could locate another syllable as she began moving.

Then it was just pure bliss.

Pure unparalleled pleasure.

Breathing became sparse, nearly impossible, as she kept moving.

Not just caught in the throes of being with a man like Graham but feeling the remnants of her gifts and its sexual leftovers, she quickly lost control. Renewed strength filled her as she quickened her pace. Grinding harder. Riding faster.

Anything to bring him closer.

To feel this bliss over and over.

She knew her energy levels and adrenaline were high, but she couldn't stop. She couldn't make sure he was okay. Based on the way he dug his fingers into her thighs tighter, and his lips fell apart, it seemed he was just fine with what she was doing.

Because she was *doing*.

Going.

Sweat beaded and glistened on them both.

She was so alive she could barely see straight as she released all her pent up energy on him, grinding and moving so quickly, bliss ravaged his face. Yet he held out. Something no man had *ever* done with her. He held out and by all accounts enjoyed every last moment of her pleasure.

They moved together incredibly well, finding a tremendous amount of pleasure in each other without any foreplay. Without seeing beyond their clothing. Their connection was potent. Undeniable.

Her energy only grew as it tried to spend itself. And all the while he stayed with her. One hand kept clenching her ass while his free arm wrapped around her lower back but that was it.

He didn't try to pull her closer.

He didn't try to steer her.

Graham let her remain in complete control while he somehow kept himself from letting go.

"I want to kiss you," she tried to say but couldn't get the words out. "But I can't stop."

"*Then dinnae,*" he whispered as his half-mast eyes stayed with hers. "*Dinnae stop until ye've had me, lass.*"

Caught by the feeling of what she knew were his thoughts within her mind, she lost it right then and there. She lost it so hard, and so fast she barely understood what hit her. Because hell if something didn't hit her square in the chest and spread through her body like wildfire in a windstorm. It happened so fast and seized every last muscle up so hard she fell forward against him.

After that, things went haywire, but at the same time, dead calm as liquid heat spread through her. It was the oddest but best sort of combination of sensations. So poignant and all-consuming, air sucked clean out of her lungs, and her body was lost to her.

Graham wrapped his arms around her and held on tight.

That's it.

Nothing more.

He didn't move. He didn't try to find his own release. No, he just held her tight and close and so damn well tears leaked from the corners of her eyes as she rested her cheek against his shoulder. Lost, gone for a good while, she came down from the best climax she'd ever had. One that seemed to go on and on and she hoped might never end.

All the while, Graham kept his arms around her and held her. Like an anchor in rough seas, he never let go. He allowed her to feel everything she was feeling without an ounce of shame. Because that was somewhat like how this feeling had been the scant few times she had taken it before. Too much, over the top, and with shame because the guy had always known he hadn't given the pleasure.

She had taken it.

Not with Graham though. It was all somehow very different with him.

A thousand times better.

"I'm sorry, handsome," she finally managed to whisper, drifting back down to reality. "That was pretty selfish of me, wasn't it?"

That's when she heard the change in his voice and felt the racing of his heart.

"Selfish? Och, nay, furthest thing from it," he said hoarsely. "Bloody hell, lass, I released *three* times!"

Chapter Twelve

GRAHAM HAD NEVER experienced so much pleasure in his life and told Christina as much. Then he just kept holding onto her. They stayed that way, totally spent, for a good while before they gathered enough strength to move again.

She wore a soft, dewy expression, as her lips curled up ever-so-slightly and she met his eyes. "Well, I'm definitely just as impressed by you, darlin'." She almost seemed a little dopey and he well understood. "It's not every guy that would be up to the challenge not only once but three times." She chuckled. "Impressive."

He met her smile and shrugged. "'Twas the least I could do considering you did all the hard work." Now it was his turn to chuckle. "I verra much like the aftereffects of your magic, lass."

"Why, thank you." She pressed her lips together and blushed. "Any chance we could wash up somewhere?"

"Aye, there's a small stream not far from here." His eyes narrowed on a nearby satchel that hadn't been there before. "I would imagine we've a change of clothes in that."

She glanced at it and arched a brow before her eyes met his again. "Grant left that, didn't he?"

"Aye." He adjusted his trousers then helped her up. "My guess is he figured you would be ready for a change of clothes after being imprisoned."

"That makes sense." She gave him a knowing look. "Among other things."

"This *did* seem somewhat planned by him," he admitted as he strapped on his weapons, grabbed the satchel and pulled her after him. *"We'll only speak within the mind now lest anyone happens upon us, aye?"*

When she didn't respond, he stopped and whispered, "Did you hear me within your mind, lass?"

She shook her head, frowning. "Should I have?"

Aye, she bloody well should have, but he didn't tell her that. "Nay, 'tis all right." He squeezed her hand. "When we talk it should be whispered just to be safe."

Christina nodded before they continued. Why couldn't she hear him but he could hear her? Especially after lying together? It made no sense. Though frustrated, he made no further mention of it as they came to the stream and began undressing. The eve was warm enough that it should not be too uncomfortable bathing.

Though there was only half a moon and plenty of tree cover, he could still make out her nude body. A trim, athletic but curvy body that made his mouth water. His eyes trailed hungrily over her high, firm breasts, toned stomach and long slender, shapely legs.

"Aren't you coming swimming?" she whispered, grinning at him. "Or am I on my own?"

His eyes glued to her the whole time, he nodded then began stripping down. In the meantime, she watched him just as avidly.

"Son of a gun," she whispered. "Just look at you, handsome." Her eyes trailed over him with appreciation, lingering on his cock before she winked. "*Every* inch the man I knew you were."

Before he could respond, she sauntered into the water, giving him the view of her backside he had wanted to see since the moment they met.

"Oh, this feels like *Heaven*," she whispered as she waded in. "I run so dang hot."

Understandable considering the energy she just exuded. By the sounds of it though, she meant all the time. He joined her, grateful for the chill as well. The water wasn't too deep. Waist high for him.

"So I suppose we should talk about what that meant back there," she murmured after she dunked beneath the water then surfaced and met his eyes. "What that meant for us."

"What do you want it to mean?" he asked, still trying to sift through his own emotions. He hadn't looked much beyond being with Kenna lately, so he wasn't sure. Before his promise to her, he had never considered commitment but enjoyed many lasses. On occasion, at the same time.

"Well, for starters, we better darn well stay friends," Christina said in answer to his question. "As to the rest, I hadn't thought much beyond steering clear of a relationship." She shook her head. "And now you know why."

"Because of your sexual prowess?" He grinned. "Truly?"

It was hard to imagine any man not thoroughly enjoying what she was capable of.

"Yeah, well, you might've taken me like a champ, but most guys can't quite handle it." Frustration and hurt flickered in her eyes. "I learned a while back, that loving 'em and leaving 'em was the best policy for me…and them. In and out." She flinched. "And I mean that literally. Half the time, it was wham, bam, thank you man on my part."

He might not be from the twenty-first century, but he understood her meaning. "I thought it was bloody amazing being with you, lass." He shook his head, never more serious. "Like nothing I've ever felt before."

"I know. You said as much." She smiled softly. "And believe me I'm thankful for the praise." Her brows drew together as her lips tilted down. "Though I'll admit having the tables turned a bit wouldn't be so bad."

"You would like to lay with a man with your stamina." He smirked. "Your extraordinary energy."

"Oh, I think I've just found a man with plenty of stamina." She smirked as well. "As to your energy levels, we'll just have to wait and see." Her brows flew up as she drifted closer. "If you're up for friends with benefits that is."

"I'm up for being any kind of friend you need me to be, lass." And mayhap more, echoed through his mind.

"Because it's just a friend thing for now, all right?" she murmured as she drifted even closer. "Until we figure out what's going on with Robert the Bruce and I guess, Bryce now." She shook her head. "Not that I see me with either of them."

Yet she did the moment Robert the Bruce came around and well he knew it. Magic was at work. As to Bryce? Never. He refused to let that happen.

"I wasn't going to mention it because I'm not entirely sure what I want it to mean," she murmured. "But we said we'd be straight with each other so you should know that I think I heard you speak into my mind once at MacLomain Castle." Her eyes stayed with his. "Then again when we were in the throes of it back there."

"Aye? 'Tis good." He offered a reassuring smile. "And it doesnae need to mean any more than you want it to."

As she nodded, he couldn't deny a spark of hope. More notably, what that hope likely said about how he truly felt. Mayhap he was not all that confused when it came to what he truly wanted.

"*But you cannae hear me now, can you?*" he said into her mind.

When she offered no response, he knew she could not. Why was this happening so randomly? Though frustrating, he supposed he should be happy that it had at least happened twice now rather than not at all.

Graham did his best to keep a light expression on his face as he took full advantage of 'friends with benefits' and reeled her closer. Almost as if she was waiting for him to do it, she wrapped her legs around his waist and her arms around his shoulders as their eyes held.

He bit back a groan at the feel of her soft skin against him as he cupped her arse. Lessening his brogue was impossible. "Bloody hell, yer well made, lass."

"So are you," she whispered, still smiling as she dropped several kisses on his lips before she groaned and a few kisses became many then deepened. He became so lost in the taste and feel of her, that he almost didn't catch the slight vibration that ran through the water.

He gently broke the kiss and peppered more along her jaw until he could whisper in her ear. "We're not alone, lass. Follow my lead and dinnae act like anything's wrong."

Clearly able to keep a level head despite the circumstances, she kept kissing him while he carried her out of the water. As though caught in the throes of passion, he lay her down close to his weapons. Then he wrapped his hand around the hilt of his blade, focused the best he could with her beneath him and whipped the blade in the direction of the intruder.

Though it was barely audible, he didn't miss a woman's grunt of pain.

"Bloody *hell*," he muttered as he leapt to his feet, peered into the darkness and thought he saw a shadow.

"Was that a woman?" Christina exclaimed as she scrambled into her dress. He didn't bother with clothes, but raced into the forest, terrified that he had hurt some lass happening through. Yet even as he ran in that direction, he knew no average lass could have stirred his magic like that.

Not one without her own magic.

A great deal of it at that.

Yet when he arrived where he knew she had been, there was no sign of her. No scent left behind or even tracks. More than that, there was no blood trail. He frowned as he stared through the woodland. It was as if she had never been here.

"Graham," Christina whispered before she came alongside him, concerned. "What's going on?"

He nodded thanks as she handed him his breeches then shook his head as he yanked them on. "I dinnae know. But there was someone here...and I hit her with my blade."

"Oh, no," she murmured, frowning as she looked around. "No sign of her then?"

He shook his head and pulled her after him. "'Tis best that we get back. I need to speak with Grant."

A short while later, he was doing just that, having woken Grant from a sound sleep.

"So 'twas a lass's magic you felt then?" He yawned as Bryce fed a small fire in the cave they were resting in. "Are you sure, Graham?"

"Aye." He nodded. "At first, I thought 'twas the warlock, but I saw her...then felt her."

Bryce frowned. "Felt her how?"

"'Twas as if..." How to phrase this? "'Twas as if I had felt her close before. As if I was familiar with her."

Christina shook her head. "I still can't figure out how I didn't know she was there from the get go." Her troubled eyes were trained on the fire. "I was there the whole time, and I didn't see, hear or sense anything." Her eyes met his. "And I'm pretty good at that sort of thing. Better than most."

Graham nodded, not doubting her in the least. "'Tis bloody odd, then."

"Aye," Grant murmured as he contemplated it. "'Twas almost as if she put out a frequency to attract Graham alone. One connected solely to water."

Christina frowned. "What's that supposed to mean?"

"It means whoever that was didnae want you to know she was there," Grant said softly as his eyes met hers. "I also tend to think she wasnae from around here."

Everyone's eyes widened at that as Bryce said, "Do you mean to say you think she was from the future?"

"Mayhap." Grant's eyes stayed with hers. "The last time you saw Jessie, she was sitting in front of the fire in New Hampshire, aye? Then there was nothing but a cryptic note."

"A picture, actually." Christina crossed her arms over her chest and nodded for him to continue.

"I wonder about your friend Jessie more and more," Grant said gently. "How much do you actually know about her?"

"Less and less by the day it seems," Christina muttered. "Care to share what you're gettin' at?"

"You know full well what I'm getting at," Grant said. "Lindsay told you everything, did she not? About her strange feeling that the healer that cared for me at the Action at Happrew felt familiar before she vanished. Then what the warlock said about a wee witch controlling him."

Graham slipped his hand into Christina's when she tensed and frowned. "Yeah, I've followed everything, and I don't know what to make of it. What I *do* know is that Jessie isn't evil." She shook her head. "She might be strange as all get out but she's not evil. Not in the least. Just different." She rolled her shoulders a little. "I tend to know these things."

Grant nodded. "Aye, I know you do, lass, and I meant no harm by my words." His eyes met Graham's before they returned to hers. "I just think 'tis best to be vigilant and not overly trust anything or anyone right now...no matter how well you think you know them."

Christina's frown only deepened as her eyes stayed with Grant's. "So you're telling me not to trust one of my closest friends if we cross paths again?"

"He's asking you to be careful," Bryce said. "And I agree with him."

Her eyes shot to Bryce. "*Agree* with him?" Indignant, her head whipped back. "You know nothing about Jessie." She shook her head again. "You might not like hearing it, but it needs to be said because I have a bad habit of saying what's on my mind whether people like it or not." Her eyes remained on his cousin. "While I'm thankful for what you did for me and what you've done for Milly and Lindsay, as a whole, I keep wondering about something."

Bryce had no chance to talk before she continued.

"Who do you really care about in all this outside of yourself and your kin?" She kept shaking her head. "Because I don't think it's so much my friends. Not beyond saving a damsel in distress. No, I think all you really care about is getting out of some marriage pact."

Disappointment flashed in her eyes as she went on. "What kind of man tries to skip out on his obligations? Who is this woman you're hurting so much? Because her feelings *have* to be hurt by your actions..." She clenched her jaw. "Unless she doesn't know, which is even worse."

Graham tensed and shifted closer to Christina, not because of his cousin's reaction but possibly the dragon within. If he were going to protect anyone, it would be her.

"*Careful, Cousin,*" he said into Bryce's mind. "*I see the beast flaring in your eyes.*"

"*Aye, but not for the reasons ye think,*" he responded. His eyes never left Christina's as he responded. "The way of dragons is verra set, lass. We have one mate, be she human or dragon."

"So it's cut in stone by some higher power?" She kept frowning. "If that's the case why would you ever agree to marry someone if you didn't know for sure they were your mate?"

"'Tis complicated," Bryce said softly as he clenched his jaw but never looked away. "And unfortunate."

Still frowning, she shook her head.

Graham bit back a sigh, knowing full well the truth behind Bryce's vague words. That he wasn't quite as callous as he sounded.

"You should get back to sleep, Uncle Grant," Graham said. "All of us should."

Grant's eyes flickered between Bryce and Christina before they met Graham's and he nodded. "'Tis a verra wise suggestion, Nephew." He settled back. "Rest well, all. May things be clearer on the morn."

That was Grant's way of saying nothing more would be discussed.

"Come, lass," Graham said softly as he spread a plaid on the ground. "Rest with me."

"My pleasure," she grumbled, still eying Bryce with distrust as she did as Graham asked. His cousin scowled, clearly not pleased as Graham lay down beside her. Yet it was also clear he wasn't all that willing to battle it out right now.

That what she had said bothered him.

"*I'm sorry, Cousin,*" he said into Bryce's mind. "*She doesnae ken...*"

"*None of ye truly do,*" Bryce muttered as he rolled over and cut off all contact.

The truth was Graham did. He knew what it felt like to be committed to another, whether or not it was truly what he wanted. While yes, in Bryce's case, it might be a bit more extreme due to an inherent need to be with his mate, it was still very difficult for anyone going through it.

Graham pulled Christina back against him, covered her with a blanket and rested his chin on the top of her head. He had never felt so content as she pressed back against him.

"*You feel amazing just like this...all wrapped around me,*" Christina's unintentional words floated through his mind. Then other words, scattered and whisper soft as she drifted off to sleep. "*I hope it's you...if anyone's meant for me...*"

In total agreement, he pulled her tighter against him, more at peace than he could ever remember as he drifted off to sleep. As he slept, he returned to the river with Christina and held her in his arms once more.

This time he sensed no other magic but brought her onto the shore as he had before but this time, nothing stopped him from coming together with her. Yet as dreams tend to do, it only came in snippets. Images of her arching in pleasure beneath him, groaning, finding release.

Then they were lying together much as they did in the cave with his front to her back as they eyed her ring, wishing it would shine the color of his eyes. No more pretending. Yet as they stared, it remained a clear gem.

Moments later, his eyes were drawn to the forest. The very spot he knew his dagger had hit a lass. Though he couldn't see her shadow this time, he could hear her whispered words. "No more pretending."

Seconds later, Christina's gem began glowing brightly.

Gold.

The exact shade of his cousin's eyes.

Startled from sleep, he bolted upright at the same moment as Christina. They frowned at each other before their eyes went to her ring.

"Oh no," she whispered. "Tell me you don't see that."

He did. Her gem remained golden.

"Even if my cousin doesnae," Bryce said softly, his eyes trained on her gem. "I do."

As if aware of the sudden discontent in the pre-dawn cave, Grant's eyes opened and he frowned at the ring. "This doesnae mean anything until it means something."

"Och, it means Christina's my lass," Bryce growled, his eyes narrowed on Graham. "And well ye know it, Cousin."

"Nothing can be trusted when it comes to the ring, and you both ken that by now," Grant muttered as he sat up and yawned. "Dinnae forget that Milly's gem glowed the color of both of your eyes at first."

"Aye, but she heard Adlin's voice in her mind first," Bryce reminded. "Just as Christina heard mine."

"Which could verra well happen if she's already found her one true love and connected with him," Grant reiterated.

"Which she hasnae because she has not heard Graham's voice within her mind," Bryce stated bluntly.

"But she has," Graham retaliated.

Grant perked up. "She has?"

"Aye, twice now," he supplied. "Surely that means something."

"Just twice then," Grant said softly, a speculative look on his face as he contemplated Christina. "Yet Graham hears your voice all the time. 'Tis strange that."

"How so?" she asked.

"I cannae be entirely sure yet but what I do know is that something is amiss." His eyes went to Bryce. "All aside, that Graham heard her within his mind first is telling. It means something. 'Tis hard to know what but seeing how they clearly desire one another, 'tis worth paying attention to." He shrugged. "And there is the fact they passed through one another under the influence of Conall and Lindsay's magic before they ever met."

Bryce frowned. "What difference does that make?"

"It could make all the difference," Grant explained. "Mayhap it scrambled their signals, and that's why Christina cannae hear Graham more frequently. Or mayhap Christina's evident brushing with a warlock within her mind when she first met the Bruce is affecting her." He shook his head. "Or it might even have to do with the residual effects of the wound inflicted on Graham by Conall and Lindsay's warlock."

Grant's eyes stayed with Bryce, his brogue thickening as he grew sterner. "Either way, ye'll not assume Christina is yers until we know for certain." Before his cousin had a chance to respond, Grant continued. "And if 'tis somehow proved she really is yer true love, ye'll do nothing about it unless she feels the same and comes to ye." His eyes narrowed. "Do ye ken, Nephew?"

"Aye," Bryce grumbled, obviously displeased.

Graham was never more grateful that Grant was here. Otherwise, things might have gone considerably different between him and his cousin.

"Come, we should travel a bit further before we double back on the morrow," Grant said as he stood. "'Tis not good to stay in one place overly long. We'll hunt and eat along the way."

As they packed up their belongings, Grant's eyes went between Graham and Christina. "I sensed you two awoke at the same time. Tell me about the dream you shared...what you saw."

Christina glanced at Grant, surprised. "How do you know I had a dream...and what makes you think Graham had the same one?"

"Uncle Grant is verra powerful," Graham explained though she likely already knew as much. "Like Adlin, he tends to know things others dinnae."

Somehow it didn't seem to shock Graham that they might have shared a dream. Yet he was curious about her take on it.

Christina's eyes met his. "I'd like to hear about your dream first if you don't mind."

"Not at all." So he told them what happened. "'Twas most certainly the same lass I may have wounded earlier though I dinnae quite ken how I know that."

"It was," Christina said softly, worry in her eyes. "Because I saw her...every feature."

"And?" Grant replied.

"It was definitely Jessie." She swallowed hard. "And she wasn't alone."

Tension made his muscles tighten. What put that sudden flash of fear in her eyes? "Who else did you see?"

"Two tall hooded figures dressed from head to toe in black," she whispered.

Bryce frowned, troubled. "So the warlock's have her?"

"No, I don't think so." Sadness and concern met her eyes. "I think *she* has *them*."

Chapter Thirteen

CHRISTINA TRIED TO keep the image of Jessie and the warlocks out of her mind, but it was nearly impossible as the day wore on. The eerie, powerful look in her friend's eyes as she peered down at Christina and Graham. The warlocks had stood behind her with their heads bowed, as though obedient, well-trained soldiers.

There had been something else though. Something she had not shared with the others and had no idea why except that it was meant for one person's ears. Bryce's. Though it should probably alarm her that she felt that way, it didn't. Almost as if it were a message being delivered that only she could carry and only Bryce could hear.

Yet how to present it? More than that, how to apologize for her rude behavior last night?

"I need to go talk to your cousin," she finally said after several hours of walking with Graham. They had chatted the whole time, getting to know one another better. Like it had been from the beginning, they got along exceptionally well. He made her laugh more often than not. Actually, they made each other laugh quite a bit.

She was surprised despite their markedly different upbringings that they had so much to talk about. But they did, and she had a feeling they always would. That time spent together would never be boring.

She told him about how her mother had died in childbirth, and her father took off soon after leaving her with Granny. How life wasn't easy, but at least she was always well-loved. He told her about his childhood too. The ups and downs of living during such a difficult era but the many happy memories of growing up with his fellow wizards. Their endless antics as they came into their powers. Most especially Adlin.

All in all, like her, he was grateful for the people he called his own and how they shaped the person he had become.

"Aye, lass, I figured you might want to talk to Bryce eventually," he said in answer to her previous statement. "Do you want me to join you?"

"Why'd you figure I might want to talk to Bryce?"

"Because you have a kind heart," he said softly. "And you need to better understand where his mind is at."

She nodded, not all that surprised he understood her so well. While tempted to say there was more to the dream, she felt she should speak with Bryce about it first. So she kissed Graham's cheek then joined Bryce who had been walking a little ways behind with Grant.

"Mind if I speak with Bryce alone?" she asked.

Grant nodded then joined Graham.

Not one to mince words, she came right out with the first part of what she needed to say. "I'm sorry about last night. I didn't mean to be so rude. I was just frustrated, and took it out on you."

Bryce nodded, his expression hard to read. "Dinnae worry, lass. All is well."

"I don't know that it is and I want to smooth things over between us which means understanding where your head's at." Her eyes went to him. "I know you're a genuinely good guy. That there's nothing you wouldn't do for your family. So I guess I just need to understand why you don't want to marry a woman if it helps your family." She cocked her head. "Because isn't that what pre-arranged marriages are? Arranged by your family? Or did you somehow arrange it yourself?"

"Nay, 'twas arranged by my Grandma Torra on her deathbed," he said gruffly. "To a lass I have never met."

Christina nodded. "Isn't that how it sometimes goes in this day and age?" She tried not to frown. "And while I still don't think too highly of you wanting to leave this girl in the lurch, I'm curious. Is your grandmother half dragon? If so, why would she want an arranged marriage for you when she knows you're supposed to end up with your true mate?"

"A question I've often asked since," he groused. "But 'twas made betwixt my grandma, grandda and parents, dragons all outside of grandda. So except for a Broun, MacLomain connection, there isnae any dodging it."

"Weird that they'd do that to you," she murmured, trying to keep things lighthearted. "So who's the lucky gal?"

"Mayhap you," he said so softly she barely caught it. "She is an unnamed lass who will always love another."

She frowned and shook her head. "What does that even mean? And why the heck would your kin commit you to someone like that?" The more she thought about it, the stranger it seemed. "And what about the Broun, MacLomain connection? Did they just assume that wasn't gonna happen to you?"

"'Tis always impossible to know what the future will hold," he replied. "If not for Aðísla's prophetic vision, I dinnae think Grant and Adlin would have created the rings, to begin with." He shrugged. "A vision the Viking foresaw *after* my marriage pact was made."

"Well, that's too bad," she said. "Did anyone ever say why this marriage was so important that you had to give up being with your destined mate, wherever she might be? That seems kind of harsh in my opinion...especially considering most of your kin are dragons themselves."

"'Tis not for me to question my elders," he said. "All I know is that this match was important for the future of the MacLeods and that's all that matters."

It was clear he was proud of his clan and had no wish to let them down. Yet... "I guess I can't really blame you for wanting out of this marriage, but the question remains. Aren't you, by wanting to be with a Broun, letting your kin down? They have to be aware of what you're up to."

"Aye, I cannae say I'm overly proud of my actions in light of just that," he conceded. "But even they know a connection such as this is necessary to save Scotland. And our country *must* come before our clan."

She supposed she understood where he was coming from. It might not seem the noblest of things, but then she hadn't walked in his shoes. What would it be like to be told you had to be with a complete stranger? Even worse, that they would never love you?

"Yet I fear despite my secret desires not to fulfill this marriage pact," he murmured, "'twill come to pass anyway."

"Why?"

"Because 'twas my twin sister, Ainsley, who shared it with Grandma." His voice was a little gruff. "A few years after she died in infancy."

Well, *damn*.

"I'm so sorry." Chills rushed through her as she remembered her dream. "I need to tell you something, Bryce. Something that might be hard to hear...or maybe just confuse things even more..."

He stopped and met her eyes, concerned. "What is it, lass?"

"There was someone else in my dream besides Jessie and the warlocks." She tried to keep her voice steady under his intense appraisal. "Someone claiming to be your sibling...your sister."

There was no missing the turbulence in his eyes at her words. "What did she say? What did she look like?"

"She was beautiful with the same golden eyes as you," she said softly. "She didn't say anything else, but I got the impression she was there to protect you...even though you weren't technically there." She couldn't stop a sigh. "One thing's for sure, she definitely seemed a whole lot less creepy than Jessie."

Bryce frowned as he seemed to mull over her news. "She has only ever appeared in Grandma's vision...then now." His eyes dropped to her ring before returning to her face. "When you awoke your gem matched my eyes." He took her hand. "'Tis telling that, aye?"

"It's something, but I don't know what that is, honey." She tried to keep her words soft and respectful. "I want to be with Graham, Bryce. I want to see where things go with him."

Funny, until she actually said the words out loud, she wasn't entirely sure.

Now she was.

Almost as if he sensed her thoughts, which he very well might have, Graham turned back and joined them. His eyes locked on their adjoined hands as he approached. She didn't need to hear his thoughts. They were written all over his face. He was wondering if she and Bryce patched things up so well that they had decided to give it a go.

Christina squeezed Bryce's hand before she pulled away and smiled at Graham. "Hey there, darlin'. Everything okay?"

His eyes went from Bryce's to hers. "I can only hope."

"Everything is well enough betwixt Christina and me," Bryce rumbled, a flicker of fire in his eyes. "Time will tell how well it is betwixt you and me, Cousin."

Graham's brows lowered, and his eyes narrowed in challenge at Bryce as he took her hand. "Aye, then."

Grant frowned at the men then gave her a pleasant smile before he waved them along. "Come on, everyone. 'Tis best to find shelter before the rain comes."

A few steps later, he stopped short. Evidently sensing something as well, Graham and Bryce stopped, and their eyes swept over the late-day forest. The next thing she knew they were ducking down behind a boulder as Bryce's words entered her mind. *"Dinnae make a sound, lass. A band of Sassenach are heading this way."*

She nodded as the men drew their blades and peeked over the rock.

"Let me help," she said. *"I can fight too."*

"Nay," Graham whispered, evidently hearing her telepathic conversation with Bryce. *"That isnae necessary."*

At first, she thought he had whispered aloud until an unusual rush went through her. *"Graham, did you just speak within my mind?"*

"Nay, he spoke within my mind," Bryce said. *"And it seems you heard it."*

She frowned at them. *"Is that normal?"*

"Aye," Grant said, joining their conversation. *"But typically only after you're well established with your one true love. Then you can speak to several of us at once. Right now, it seems, Bryce is a conduit betwixt you and Graham."*

"Or Graham is just intruding on a conversation he doesnae belong in," Bryce muttered.

"I think I belong in a telepathic conversation with my lass before ye do," Graham shot back.

Bryce's brows shot up. *"Yer lass?"*

"Enough!" Christina exclaimed before Grant had a chance to. *"Don't you guys think we should worry more about the bad guys right now?"*

"*I couldnae agree more,*" Grant added. "*Because 'tis a good sized band. At least fifty.*"

Graham and Bryce might be at odds with each other, but in the face of danger, they began to work very well together.

"*There is a chance they might pass without detecting us,*" Bryce began.

"*But 'tis best to assume otherwise,*" Graham continued as he handed her a blade despite his reservations. "*'Twould be best if you stayed with Grant, lass. He isnae as young as he used to be and has been injured recently.*"

"*Och,*" Grant muttered. "*I can fight well enough if need be.*" His eyes went between the men as it began raining. "*Unless your life's on the line, dinnae use magic. 'Tis far too risky.*"

They nodded as Bryce peeked over the edge again. "*They're nearly here.*"

After that, it became a waiting game as the English slowly but surely began passing. Christina held her blade tightly and barely breathed the entire time. Every once in a while, her eyes would go to Graham who always offered a look of reassurance. He was remarkably calm, and it did her pounding heart good.

It was one thing being dragged into that courtyard back at the castle. She had no time to think just act. This time it was different as her gift ignited. She heard every last horse hoof. Every clink of armor. Each man's heartbeat and every breath they took.

Considering what she could hear, she wondered if Grant's count was off.

"*I would say their number is closer to sixty-five,*" she said into their minds. "*Because there are more further out...*"

No sooner did she relay her message than one of those men appeared in the forest directly in front of them. She didn't think but acted on instinct and whipped her blade. Surprisingly enough, it landed neatly in the man's throat.

"*Bloody hell, lass,*" Graham and Bryce said simultaneously, clearly impressed before another man appeared behind him and things started to spiral out of control. Bryce took him out with an arrow but not before he sounded the alarm that they were under attack.

"Give her your spare sword, Graham," Grant urged.

"I have no idea how to use one," she began before Grant's eyes met hers, and he interrupted her. "I think, mayhap, you will find that you do, lass. And if you dinnae, simply toss it aside, aye?"

"'Tis a heavy blade not suited to her size," Graham argued, but Grant cut him off too.

"Give her the blade, lad," he said again. "And let her ancestry decide whether or not she can handle it."

Graham's eyes met hers, his concern obvious as he handed over one of his swords. "Be careful, lass."

She nodded, testing its weight. It certainly wasn't light.

No more words were needed after that. They had been down this road before. Moments later several more men appeared, and all hell broke loose.

"Dinnae worry about me, lass," Grant roared as he crossed blades with an oncoming soldier. "Take care of yourself!"

Like hell. She would do exactly what was asked of her. Stick close to Grant and protect him if need be. So she tested the weight of her blade again and got a better grip. While heavy, she knew she could handle it. That she *would* handle it. So though she was frightened initially, she jumped in and started fighting.

When she did, all fear fled.

Exhilarated, she began battling. Where she could hold her own with her fists and feet and grunge fight without a problem, this was much different. The sword suddenly felt like an extension of her arms. As if it was part of her. When that happened, a bizarre but enlightening feeling rolled through her. She felt as though she had fought with a blade like this countless times before.

As such, she began fighting with it as if she had wielded it all her life.

She parried with the first warrior that came at her, her adrenaline rushing as she met his every thrust. It was odd, surreal almost, and damn addictive. Half a breath later, she sliced his throat open. Satisfied, caught in the rush, she battled the next then the next. On occasion, she would side kick someone then twirl away, and fight another only to twirl back and end the first guy.

Blood poured as readily as rain, but she kept going.

Every once in a while, she would catch Graham out of the corner of her eye and chuckle. Mainly because he was chuckling as he fought. She realized it was his calling card in battle. A way to disarm his opponent. But she also realized he found true enjoyment in downing his enemy. That every swing of his blade had purpose.

Christina could relate to a degree. She had felt the same way every time she ran and raised money for charity. Every step would help feed someone or help battle some disease. Every step put money where it was needed most.

As she continued fighting, it almost felt like a choreographed dance. One that she had always understood. It had rhythm and balance and timing yet it freed her in a whole new way. It was creative yet methodical. Wildly addictive. She never stopped or slowed but kept thrusting and slicing and fighting with everything she had.

It wasn't until she turned with a roar on her lips and had no one left to fight that she realized the battle was over. Every last man had fallen. Sword at the ready, breathing heavily, she eyed her surroundings, shocked by what she saw.

Death.

Carnage.

What *she* had left behind.

That's when everything slowed before it came crashing down around her and her high fled.

"Oh dear God," she whispered, as she dropped the blade and began trembling. "Oh, God, what have I done?"

"'Tis all right, lass," Graham said softly, suddenly there and gripping her shoulders. "Focus on me, not them, Christina."

So she did, grateful for the immediate comfort she found in his eyes.

"Ye did verra well," he said gently, his brogue thicker than ever. "Ye never stopped protecting Grant. Now 'tis time to protect yerself and come with me, aye?"

She nodded, trusting him without question as he pulled her after him. Somewhere far outside her mind in what had to be shock, she heard thunder rumble across the sky and saw flashes of lightning. After that, all she could focus on was putting one foot in front of the other and following Graham.

At some point, he sat her down in yet another cave and urged her to close her eyes as he covered her with a blanket. As her eyelids drifted, she saw other things. Lindsay. More lightning flashes.

Conall and Kenna. More flashes. Then Sven crouched in front of her, a fierce but respectful look in his eyes.

She thought for a moment she might have even seen Granny. Guiding, comforting her, welcoming her as she finally, truly embraced her *lightn'*.

Telling her to forgive herself for what that meant.

Then utter darkness fell.

When she opened her eyes again, wind gusted, and thunder still rumbled but a crackling fire burned. As far as she could tell, everyone was here, alive and well. Yet it was Graham her eyes went to first. Her head had been resting on his lap.

"I fell asleep, didn't I?" she murmured.

"Aye," he murmured back and brushed the pad of his thumb gently down her cheek. "How do you feel, lass? Hungry? Thirsty?"

"Very," she said hoarsely, her throat parched as she sat up. Clearly anticipating her answer, he handed over meat and a skin of water. She nodded thanks and downed nearly all the water. She managed a small smile and nodded hello to the others before she dug into her meat.

Lindsay sat on her other side and waited until she was finished eating before squeezing her shoulder in comfort, her words gentle. "How are you doing, darling?"

How *was* she doing? Truly?

"I think I killed a lot of people, Linds," she finally managed to whisper, shaken. "I'm pretty sure I've just become a serial killer."

"You've become no such thing." Lindsay shook her head. "You've become a warrior who defends and protects her people." Pride lit her eyes. "One who did so with an amazing amount of talent."

"Talent?" she whispered, not sure about that in the least. Now that everything was said and done, she pretty much felt like she had flailed about while fighting. It almost felt like a sloppy dreamlike dance.

"'Tis a rare day I get to see the likes of you fight," Grant said softly as he crouched in front of her. "Thank you, lass. Both for fighting to protect me and for embracing the warrior within with such courage. 'Twas most extraordinary."

"Oh, c'mon," she whispered because she had no idea how else to respond. "I wasn't all that."

Yet as she looked from Graham to Bryce, then from Conall to Sven, she saw the respect and pride in their eyes. That's when she realized she must have done all right. But at what expense?

"How many did I kill?" she murmured, afraid to hear the answer.

"As many as you needed to, lass." Grant squeezed her hand, his eyes level with hers. For a flicker of a moment, she swore Granny might have been in there somewhere giving her approval as well. "As many as you needed to in order to protect those you cared about." He shook his head. "That is all the answer you will ever need, do you ken?"

It almost felt like a soothing balm poured over her raw nerves as their eyes held. Peace filled her where moments before there had been turmoil.

"Do you ken, lass?" Grant repeated.

"I think so," she murmured as things slowly became clearer...as she felt surer of herself and her actions. "I did what my ancestors would have expected of me. I embraced my gift and became a warrior."

"That's right." Grant smiled. "Every inch a warrior and an honorable one at that."

Honorable? Though not so sure, the way he said it and the warmth in his eyes made it seem okay. Plausible. True.

"When you're ready, Graham and Lindsay will go with you so you can bathe," Grant said softly. "Meanwhile, enjoy some whisky and eat all you like. I had the lads hunt extra game."

Never more grateful, she nodded. "Thank you, Grant."

After that, she did exactly as suggested and drank some whisky while she kept snacking. Apparently, Lindsay and the others had joined them near the end of the battle and helped them polish off the enemy. By all accounts, it had been one heck of a battle, and none got away. Or so they hoped.

Though everyone said it was a good thing the others showed up when they did, she got the impression they weren't entirely truthful. If anything, as the men cast her approving glances every once in a while, she got the feeling she fought extremely well and left little behind. In the end, she suspected help wasn't all that needed.

"I dropped your sword." Her eyes went to Graham. "Did you get it back?"

"Aye, lass, I got it." He nodded and offered her a reassuring smile. "Though you fought well with it, you deserve your own blade. We will have our blacksmith forge you one to your specifications."

Now here was a conversation she never thought she would have.

The whisky must be going to her head because she replied more boldly than intended. "So you want me to stay then, handsome?"

"Verra much," he replied, surprising her with his words before he doused the flames a little. "'Twould be good to have a chance to get to know each other even better, aye?"

Lindsay had been talking to Conall but sort of trailed off and rolled her eyes at Graham.

"It *would* be nice," Christina acknowledged then shrugged, in no mood to take things too seriously right now. If he was not overly interested, she wouldn't pressure him. "I guess we'll just see what happens." Her eyes landed on Kenna who seemed rather well across the way. In fact, she was smiling and laughing.

Christina turned teasingly sympathetic eyes Graham's way. "Besides, you were just dumped. That's gotta leave a guy a little gun shy."

Lindsay chuckled before focusing on Conall again.

Meanwhile, Graham offered Christina one of those charming grins he used when he knew she was messing around. Sort of. Because they both knew her lighthearted words had some mixed messages. Ones that didn't seem to overly bother him. Rather, he seemed more comfortable with her than most men. Comfortable enough to say what he said next.

"How are you feeling, lass?" His brows rose slowly as he addressed the residual effects of her gift. "You have slept, eaten and drank your fill of water." The corner of his mouth curled up. "Is there anything else you might need taken care of?"

She met his grin. "I like the way you think." Because hell if she wasn't aroused. Yet still. Was it right? She frowned. "But what about…" She tilted her head slightly in Kenna's direction. "You know."

Based on the way Kenna was looking at and flirting with Sven, she knew his response before he said it.

"I think Kenna might verra well be relieved to be free of we MacLomains," he replied softly. "At least in a romantic sense."

That fast? But it certainly seemed that way. All aside though, Christina was covered in blood and needed to bathe. A few minutes later, as they headed deeper into the cave, she wondered how this might go with her friend along.

"Don't worry," Lindsay finally said as they came to an exit a short time later. "I intend to stay in here where it's dry."

Christina almost denied Lindsay's insinuation but based on the knowing twinkle in her eyes, her friend wouldn't buy it.

"I'm not comfortable leaving you here alone," Christina argued.

"She isnae alone," Conall said, appearing out of the darkness.

"See." Lindsay winked. "And we could really use some time alone." Her eyes went to Conall. "Traveling with others puts a damper on things."

"It's been less than two days," Christina remarked.

"I know! Nearly a century." Lindsay smiled as her eyes went from Graham to Christina. "You'll understand once you sleep with your MacLomain."

Oh, she understood all right. Or at least she understood she wanted more of what Graham had to offer whether or not he was hers.

"Come then, lass," Graham said before he swung her up into his arms and grinned. "I think 'tis time you got as well as you gave, aye?"

Before she had a chance to be astounded he had said that in front of Lindsay and Conall, they were out in the rain and heading through the forest. Soon enough they stopped beneath thick tree cover beside a river. Thunder still crackled, and lightning flashed, but all became obsolete as he set her down.

That's when she learned, much to her amazement, that Graham could offer something no man before ever had.

Chapter Fourteen

THOUGH GRAHAM HAD debated whether to bring Christina to another river after what happened before with their dreams, Grant had felt it would be all right. Between the storm and the river itself, they should be protected well enough.

"So you're saying we're safe because there's so much of your element going on," Christina murmured as their eyes held. "That the rain and river and all the water molecules in between protect us?"

"Aye," he whispered as he came behind her and untied the strings on her dress. He slowly pulled the material off one shoulder then the other. Her head fell back as he nibbled the soft, smooth flesh on the side of her neck.

"That feels *so* good," she groaned as she pressed her backside against him and her breasts spilled free.

"I couldnae agree more," he said, his voice gruff and his cock eager as she ground against it.

While determined to take this slow, or at least make it into the water, he couldn't. Instead, he yanked off his tunic and walked her forward a few steps. "Put yer hands against the tree, lass. Brace yerself."

Breathing just as hard as him, she complied as he pulled the dress down until it pooled around her feet. As he untied his breeches and freed his cock, she kicked the dress away entirely but didn't bother with her boots. Neither did he as he pressed her legs apart, grabbed her hips and thrust deep.

She shuddered and cried out in pleasure as she dug her nails into the bark.

After that, it was fast and passionate and without pause.

Reveling in the feel of her tight heat, he never slowed. With his element all around him, he had no need of magic to show her how good endurance and a strength to match hers could feel. How powerful and wonderful.

Because it *was* just that.

While he knew full well what it was like to be taken by her, it was equally fulfilling to offer her the same enjoyment in return. To draw sounds of pleasure from her. To show her that she could relax into pleasure and not have to work so hard to find it.

This night, beneath the rain and beside the river with a faster current than usual, he possessed extra strength and most especially stamina. Enough to drive her to release not once but twice.

When her knees gave way after the first climax, he spun her, protected her against the bark with his hand, and kept going. Eventually, through her moans and groans, she found the strength to wrap her legs around his waist and take him even deeper. Not long after came her second release.

Yet he owed her a third before he released as well.

First, though, they would wash away the battle. So he sat her on a rock, removed her boots then swiftly took off the remainder of his clothing. All the while she watched him from beneath drowsy lids, a soft smile curling her lips. Approval lit her eyes as she looked him over as though this were the first time. He well understood because he was doing the same to her.

"'Twill be a bit rough," he murmured as he scooped her up and waded into the river. "So hold on tight, lass."

"You bet I will," she promised, delighted.

He braced himself against the current as he lowered her.

Revived within moments by the cool water and the rush of excitement, she laughed with pleasure as she wrapped her arms around his shoulders and he released her legs. Lightning flashed, and thunder boomed across the sky as he brought them into the water entirely. Though he couldn't release her so she could scrub herself clean, the pressure of the water would take care of things.

"This is unbelievable," she whispered as her eyes went from the pines towering over them to the rambunctious sky beyond. Then her gaze dropped to his. "You were too…thank you…"

He knew she wasn't just talking about his endurance but the battle they had fought together. Then those terrible moments afterward. In all his long years warring and fighting, he had never seen a warrior do what she did. While he had glimpsed a fraction of it at the castle, it was nothing like what she embraced earlier today.

She had been every inch a warrior goddess as she and his sword became one. As she cut down men before they ever saw her coming while toying with others. Her magic—subliminal and wrapped up in her DNA enough so that it likely remained undetected by the warlock—was breathtaking.

She was breathtaking.

Christina fought better than any warrior he had ever seen, which said much considering he was related to some of the best fighters in Scotland. It said even more, considering she did so in a *dress*. Yet she did and impressed them all including Sven, which he suspected was rare.

Caught between the memory of her beauty, both then and now, then the fear he had felt for her despite her talent, he held her more firmly, cupped her cheek and kissed her. Not hard but with everything he felt. Hell, he suspected he kissed her with everything he had *yet* to feel he wanted her so bad.

As their tongues twisted, she wrapped her legs around his waist, and her thoughts brushed his. "*I want you too.*"

Fueled by that, fueled by everything about her, he had them out of the river in no time and her beneath him on the grass. Battered by wind and rain, it wasn't a particularly sheltered spot, but that didn't matter to either of them as he continued to kiss her. As she kissed him back just as passionately.

What he made her feel now as he thrust would be tenfold what they had just shared against the tree. She dug her nails into his back just as deeply as she had that bark as he moved. Again and again, over and over, he thrust, his energy levels high. His pleasure even higher.

He lost all track of time and awareness as they moved together.

He knew she released and locked up with pleasure, but still, he went until it all became too much. Too extreme. It was then, at that moment, mixed with her wails from yet another release, that he finally let go.

Neither moved for some time as he spent himself in her.

As he lost himself in her body.

"Graham," she whispered at some point but said nothing else after that as she ran her hands languidly over his back and arse.

While tempted to start all over he knew better. She might run hot, and he might be in his element, but remaining out in this weather for too long wasn't a good idea. So he carried her back to the thick pine then rifled through the satchel Grant had sent along.

"It looks like your days of dresses are over for now," he said, amused as he pulled out a pair of women's trousers.

"Not complaining," she said as she pulled them on. "Perfect fit too!"

He grinned as he eyed her long legs and firm arse made clearer by the trousers. "Nor am I, lass."

Already wanting to rip her clothes off again, he couldn't help but speculate on her outfit. It was far better suited to battling than her previous clothing. He could already see her with weapons strapped here and there. She would be fierce and bonnie and mayhap *all* his.

"What's that look in your eyes, Graham MacLomain," she murmured as she pulled on her boots. "Because it's another whole type of arousal if I were to guess."

He grinned as he yanked on his boots as well. "I like you in clothing like that. It suits you better." He eyed her up and down again with appreciation. "Verra much…not to say you werenae bonnie in a dress but now…well," he chuckled, "let's just say you'll be verra distracting in battle."

"Why thank you…I think." She grinned. "If you like these clothes then you'd probably like my clothing back home."

"I like what I already saw," he conceded. "Twenty-first century clothing leaves less to the imagination, and that is just fine with me."

"Would you want to live there?" she murmured. "In the future?"

"Nay," he said honestly as he met her eyes. "I wouldnae want to live apart from my kin."

She nodded. "I get that."

Sadness rolled over him as her thoughts skirted his. If all her friends remained here in medieval Scotland, she would be alone in the twenty-first century. That's when he realized her granny had already died. Something he wasn't entirely sure about until now.

"I'm sorry, lass," he said, joining her as she leaned against the tree. "You must miss your granny verra much."

"I do." Christina didn't seem surprised in the least that he had read her mind so easily. "She was all I had until my friends came along."

He might have treaded delicately around this subject with any other woman and remained quiet, but Christina was too important. Getting to know and understand her better was too important.

"What happened, lass?" he said softly. "How did you lose your granny?"

She shrugged. "Nothing overly complicated. Not cancer or any other kind of illness." Her eyes drifted to the river, damp though she tried to blink the moisture away. "I just tucked her into bed one night, and she didn't wake up to join me for coffee the next morning."

He considered her as he caught snippets of her thoughts. "She helped you navigate your gift quite a bit when you were young, aye?"

"She did actually." She twisted her lips and flinched. "And it wasn't always pretty."

"Nay, I imagine not." He shook his head. "Coming into our gifts can be difficult." He offered her a sympathetic look. "Especially in the twenty-first century, I would think."

She nodded. "It sure was. I tended to use my gift most when getting into fights as a child. Mostly defending kids who couldn't defend themselves. But that didn't much matter at the end of the day. Not when Granny had to deal with another call from school and yet another suspension." She snorted. "Eventually she just ended up home-schooling me to keep me out of trouble."

Before he could respond, she held up her hand and shook her head. "I know, it sounds like I had some serious anger issues, but it wasn't really like that. I just had this extra strength and using it on bullies seemed like the thing to do."

He nodded, in agreement with her logic. Still, it had to have made for a choppy childhood. "So your granny didn't get overly mad at you?"

"Ha! Did she ever." She chuckled and shook her head. "'Violence never gets you anywhere, child,' she'd say time and time again."

"'Twas better after she started homeschooling you though, aye?" he asked.

"You'd like to think, but not so much." She looked a little guilty. "Not for a few more years."

When he tilted his head in question, she explained. "Well, Granny had a kind heart. So kind that she tended to put what little money we had anywhere but into our bills." She shrugged. "So rather than get a normal job, I did what any cocky, ignorant teenager would do with magically enhanced strength. I started fighting for easy cash."

"Och, lass," he murmured. "Your granny couldnae have been happy about that."

"That's an understatement," she said softly. "But she stood by me, and we got through it. She helped me see the error of my ways and eventually, inspired me to put my gift to good use. That's when I began running for charities. I returned the favor by keeping a steady job, and helping her manage her finances better." A nostalgic smile ghosted her face. "In the end, everything worked out just fine." She sighed. "But I miss her like you wouldn't believe."

"Aye, 'tis understandable." He rested his shoulder against hers, remembering all too well the pain of losing Grandma Cadence. Though Grandda Malcolm was well enough in his old age, he hadn't been right since losing Grandma. It was only a matter of time before he died of a broken heart if nothing else.

"And I'm sorry about your grandmother," she murmured as her eyes met his.

She was picking up his thoughts more and more by the moment which *had* to mean something. "Thanks, lass. Uncle Grant tries to keep Grandda going but 'tis not always easy."

"Because Grant is actually your great uncle, right?" she said. "Malcolm's brother."

He nodded. "Aye, but my cousins and I have always just called him Uncle Grant. 'Tis easier."

"I get it." She sighed. "He's a good guy. Everyone I've met is." She cocked a grin at him. "Even your mom."

He chuckled and shook his head. "Mayhap you really are the lass meant for me then."

While he thought the moment the words slipped out of his mouth, he would regret them, he didn't. Not at all.

"Maybe I am," she said casually as she stretched and yawned. "And maybe I'm not."

"Time will tell, aye?" he murmured, watching her closely. How much did she really want this? How much went beyond friendship and sex?

"Yep, time usually does tell." She slipped her hand into his. "Ready for bed?" Despite all they had done intimately, she still blushed as she smiled. "You done wiped me out."

Sleep sounded great considering what day tomorrow was.

June twenty-third.

The first of two days that made up the infamous Battle of Bannockburn.

He warned Conall that they were returning but heard nothing back. Not worried, he and Christina joined the others. All of whom were asleep except Sven. He never cast a glance in their direction but stared out into the night as if deep in thought about someone long gone.

The next morning dawned bright but quiet and windless. As though time stood still, waiting to witness history. A history that was about to be made with no help from Adlin and Milly. Where were they anyway? Trapped in limbo with Aðisla again? Doomed to appear at the last minute?

"So what is our plan, Uncle Grant?" Bryce asked when he returned with a carcass, and he and Sven began skinning it. "As far as Robert the Bruce knows, Christina is still in Stirling Castle, and that is important, aye?"

"Aye," Grant replied. "'Tis why he has rerouted his plans closer to the castle though still down the road a ways. Her kidnapping made him rethink his battle plans and 'tis a bloody good thing."

"So what will make things unfold as they should today," Conall asked. "What will make him take action?"

"Rumor, lads. Sent by us to his men about Christina." A clever grin slid onto Grant's face. "'Twill prompt him to act on this verra morn as history says he should. When he does, 'twill be a means to draw the enemy out and distract them so he can try to infiltrate the castle and save her." He appeared quite pleased. "Yet she willnae be there anymore but escaped and returned to him."

"How will she have escaped though?" Graham frowned, confused. "When the castle is watched so closely by the Scots on the outside, and I'm sure enough Sassenach on the inside despite our battle there."

"Aye." A mischievous gleam lit Grant's eyes. "But tis a mighty haunted castle now too or so rumor has it." He made the sign of the cross over his chest and winked. "After all, 'twas just a few nights ago that wails were heard within its walls. Haunting sounds of warfare and pain." He shrugged. "So 'tis not such a far-fetched idea that they threw poor Christina to the wolves, thinking mayhap she brought the evil beasties out." He shook his head, baffled. "'Tis hard to know why no one saw her beyond the castle walls but haunted grounds are capable of anything, are they not?"

While the story could be told many ways, Graham got the gist of it as did they all. Not only their actions in saving Christina but likely her own before they arrived had created sound aplenty.

Enough to cast rumors far and wide.

So Christina had an excuse for getting away. She was also the very reason Robert had changed his battle strategy. No, that wasn't quite right. The warlock was the reason for all of this change, and they needed to remember that.

"A warlock that almost seems to be helping us," he murmured without realizing it.

"Aye, and something to remain aware of and vigilant of," Grant said. "For now, 'tis time to make our way back to Robert's encampment to ensure day one of the Battle of Bannockburn goes as it should so that there can be a day two, aye?"

"Aye," Graham and his cousins replied before they ate then set out. The air was slightly cooler than the day before, but visibility was good. Just the sort of day Robert the Bruce would need to be seen from afar.

Just the sort of day to launch one of the most historical battles in Scottish history.

"So what can we expect today?" Christina asked. "What is Robert supposed to do?"

"As far as history tells it, incite the enemy," he provided. "But as we now know it, initially draw the Sassenach out to battle so he can take Stirling Castle and save you." He shook his head. "Which willnae happen because you're going to show up before he does."

"Which will somehow lead to day two of this battle?"

"Aye." Graham nodded. "How that happens precisely is yet to be seen but 'twill be one of two ways."

Her brows rose. "And those are?"

"Either the Sassenach will do as history told and get caught unaware, then disheartened by today's events and back off," he said. "If that doesnae happen, I imagine we will have to find a way to make sure he attacks on the morrow regardless."

"You mean *I* will need to make sure," she said softly.

"Och, lass, you arenae in this alone." He stopped and cupped the sides of her neck, making sure she paid attention as their eyes held. "You might be a fierce warrioress and able to hold your own, but you'll never be alone." He shook his head. "Not so long as I'm around. Or any of my kin for that matter."

"I know," she replied. "But I still get the feeling I'm stuck right smack dab in the middle of all this and in the end, it's gonna come down to my actions." She bit the corner of her lip and shook her head. "Because let's not forget Robert's determined to make me his wife and..." an unsettled expression flickered across her face, "and, well, when I get around him I don't tend to think straight."

Graham knew as much and was glad that she seemed to as well. That she wasn't sitting here days later still swooning over the Bruce. While he could champion himself on having done a stellar job keeping her mind preoccupied, he found satisfaction in it for a much better reason. This meant that it was as he thought and dark magic was at work. That her romantic feelings toward Robert the Bruce were not genuine.

Yet like Grant had to be wondering...where did Robert's wife fit into all this?

How did they make sure that marriage actually happened?

Bryce had gone out scouting earlier and reported back exactly what they had hoped to hear. The Sassenach, as well as the Scots, were ready for battle and in the proper location just over the Scottish border southeast of Robert's army. Banners were flying, and a great deal of men were amassed.

"I would say the Sassenach have around two thousand horses and thirteen thousand infantry, some clearly from Ireland and Wales," Bryce said. "Robert's men total around six thousand I'd say. Far less on horseback."

"Even so, the odds are better at this battle than they were at Stirling Bridge," Conall remarked. "Though the men under Wallace and Moray fought well, now we've an army led by three seasoned commanders and men with eight years of successful guerrilla warfare behind them. Much of which took place in the north of England." Pride lit his eyes. "They're experienced and battle-hardened."

Graham and Bryce nodded, as pleased as Conall.

"We're drawing close," Grant said as they came to an area looking down on where the battle would take place. "We should stay out of this if possible."

Yet it seemed Fate had another plan.

Christina.

Though they had tried to stay out of sight, the clear day aided them in yet another unexpected way. Robert the Bruce had, against all the odds, locked eyes on Christina despite the distance. When he did, whether to get to her faster or keep the enemy from seeing her, he set history in motion.

"Bloody hell..." Grant murmured, as things went exactly as they should.

Grant had planned on Robert seeing Christina toward the end of the battle where instead he had seen her at the beginning. Either way, things were going precisely the way they were meant to as Robert the Bruce proceeded to make his infamous first move.

He sent a group of his soldiers fleeing into the woodland in such a way that they would be seen. As planned, the Sassenach vanguard, made up of heavy cavalry, charged. As they clashed with the Scots, an English knight, Sir Henry de Bohun, spotted Robert the Bruce. That, as it turned out, was exactly what Robert had hoped for.

With sights set on greatness, de Bohun knew if he killed or captured the Bruce, he would become a chivalric hero. So, spurring his warhorse to the charge, he lowered his lance and boar down on the king. Robert, an experienced warrior, showed no signs of fear, but mounted his horse, known as "Ane palfray, litil, and joly" and met the charge. Dodging the lance, he brought his battle axe down on de Bohun's helmet, striking him dead.

Elated, the Scots forced the English cavalry to withdraw.

As foretold, two of King Edward's experienced commanders, Sir Henry Beaumont and Sir Robert Clifford, attempted to outflank the Scots and cut off their escape route...and it nearly worked. At the last moment, however, Thomas Randolph's *schiltrom*—a compact body of troops forming a battle array—dashed out of the woods and caught the English cavalry by surprise.

After that, a ferocious melee ensued.

Men died on both sides.

But without archers, the Sassenach cavalry found they were unable to get through the dense thicket of Scots spearmen. They even resorted to throwing their swords and maces at them, until the Scots pushed them back and forced them into flight.

What Graham and his kin had not foreseen, however, was that the battle would spread out more than expected and that they would become part of it. Though they saw men heading their way, there was little time to flee, so they stayed and fought. While he and his cousins would never admit to it, some small part of them had wanted this from the beginning. Blood on their blades as they assisted Robert in such an important battle.

Graham handed Christina the same blade from yesterday. "This time we must protect both Grant and Kenna, lass."

She nodded. "You got it."

"Be careful," he said softly, worried about her despite how well she fought. He imagined he always would be.

"You too," she replied.

He had just enough time to give Kenna a dagger as well. "Stay close to us, lass." He gave her a look of reassurance. "We will protect ye."

"Aye." She nodded, confident. "Dinnae worry about me."

As their eyes held, he saw something new in her. An inner peace that had not been there before. What had Sven said to her the previous night? Or had it even been the Viking? Mayhap, like he surmised, she had simply found what she was looking for when she let Graham go. He didn't get the chance to ask her because moments later retreating Sassenach soldiers were everywhere.

Then it was utter chaos.

While many simply flew by them, others engaged and they had their own mini war right there in the woods. It was ferocious and fast and disheartening in ways he never saw coming. Unlike a man going into battle, angry and righteous, these Sassenach warriors were desperate and fleeing for their lives. Such a position made men more vicious than usual and tended to give them extraordinary strength.

Therefore, they put up more of a fight than anticipated.

That in combination with something unexpected turned things for the worst very quickly.

While Christina certainly fought with the same passion and vigour as the day before something was slightly different. More enhanced if possible. Vivacious. Eye-drawing. Something was amplifying her magic. As he crossed swords with two men, he was only able to catch snippets at first.

The golden shine of Christina's gem.

How it grew brighter as she and Bryce moved closer and battled alongside each other.

How their moves nearly synchronized and became almost more than magical. Powerful. A true force to be reckoned with. By all accounts, it appeared they had ignited the power of the MacLomain, Broun connection.

Disarmed by how well they fought together, how intimate it seemed in some strange way, Graham nearly got run through with a sword but dodged just in time. As he battled another Sassenach, he realized that Christina and Bryce were becoming aware of it as well. That it was throwing them off as they adjusted to fighting even better than they had before.

It wasn't just throwing *them* off either but ended up distracting everyone—including him—so much so that a Sassenach managed to get past all of them.

Moments later, he heard Kenna scream.

Horrified for her, Graham ended the man he had been fighting and raced in her direction, but it was too late.

The enemy pulled her back against him, put a dagger to her neck and shook his head. "Back away rebel or she dies."

While the blade worried him plenty, the wild look in the man's eyes and the shakiness of his voice concerned him ever more. The man was terrified and more than unstable as he walked her backwards. Kenna, thankfully, was calmer than anticipated.

She trusted Graham to save her and he would.

In retrospect, it was unfortunate that the last of the enemy fled at that moment and far too much attention turned their way. Between him and his kin and Sven, the frightened man was facing off with far more trouble than he bargained for. Before anyone had a chance to use magic, Grant included, the panicked warrior took immediate action.

He distracted his opponents then ran.

Graham blinked several times, barely processing what had just happened as Kenna fell to her knees. The soldier hadn't sliced her throat but ran her through with a sword, likely to lose the extra weight before he began his sprint to safety.

A sprint that ended seconds later as Graham whipped his blade into his back then raced to Kenna. He fell to his knees in front of her before she toppled forward. Conall, thinking more clearly than him, moved fast and managed to pull the sword free first so it wouldn't harm Graham as well.

Though Kenna initially whimpered in pain, she soon quieted as shock set in.

While tempted to scoop her up, rush back to the encampment and find the healer, he knew it was already too late. She had been fatally wounded.

"Och, lass," he whispered, torn up with grief as he held her head on his lap and stared into her eyes. "I'm so verra sorry."

"Nay," she whispered as blood trickled out of the corner of her mouth. "Dinnae be. 'Twas not yer fault."

But it was.

He had led her to this precise moment.

He had *somehow* caused this.

This should not have happened.

"Be happy, Graham. Ye deserve it. And when ye see Fraser..." she whispered. Her voice was a weak croak now, and her eyes were beginning to glaze over. "Tell him...that I only wish him peace...that there's light beyond the darkness..."

"Aye, lass," he replied, willing to say anything she needed to hear. "I'll tell him."

"Aye, then," she managed, her voice fading as their eyes remained locked. "May we meet again someday, my frien—"

Sadly, that's all she got out before the life left her eyes and she was gone.

Chapter Fifteen

ALL CHRISTINA COULD do later that day was sit in Robert the Bruce's tent and hold her head in her hands. What had she allowed to happen?

She had let everyone down.

Most especially Kenna.

A tear slid down her cheek as she recalled the pain on Kenna's face then the pain in Graham's eyes as he watched her slip away. Christina wasn't sure she would ever get either image out of her mind.

It was her fault.

She could have stopped it somehow.

Robert handed her a mug of whisky when he entered, concern in his eyes as he sat beside her and took her hand. "I'm so verra sorry, lass. Sorry that ye were taken prisoner by the Sassenach then even sorrier that yer friend met her end today." He shook his head. "'Twas not right."

"No it wasn't," she whispered then sighed as her eyes drifted to the whisky though she didn't bother drinking it. "She was a strong woman in so many ways. She kept my head on straight when we were taken."

"Aye and for that I will forever be indebted to her," he said, his voice still soft and respectful.

Christina nodded and managed to pull herself out of her own stupor and be decent. "I'm sorry for the men you lost today too."

While it was on the tip of her tongue to do so, she refrained from calling him sweetie. Anything that might be considered an endearment. Because whatever spell she had been under before when it came to him no longer seemed to apply.

At least not on her part.

Robert nodded his thanks to her comment. "The bodies are being buried and my men commencing outside will say a final farewell. Kenna will be amongst those mourned." His eyes stayed with hers as he wiped away yet another silent tear rolling down her cheek. "Would ye care to join me, lass?"

"I would," she whispered and nodded.

Though there was a certain sense of victory in the encampment as they exited, there was also a somber feeling as friends said goodbye to the fallen. A fire had been built a ways out from the graves, and by the looks of it, all had been buried.

It wasn't difficult locating Lindsay and the rest. They stood together talking softly.

"I need to go be with my friends for a bit," she murmured.

"Aye, lass." He touched her shoulder. "Come find me when yer ready."

She nodded and headed toward Lindsay and the others only to veer off without knowing where she was going. Soon enough, she realized her instincts were bringing her to Graham. He was crouched at the foot of a mound of dirt with his head hung.

She was still a good twenty feet away when he shook his head without looking up and murmured, "Nay, lass. Dinnae come any closer. I wish to be alone."

Pained by his rejection but understanding it she stopped but couldn't seem to walk away. Instead, feeling his pain as if it were hers, she sank to her haunches and stayed that way. She wanted to go to him and say how sorry she was. More than that, she wanted to rewind time and make this all better.

Because she *could* have.

She *should* have.

"I'm so sorry, Graham," she whispered. "I never meant to let you down."

Though she imagined he likely heard her, he never raised his head and never said a word. How did she help him from here? How did she offer comfort? What could she do?

"Nothing, lass," Grant said softly as he came alongside and held out his hand. "You've been out here long enough. Come join us and let Graham work through his emotions."

"I don't want to leave him," she murmured even as she took Grant's hand and went with him, glancing back at Graham until she couldn't see him anymore. "He's taking this real hard, and he has every right to." She clenched her jaw and wiped away yet another stray tear. "I let him down, Grant. I let her die."

"You did no such thing," Grant said, his voice sharp enough to yank her eyes to his. "You protected her the best you could. You fought hard." He shook his head and stopped. "'Twas her time, Christina. 'Twas Kenna's time and she knew it."

She frowned. "Why does that almost sound like you mean it literally?"

"Because she spoke at length with Sven this morning apparently," he said softly. "It seems she dreamt that her death was close." His eyes were moist as he paused then continued. "She was not afraid but instead had a new sense of hope. Things were going as they should, and her renewed hope was for both Scotland and her people... and most especially her friends, old and new."

"Why did she only tell Sven about this dream?" She kept frowning and shook her head. "We might have been able to help her somehow... save her."

"'Tis not for us to question why she told Sven," he murmured. "All that matters is that she felt comfortable enough to confide in him. More than that, she likely realized he would share with us, and that was precisely what she wanted. To give us a sense of peace when we lost her and mayhap a fresh sense of hope for our country as well."

Christina released a choppy sigh, so darn sad she couldn't see straight.

Grant cupped her cheek. "As to letting Graham down, no." He shook his head, his eyes pained. "He's just coming to terms with things. Blaming himself when he shouldnae. But he's not blaming you. Graham would never blame you for anything."

"How do you know?" she whispered. "I might if I were him."

"He cares for you too much, lass." Grant's eyes stayed with hers. "He loves you, Christina."

"*Love?*" She widened her eyes, and shook her head, long past playing any part now. "No, we're not nearly there. Just good friends is all."

"Aye, I hope 'tis true," Bryce said as he joined them, met her eyes and finally put voice to something she had pushed to the back of her mind. "Because if I'm not mistaken, 'tis our magic together that helped today's battle. 'Twas magic born of a MacLomain, Broun connection."

"Yet it didn't save poor Kenna." Christina kept frowning as she looked from Bryce to Grant, remembering all too well what had happened. How they fought together. While she might not want to ask her next question she had to. "Was it then, Grant? Was what Bryce and I did together part of some greater true love connection?"

"I cannae imagine how when you're in love with Graham, Christina," Grant remarked.

"*What?*" both she and Bryce said at the same time.

"No, I'm not," Christina denied as Bryce pointed at her gem and spoke.

"It glowed bright golden when we battled together and created unbelievable magic," he reminded. "There must be a great connection betwixt us for that to have happened."

"Aye," came a familiar voice before Adlin appeared through the night with Milly. His expression was uncharacteristically grave as his eyes flickered from Christina to Grant. "And 'tis a connection that we shouldnae ignore."

Disgruntled surprise flashed in Grant's eyes as if he suddenly understood something.

"Mil," Christina exclaimed before she gave Milly a big hug. "I can't tell you how happy I am to see you."

"Same here." Milly's smile seemed strained as she embraced the others. "I wasn't sure we'd make it." Her eyes slid to Sven then back. "Though I'd say by the looks of things, Aðísla was right not to tag along."

"Where is my aunt?" Sven's eyes narrowed. "Why does she avoid me and our kin?"

"Milly didnae *quite* say that." Adlin patted Sven's shoulder. "We will talk in private, aye?" Then his concerned eyes went to Milly. "But first, are you sure you don't want me to stay with you and help explain things? Because you know I will."

"No, go ahead with Sven." She gave him a reassuring look. "I've got this."

What were they talking about? And why did she get the sinking feeling it had to do with her?

Milly's eyes went from Christina to the direction of Graham. It seemed she was caught up on things based on her next question. "How's he doing?"

"Not good," Christina said bluntly. "In fact, pretty crappy."

Milly nodded and looked toward the tents. "Is there somewhere we can talk in private?" Her eyes went to Lindsay then back to Christina, her expression troubled. "Just the three of us?"

Lindsay nodded. "Conall and I were given our own tent. That might be the best choice."

Christina couldn't agree more considering Robert might very well walk into his tent at any moment. And she wasn't quite comfortable going to the one she and Graham had shared until she knew if he was upset with her or not.

"So what's going on?" Christina asked, edgy the moment she entered the tent. No, edgy the second she walked further away from Graham.

Milly said nothing at first but eyed Christina, clearly seeing what she expected to as she murmured, "You've really truly fallen for him, haven't you?"

She frowned. "Fallen for *who*?"

"Graham."

"No."

"But you have, sweetheart," Lindsay said softly as she lit a fire and urged them to sit. "Since the moment you met him in New Hampshire." She gave Christina a knowing look. "All games aside."

"The ring never shined the color of his eyes, did it?" Milly asked. "That was all a charade."

"No," she began to lie but instead sighed, plunked down in a chair and muttered, "Yeah, it was a lie."

"A lie built on what turned out to be the truth," Lindsay added. "So not really a lie at all."

"A total lie if the gem never shined a color yet they said it did, Linds." Milly shook her head before her eyes met Christina's. "Not to say I don't see the underlying truth in Lindsay's defense. Still, it might not be enough…"

"What do you mean, *enough*." Christina frowned. "What's going on?"

Milly eyed her again, clearly not sure how to word things until she came right out with it. "I mean we need to strongly consider you...and Bryce."

"There is no me and Bryce beyond friendship," she said bluntly. "I'm sorry. He's hot and great and all that, but the sparks just aren't there. It's not gonna happen." She shook her head. "Not like that."

"I understand," Milly replied. "I really do." She hesitated. "Yet the sparks *are* there. Or so said the battle earlier today."

"So we fought well together." Christina shrugged, still amazed by what had happened. "That doesn't spell love in my book."

"From what I heard, it was more than just fighting well together," Milly murmured, watching her closely as she sat. "And I think whatever it was blew your mind a little."

"And distracted me long enough for Kenna to be killed," Christina spat before she could stop herself. "What kind of warrior lets that happen?"

"You can't blame yourself for that, and you damn well know it," Milly said. "You did your best." Her eyes stayed with Christina's. "And let's not forget you were fighting alongside several well-trained Scottish warriors that were trying to protect her as well. Yet she *still* died." Her eyes narrowed. "Now tell me about this feeling you had when you and Bryce fought together."

"Why, so you can relay it back to Adlin?"

"Yes," Milly readily confessed. "He wanted to speak to you about this, but I told him I would prefer to. That you didn't know him well enough yet." She sighed. "He helped create these rings so the more he knows about what happened between you and Bryce, the better. That way, we can get to the bottom of things. Wouldn't you agree?"

Well, when she put it like that. Christina frowned and took a deep swig of whisky before she finally answered. "Whatever happened between us, it was one helluva power trip and hard to explain."

"Did it feel sexual?" Milly asked. "Were you aroused?"

"No," Christina answered honestly, not overly shocked by the question. "It was more like..." she searched for the right words, "more like we knew exactly what the other was going to do and complimented it." She shook her head. "And I don't mean by reading each other's minds. It was more like we had been practicing

192

it for ages and everything just worked out perfect. Like we were invincible together."

"Hmm," Lindsay murmured, considering what she had said. "I think I know what you mean but to a lesser degree." Her eyes went to Milly's. "When Bryce and I held off the English at the village in Happrew, he as a dragon and me as an enchantress, it felt very intense. Powerful."

Christina looked between them. "So are we thinking this is dragon related?"

"It could be," Milly conceded. "Yet you and Bryce seem to be making a much stronger connection even though Lindsay literally saved his life."

Milly's eyes never left Christina's as she continued. "When Adlin and I arrived here, he sensed the magnitude of the connection you made with Bryce. Soon after Grant did too. It's likely they didn't sense it sooner because they weren't in the same era together." She shook her head. "Anyway, they're certain your connection with Bryce is *not* warlock related. It felt directly connected to the MacLomain magic used when the rings were created." Her voice softened as she delivered news that made Christina's chest tighten. "The magical connection that sparked between you and Bryce was without a doubt for the greater good of our clan and Scotland, not against it."

"Perhaps it also happened because Christina is a warrior and a part of Bryce can relate," Lindsay volunteered, clearly trying to come to Christina's rescue. "Both the man and likely even the dragon."

Milly nodded. "It could be." Her eyes stayed on Christina. "But the fact remains, three things now tie you to Bryce and what just happened between you two is pretty big…"

When she trailed off, Christina frowned and finished her sentence. "And nothing ties me to Graham except attraction," she perked her brows, "*and* him hearing my voice in his head before anyone else did… and then the scant few times I heard him." She rolled her eyes. "Which is evidently not enough."

"I have to ask you a personal question, sweetie," Milly said, not commenting on what Christina had just said.

Somehow, she just knew what her friend was going to ask next, so she beat her to it.

"Yeah, we've already slept together," Christina muttered. "Have you *looked* at him?" She took another swig and shook her head. "I know, shame on me considering poor Kenna."

"Ah, the woman he was going to marry to save her clan," Milly said softly. "That was noble."

Christina eyed her for a moment before she murmured, "So Adlin knows."

"Not much gets by him," Milly responded. "But yes, he's known for some time."

"Why didn't he tell Graham?" She frowned, bewildered and a little frustrated. "Why not tell him that the MacLomains would offer Clan MacLauchlin protection so that Graham didn't feel the need to marry Kenna?"

"Like Grant, Adlin tends to let things play out as they will," Milly said. "He doesn't like to mess with destiny or Fate overly much."

While that seemed plausible enough, sometimes she got the feeling that Adlin and Grant did the very opposite. That they worked together to steer destiny and Fate right along.

"I'm sorry, but this seems pretty cut and dry." Christina crossed her arms over her chest, cocked her head and remained focused on Adlin's silence when it came to Graham and the MacLauchlins. "Ensure a clan protection and help your cousin out."

"I can pretty much guarantee that Adlin was doing just that," Milly said. "Though it might not be entirely clear to us how yet."

"What's that supposed to mean?"

"It means Adlin's as powerful as Grant," Lindsay reminded. "Which means he's very much a forward thinker and likely sees things nobody else can."

"Alrighty then." Christina sighed and took another swig of whisky, knowing full well she would likely never get a straight answer. Truthfully? She wasn't sure she wanted one.

"So, I have to ask." Lindsay's eyes went to Milly's before they returned to Christina's. "*We* have to ask." Her brows rose in question. "How was the sex, darling?"

"With *Graham?*" Christina snorted and looked between them. "How the heck do you think it was?"

"You tell us." Amusement lit Milly's eyes. "Details aren't necessary. We just need to find out if...well...if it was the sort of sex it should be if he's your one true love."

"Enough with the one true love thing, y'all." She rolled her eyes again and finally managed a grin. "But as sex goes, it was top notch."

Lindsay slanted her head. "*Just* top notch?"

"Yeah, top notch. The highest rung on the totem pole. Doesn't get any better." When they looked at her dubiously, she chuckled then gave it to them straight. "Okay, ladies, it was the most amazing sex of my entire life. He could handle me. I've never felt anything like it..." Her voice softened and thickened with unexpected emotion. "And I know I never will again."

Silence fell as they stared at her.

"Hell," Milly whispered. "Then this really sucks."

"What?" Christina said.

"What I came in here initially to tell you." Milly sighed, her eyes pained as they stayed with Christina's. "If nothing else, we need to make sure we save Scotland's history, wouldn't you agree?"

She frowned. "Well, *yeah*, of course."

"That means doing everything in our power to make sure that happens," Milly continued. "Which means harnessing the power of these rings."

Christina narrowed her eyes. "Your point?"

"My point is you need to listen to that ring, Christina," she replied, obviously upset but still determined. "And you need to give Bryce half a chance because, despite everything, it's looking more and more likely that he might be your MacLomain."

"This sounds an awful lot like what I went through," Lindsay kicked in. "I was told to pursue man after man though I was always meant for Conall."

"Right, but now we all know Adlin and Grant were steering you two together," Milly reminded. "Because you were determined to remain apart."

"True," Lindsay conceded as hope sparked in her eyes. "So is that what this is then? Do Adlin and Grant know something we don't and however opposite it might appear at the moment, they're actually pushing Christina and Graham together?" She shook her head and frowned. "Because I can tell you from experience it's not all that fun

195

going from guy to guy, even if it *is* designed to steer you into the arms of the man you're meant to be with."

"At least Adlin's only asking Christina to be with *one* man," Milly said softly. "Bryce." She shook her head. "And as far as I know this is no grand scheme to get Christina and Graham together."

"So is Adlin *ordering* or *asking* me to be with Bryce?" Christina kept her tone not just incredulous but sarcastic as she stood and planted her fists on her hips. "Not that it really matters because it's bullshit." She looked skyward and whispered, "Sorry for swearing, Granny."

"Don't get too upset, Christina," Lindsay said, evidently focusing on the one thing Milly said that offered any hope at all. "Like Milly just reminded, Adlin and Grant are known to play games to move Fate along."

"Yet she also said she didn't think they were scheming this time." Christina scowled at Milly as she faced the cold hard truth. "So you're telling me if I don't hook up with Bryce, I'm going to destroy Scotland?" Her eyes widened as her voice rose. "Are you *seriously* telling me that?"

"Yes," Milly said, her voice firm but her eyes worried. "That's exactly what I'm telling you." She stood as well. "So no, you don't have to listen to Adlin's request but consider this if you don't. Scotland ceasing to exist in the future and what will happen to its people between now and then to see that through. All the death and loss."

Christina blinked back moisture, shocked by the words coming out of her friend's mouth. Shocked that she was being guilted into this. Worse yet, that it might actually be true. That her desire to be with Graham could ruin so many lives…an entire country.

She sank into her chair and stared at the fire, baffled and angry but most of all, frightened. Scared that so much was being put on her. So much depended on her.

"What about Robert," she said absently as her thoughts churned. "He's determined to marry me."

"*What?*" Lindsay and Milly said at the same time.

"I mean he mentioned it a while back, so I figured I better let you know, all things considered."

They stared at her a moment in utter shock before Milly finally said, "Details would be good."

"But pointless," Christina remarked and shrugged. "Seeing how I've been *ordered...*" she shook her head, "I mean *asked,*" she snapped her fingers, "dang, I meant *requested* to be with Bryce, I don't see how it matters."

Milly narrowed her eyes. "Don't be a wiseass."

"I'll be whatever I damn well please," she shot back. "Until I wrap my head around everything you just shared."

"I'm sorry," Milly said, her voice soft and her eyes genuine. "I really am."

A few moments later, Conall ducked in followed by Adlin and Grant.

Miffed and not much in the mood to talk she stood only for Grant to shake his head. "Sit, lass. Please. We need to discuss a few things."

"I tend to think enough's been discussed," she replied, saddened that he might be in on this. "Are you aware of what Adlin wants from me?"

Grant nodded. "I'm afraid I am." His eyes stayed with hers. "And I agree with him."

"Well, that's a shame." She shook her head. "Didn't you just say before Adlin arrived that you thought Graham and I loved each other? Why say that if you didn't believe it?"

"What I believe isnae important anymore, lass," he said gently, sadness in his eyes. "I didnae mean to..." He sighed, distraught. "I didnae mean to lead you in one direction only to ask you to go in another. I'm verra sorry."

She knew full well he didn't have a better understanding of she and Bryce's connection until Adlin arrived but still. The whole thing stunk. Her eyes went back and forth between the two arch-wizards. "Does Bryce know? Graham?"

"Aye, we've spoken with them," Adlin replied softly, clearly as upset as Grant.

"Real nice," she muttered. "Poor Graham. He's having a heck of a day, isn't he?" She took another swig of whisky and sank into a chair again as she gave it more thought. "Or maybe he's just grateful considering I failed to protect Kenna."

"I told you how I felt about that and 'tis the truth, lass," Grant said, his voice gentle yet firm and final. "For now, we've other things to worry about as a group, from Robert's intent to marry you to talk of Fraser."

"Talk I bloody well intend to be part of," Graham growled as he stalked in. His eyes lingered on hers for a moment before they swept to Adlin. "We saw Fraser die in battle. Conall was right in front of him. His life was lost. His heart stopped beating. Why then, was Kenna so convinced he might still be alive?" His jaw tightened. "So much so that she would devote her last words to saying as much."

"I stand beside Graham entirely with this." Conall shook his head, troubled. "Fraser received multiple fatal wounds and died." His brows snapped together in confusion as his eyes went from Adlin to Grant. "Yet when we went back for his body it was gone. We assumed the enemy had disposed of it. Do you know otherwise? Have you been keeping the ultimate fate of our cousin from us these long years?"

Both shook their head as Grant responded. "No, Grandson. I swear on your grandma's life that nothing was kept from you and your cousins. Kenna's revelation, such as it was, is new to us."

"Could he be trapped like Da was in some other dimension?" Conall asked, his voice hoarse with emotion.

"No," Christina murmured and shook her head. "Kenna said no, and I believe her."

She again relayed their vague conversation when in captivity so that everyone could hear it firsthand.

Silence fell afterwards as her words sank in. When her eyes drifted to Graham, he was staring into the fire, as lost in thought as everyone else. She needed him to look at her though. She needed him to know how sorry she was about everything.

Kenna.

Bryce.

Fate.

"We'll have to wait and see then," Grant finally said. "But we will not ignore Kenna's last words, may she rest in peace. And we will not give up hope that mayhap somewhere out there, Fraser is still alive."

Before he could continue, Bryce ducked into the tent as well, adding that extra body that made things start to feel a little tight. His eyes went to Christina's, and he nodded before he urged Grant to continue. She sensed by his expression that he had likely caught the discussion about Fraser though he wasn't here.

"What we need to figure out next is how to get Robert the Bruce to stop desiring you so much, Christina," Grant said. "No matter how well it served our purpose today." He shook his head. "That he desires to marry you isnae good."

"No, but at least I don't desire him anymore," Christina said. Though frustrated with Grant and Adlin, she focused on the bigger picture. "That's halfway to what we want, right?"

"Aye." Adlin nodded. "'Tis verra good."

Graham still wouldn't look her way, yet she sensed he wanted to. That this was as hard on him as it was on her. Or maybe that was just wishful thinking.

"So should we assume that half the spell cast on Robert and Christina has lifted?" Lindsay asked. "And if that's the case, what do you suppose caused it? Because if we figure that out, it stands to reason we might be able to replicate it and perhaps lift the curse entirely, right?"

"A sound deduction and equally good questions, lass." Grant looked at her with pride before his eyes swept over everyone else. "Naturally, 'twould have had to be something that happened betwixt the last time Robert saw Christina and now which could be a number of things."

"Aye, it *could* be a number of things," Graham said, that same frustrated growl in his voice as his eyes narrowed on Adlin and Grant. "Mayhap because she has embraced her gift in its entirety or because history is starting to correct itself with today's battle."

Then his eyes leveled with hers, and he said the last thing she expected. "Or mayhap 'tis because I've truly fallen in love with her."

Chapter Sixteen

STUNNED SILENCE FELL as Graham's eyes stayed with Christina's. Though this was the most inappropriate time to declare his love for her, he meant it. He didn't want to lose her. Yet he knew he had just spoken impulsively. That he was being selfish considering the fate of his country was at stake.

When he was told that he had to step back and allow a relationship to grow between her and Bryce, he nearly snapped. How was he supposed to do that? How was he supposed to let her go now that he realized how strongly he felt? Yes, some might say that because of what he was going through at the moment, he wasn't seeing clearly. Yet deep down, he knew he was thinking more clearly than ever.

"I…" Christina began, then clamped her mouth shut, her pained eyes with his before she finally managed to get more words out. "We need to talk, handsome…I mean Graham. Alone."

When Adlin shook his head and began to say something, Grant interrupted him. "I think that would be a good idea." His eyes went to Adlin. "We cannae order them to be apart any more than we can keep them from speaking alone. They know where things stand now. Trust in them to take that into consideration."

"I agree." Milly nodded as she looked at Adlin. "Grant's right."

Not waiting for *anyone* to decide whether he could talk alone with his lass, Graham ushered Christina out. They walked away from the bonfire and graves, not saying a word until they were free of the encampment altogether. The moonlit night was warm, breezy and peaceful. At complete odds with the day he'd had and the emotions churning inside him.

"I didn't see that coming," she finally murmured.

"Nor did I," he said honestly. "But I couldnae just let them take you away from me."

"Take me away?" She stopped and frowned. "I know things have been happening pretty quickly and we enjoy each other's company in all the right ways but..." She narrowed her eyes. "When did you decide I was yours? So much so that you were gonna declare something as important as love to keep anyone from taking me away?"

"Tonight," he murmured then shook his head. "Nay, before that."

"Before that?" Pain flickered across her face. "Honey, I let your friend get killed today. You *do* know that, right? You asked me to protect her, and I failed, and now you think you *love* me?" Her brows slammed together, her frustration evident. "C'mon! Love's about the last thing you should be feeling."

"You think I think that about you and Kenna?" He scowled, disturbed by her assessment, his brogue thickening with aggravation. "Ye think ye failed me? That 'twas yer fault Kenna was slain?"

"Everyone says it isn't," she shot back, wiping away a stray tear. "Except I feel like it must've been and you haven't said otherwise." She clenched her jaw and shook her head. "And yours is the only damn opinion that matters."

"I would *never* blame ye, lass." He pulled her into his arms and held her as she rested her cheek against his chest and trembled. "If anyone was to blame 'twas me. I told her I would protect her and I didnae."

"Did Grant tell you what she shared with Sven?" she murmured. "What she dreamt about last night?"

"Aye," he whispered, frustrated that she had not shared it with him as well. He might have done things differently. But as Sven said, more comforting than expected, Kenna had chosen her own path. That for the first time in her life she was in control of her own destiny. It was her choice. And that apparently gave her newfound strength and peace.

Yet there was more.

Something else that gave her purpose and courage.

"What?" Christina whispered, obviously following his thoughts.

"She told Sven it was part of the prophecy," he said softly. "That her death would not be in vain but would have great purpose. That she was along on this journey for a reason."

She pulled back slightly and met his eyes. "What reason? What purpose?"

"To steer this country in the right direction and help save it," he murmured. "So that someday it would be a better place with less poverty and warfare. A Scotland that didnae treat their women like chattel but gave them the freedom to live their own lives the way they wanted to."

She nodded, fresh tears in her eyes. "That's a good cause if ever there was one." She frowned. "Did she ever say specifically how her death was going to achieve that?"

"Nay." He shook his head. "Though Sven got the impression it had to do with you and me. That what we found together was going to make all the difference."

Yet what difference could they possibly make if they weren't together?

"Well, why'd she have to go and die for that?" she said, her voice thick with emotion as it occurred to her how that might have sounded. "You know what I mean." Clearly struggling with everything, she released a shaky breath. "You and I might have hooked up regardless."

Might have.

The hardest words he had ever heard because hope was dwindling for them now.

"I wish I had more answers, lass," he said softly, "but she only told Sven so much."

She nodded then rested her cheek against his chest again.

As he stroked her hair and tried to soothe her, he murmured, "Whatever else came from today, Christina, please know that I was verra proud of you. I've been proud of you since the moment we met."

"Not sure why," she mumbled through sniffles, finally letting go. "God, I'm just so sorry, Graham. I'm so sorry about Kenna. She didn't deserve that."

"Nay, but she was at peace in the end, lass," he whispered. "I saw it in her eyes."

She didn't say anything else for some time just sobbed quietly as he held her. It had been a very hard day on many fronts. Losing Kenna like that had been terrible.

Now, this.

Losing Christina.

As if she sensed his thoughts, she pulled back and looked at him again. They stood like that for some time, gazing into each other's eyes and coming to terms with the reality of their situation before she finally whispered, "This is it, isn't it? What happened back there, telling me you love me, was your way of letting go the only way you knew how. Telling me how you really felt then doing the right thing and putting your country first."

Until she said it, he didn't realize that was exactly what he had done.

What he *had* to do.

He didn't answer her questions right away but asked his own.

"What about you, lass?" he said softly. "What do *you* want to do now? Listen to Adlin and Grant or throw caution to the wind and be with me?" His voice dropped an octave. "Love me."

"I think we both know the answer to that." Several emotions flashed in her eyes. Pain. Fear. Desire. But mostly acceptance as she stood on her tip-toes, and kissed his cheek. Her breath was choppy with need as her lips hovered close to his before she pulled away. "I can't live with knowing I might be responsible for ruining Scotland and its people any more than you can."

He nodded and swallowed back a denial.

If this was what they had to do, they would do it.

"Again, I'm verra proud of you, lass," he murmured. "You arenae just strong physically but mentally. I'm honored to know you."

"Back at ya," she whispered, her hand still in his as their eyes lingered on one another's and they remained close. "And just so you know, I'm not going to kiss him or have sex with him to ignite some magic just..." She shrugged, struggling. "Be friends for now I guess."

He knew very well she was talking about Bryce and ignored the tightening of his chest at the thought of them together. Her in his cousin's arms. He couldn't get much beyond that image, never mind them lying together fully.

"Aye, lass," he said gruffly. He should tell her to open herself up to getting to know Bryce better because he was a good man, which he was. But he just wasn't there yet. Not nearly.

"Christina?" Robert called out. "Is that ye? Are ye all right?"

Here came the other ongoing problem.

The famous king determined to marry her.

Bloody hell.

"I'm here," she called out, holding Graham's hand until the last moment as they headed back.

The wary look on Robert's face was telling as he nodded at Graham then offered Christina a dashing smile as he held out the crook of his elbow. "Might we have some time together, at last, lass?"

She nodded, tossed one last shaky smile at Graham then walked off with Robert.

In a dismal mood—the sort he had refused to feel for a long time—Graham stalked back. He nearly spun and walked in the opposite direction when he spied Bryce heading his way.

"We should talk, Cousin," Bryce stated as he handed him a mug of whisky and gestured that he follow. "Alone."

Graham sighed and reluctantly complied if for no other reason than Bryce was kin and before this, they had always gotten along well. They didn't go far but stopped at a small fire with a few men around it. Those that were there barely paid them any mind they were so focused on the whores meandering about.

"We cannae have this strife betwixt us as we move forward," Bryce led out. "We need to come to some sort of understanding so that I know I still have yer sword at my back in battle." His eyes met Graham's. "So that I know I can trust ye."

"Ye'll always have my sword at yer back," Graham scoffed and frowned. "Yer my bloody kin."

"Aye, kin with an eye toward a lass ye just declared ye love." Bryce clenched his jaw and shook his head. "That is no small thing." His eyes met Graham's and his brows swept down. "Did ye truly mean it? Are ye in love with Christina?"

"Would it make any difference?" Graham grumbled. "Ye've known for days that I desire her, that we were together, yet ye keep with yer advances."

"And for that I am sorry," Bryce admitted, surprising him. "I've been trying to run from my commitments however shameful my actions."

Even more surprised, Graham cocked his head. "Ye mean that aye?"

"I do." Bryce's eyes went to the fire. "For some reason, talking with Christina made me realize..." He paused and sighed. "I realized that my actions havenae been as honorable as they should have been when pursuing these Broun lasses. That in my selfishness, I have been unfaithful to my clan. To my grandma's prophetic vision." He shook his head. "Yet now that I see the error of my ways, the bigger picture remains." His eyes returned to Graham. "My country *must* come first."

While some might be inclined to think Bryce had thought up a creative albeit admiral defense to justify being with Christina, he was being honest. It was in his eyes. In the genuine regret that he had no choice but to do as Adlin and Grant requested.

Whatever it took to save Scotland's history.

"Aye, then," Graham murmured before he downed half his whisky. "I suppose if I had to see her with any lad besides me, 'twould be ye."

Though tempted to mention she had no intention of kissing or lying with Bryce, he finished off his whisky instead. The truth was if he said those things, it only proved he didn't support this. And if she didn't eventually do those things with his cousin, what hope was there that they would come into their full power together and save Scotland?

Then there was Bryce's grandmother's prophetic vision. Didn't she say Bryce was destined to marry a lass who would always love another? Could that be Christina? Yet how to spark the ring's magic without true love? He shook his head. Visions and prophecy were tricky and could sometimes be unclear. Mayhap she got the first part right and the second would happen eventually. Bryce and Christina would, indeed, find love.

Though loathed to admit it, they might have already ignited her ring's power when fighting together and the rest would soon follow. On that premise, mayhap Bryce's grandma's vision couldn't see beyond something so powerful as the ring's gem igniting. Mayhap its magic somehow obscured the future.

Grumpy though he tried to keep a cordial expression on his face, Graham bid Bryce goodnight. While tempted, he didn't look back to see where Christina and Robert might be. Better yet, if Bryce was heading in their direction so he could spend the eve wooing her. Instead, he tried to put her from his mind and ducked into his tent only to find Conall sitting in front of a small fire waiting for him.

"Och," he muttered as he plunked down in the chair beside him. "Ye dinnae need to be here comforting me when ye should be with Lindsay. The lass shouldnae be alone in this encampment, and well ye know it."

"She's with two arch-wizards and a lass who is powerful enough to reincarnate herself," Conall reminded, handing over another mug of whisky. "So I am not all that worried."

Graham eyed him, seeing the truth of it. "Nay, 'tis Lindsay's ability to protect herself that makes ye so confident. Even despite what happened to her hand."

"Aye," Conall conceded and grinned, pride in her written all over his face. "She's something else when she sets her mind to it."

"She is," Graham agreed, content to settle back and enjoy Conall's company. Yet he wasn't so foolish to think his cousin was here solely to be a shoulder to rhetorically cry on. "So what brings ye my way, Cousin?"

"You mean what brings *us* your way," Lindsay murmured as she ducked into the tent. She touched Graham's shoulder in passing and offered a soft smile before she sat beside Conall.

"Ah, so you couldnae bear to be apart after all," Graham teased.

"We can when and if we have to." A fond look passed between Lindsay and Conall before her eyes returned to Graham. "Though we tend to work better as a team."

Graham nodded, not doubting that in the least. "So then, what brings you both here?"

Lindsay smiled. "Look at you saying 'you' instead of 'ye' now." One brow lifted. "That's very telling."

Not much interested in analyzing changes in his speech patterns, he shrugged. "My apologies for not doing so sooner, lass."

"My goodness, don't apologize," she scoffed. "You're allowed to speak however you like. I was just noting the change."

Graham looked from Conall to Lindsay then sighed and took another swig of whisky. "So you're here to seek out the same answer Bryce just did, aye?"

"Whatever do you mean?" Lindsay asked innocently as Conall shrugged and came right out with it. "So do you really love her?"

"Aye," Graham said without hesitation.

"How do you know?" Conall asked.

He frowned. "What do you mean how do I know?"

"He means what makes you love Christina compared to all the other women you've been with?" Lindsay provided.

"You've both met Christina, and you're one of her closest friends, Lindsay." He shook his head, baffled. "So how can you ask such a question?"

"So that's it?" Lindsay grinned. "That's all you've got?"

"All I've *got?*" Graham looked at her, astonished. "Her astounding skills in battle and selfless need to protect others aside, just look at the length she'll go to help people, kin, and strangers alike. She is a truly admirable and kind person." He shook his head. "But you already know that so why ask?"

"Well, I just..." Lindsay whispered before she trailed off, with a wistful smile on her lips and moisture in her eyes.

Conall picked up where she left off. "What she means to say is she's verra happy for both you and Christina. That 'tis good to see true love was found betwixt you." He clasped Graham's shoulder and nodded. "I feel the same, Cousin."

Confused, Graham set aside his mug, crossed his arms over his chest and narrowed his eyes at him. "You *do* know I've just given her up to Bryce. That *they* are to be together."

"Maybe," Lindsay said airily, the devil in her eyes.

"Definitely." Graham shook his head. "We both agreed Scotland was more important than how we feel about each other."

"So Christina admitted she loved you too?" Lindsay exclaimed, her eyes wide and hopeful.

"Well, nay, not in so many words," Graham began before Conall interrupted him.

"It can be that way at first." He winked at Lindsay. "Our Brouns can be vague even though they love us from the start."

Graham eyed Conall, still trying to get used to having his cousin back to his old self. A man he hadn't seen since Fraser's death. A more jovial, upbeat version. Yet Lindsay came into his life, his father returned, and now their cousin *might* just be alive somewhere, so it made sense.

"That's right," Lindsay said, echoing Conall's sentiment. "We Brouns *do* love you MacLomains from the start though we might not admit it."

"Aye, well, 'tis good that," Graham muttered and returned to his drink. "Either way, whether she loves me or not, our paths can no longer be connected outside of friendship."

"Aye, friendship." Conall nodded. "Something that is already strong betwixt you."

"Very strong," Lindsay agreed.

"And were we not friends long before love found us?" Conall asked Lindsay.

"We were," she concurred.

"Bloody hell, just come out with it already," Graham grunted before he drank more whisky. "'Tis clear you two arenae quite on the same page as Adlin and Grant though you should be."

"We should," Lindsay agreed.

"Aye," Conall said. "But we're not."

"Nope." Lindsay's eyes met Graham's. "We're on your and Christina's page."

"A page that ends with this country in ruins," Graham reminded. Though already set on his path, he couldn't help but be grateful. It meant a lot that someone else believed in what they had. What they had found.

Something that could no longer exist.

"While I truly appreciate your support," Graham began, but Conall cut him off.

"'Tis not just support, Cousin." His eyes were deadly serious as they met Graham's. "We believe you and Christina have found the same love that Lindsay and I share and intend to make sure it doesnae end before it has a chance to begin."

"That's right," Lindsay said.

"And how do you intend to do that without driving our country into ruin?" His eyes went from Conall to Lindsay. "Because this is every inch your country now too, aye?"

"Absolutely." She nodded. "While we haven't got all the details worked out yet, we've got a plan starting tonight." She shrugged. "Hopefully, after that and the battle tomorrow it won't matter."

"And what's your plan this eve?" he asked, intrigued.

"Simple," Conall said. "Divide and conquer."

"Or at least divide," Lindsay stated as they stood. "Not sure about the conquer part, but something is better than nothing, yes?"

Graham shook his head, still not following.

"We're going to see that Christina sleeps alone tonight, sweetheart," Lindsay murmured, her hand on his shoulder again as her eyes met his. "She will be with me, and Conall will make sure Bryce steers clear. As to Robert the Bruce..." She shrugged. "He won't be with Christina, and that's all that matters."

"Ye shouldnae," Graham murmured. "'Tis wrong and ye know it. If Bryce and Christina are meant to come together to save Scotland, then nothing should stop them."

Neither responded just left.

He sighed and stared at the fire. Though he should not be, he could admit to a sense of relief at their mission even if it was only temporary. While, yes, Bryce and Christina might very well be meant for one another, an extra night apart wouldn't do any harm. Not in the scheme of things.

Or so he hoped.

Not in the mood to sit alone and dwell, he went to bed and tried to stop thinking about not only Kenna's death but Christina's absence. Thus far, nothing had gone as it should. Aye, history seemed to be correcting itself but at a great toll.

Sleep didn't come easy. When it did, it was filled with flashes of battle. Losing Kenna all over again. Pain and heartache. Then realizing how much he wanted Christina. How he had let her into his heart in a way he never meant to.

Suddenly, he was with her again after she first ran through him at the beginning.

Their eyes met then he was somewhere else.

Her dream....*before* she met Graham.

Or was it at the same time?

He couldn't tell. All he *did* know was that she was face to face with Robert the Bruce in the stone dwelling at Mystery Hill. A younger Robert. The age he had been at the last battle. The age he was when he first dreamt of Christina.

Then, strangely enough, she was in two places at once. With the Bruce and beside Graham.

"What's going on, Graham?" she whispered.

"I dinnae know," he responded. "If I were to guess, I'd say we're viewing the dream you had before you traveled back in time."

She nodded. "It's odd seeing myself like this."

"Aye," he murmured and slipped his hand into hers as they watched.

She and Robert stared at each other, at first seemingly unfamiliar, before he said, "I'm promised to ye, aye?"

"I think so." She nodded. "And I'm promised to you..." A frown settled on her face as her eyes swept over something they couldn't see. "We'll make history...change history."

"Aye." Robert nodded. "Just as long as ye stay promised to me."

"I will," she assured before a startled expression flickered across her face, and her eyes shot to Graham. "Unless I'm already promised to another."

By the time Graham glanced from the Christina standing next to him to the one caught in a dream, her other self had vanished.

"That was weird," she whispered. "Why are we seeing this?"

Seconds later, he knew as he caught something out of the corner of his eye. A dark shadowy figure was fleeing the stone dwelling. Worse yet, it appeared to be scrambling obediently after a petite figure he recognized as Jessie.

Half a breath later, his eyes shot open and he awoke from his dream.

"Oh, God," Christina whispered. "We were at the Stonehenge in New Hampshire again, and that was Jessie, wasn't it?"

"Aye," he replied and nodded, only to realize morning light was filtering through the tent opening and Christina was *not* with him. Yet she still heard him. Or was that just remnants of the dream?

"*Christina?*" he said into her mind as he sat up. "*Can you hear me, lass?*"

"*I sure can!*" There was no missing the smile in her internal voice. "*What does this mean?*"

He grinned even though she couldn't see him. "*I dinnae know, but it cannae be all bad, aye?*"

Beyond hopeful, he dressed and went in search of Adlin or Grant.

Though Christina didn't reply he could still feel her mind brushing his even more than before. She was with him in a whole new way. Sadly, as he found out a short time later, that didn't mean as much as he had hoped it would. At least not at first.

"While 'tis certainly interesting," Grant said, speculative as they broke their fast in his tent. "I dinnae think 'tis quite enough, lad."

"We've true love betwixt us," Graham argued. "*That* alone should be enough."

He didn't care if he was presumptuous about her loving him too. She could deny it telepathically anytime she liked.

Grant looked hopeful. "So she's admitted she loves ye then?"

"Well, not in so many words," Graham began before Grant cut him off with a potent reminder.

"Only the power of her ring can defeat the next warlock."

"*Well, that sucks,*" Christina murmured into his mind. "*So what's the point of us being able to communicate like this now, then? Not that I'm complaining. You feel pretty good inside my mind.*"

He almost smiled but kept a scowl on his face for Grant's benefit as he asked the same question she just had.

Grant shook his head before something occurred to him, no doubt a more direct connection to Conall's mind than most. "My grandson and Lindsay visited ye last night, aye?"

Though tempted to evade the question, he knew better. "Aye, they were a great comfort."

"I'll bet they were," Grant murmured, a curious look in his eyes as they stayed with Graham's. "Pray tell, what did they say to comfort ye?"

So he shared all but the part about them believing true love existed between Graham and Christina.

"'Twas just a simple kindness really to keep Christina with them." Graham shook his head. "Whilst Christina fully intends to put Scotland before all else, ye cannae blame the lass for not wanting to share a tent with anyone but her close friend, Lindsay."

"Nay, I suppose I cannae." Grant's eyes narrowed on Graham. "They're conspiring to bring ye and Christina together, aye? They believe ye love each other?"

"We do," he replied hotly. "At least I do."

"And they believe it as well?" Grant said. "Truly?"

"Aye," Graham confirmed, finally confessing. "So it seems."

"Well, bloody hell." A small smile tugged at the corner of Grant's mouth. "It seems mayhap the telepathic barrier betwixt ye and Christina might have been directly related to being caught in Conall and Lindsay's magic after all." He shrugged, bemused. "It also seems they arenae just giving ye the benefit of the doubt but really *do* believe in the love betwixt ye two." He shook his head. "'Twould be the only way for the spell to lift."

Graham frowned. "Ye mean they cast Christina and me under a spell?"

"Not intentionally." Grant chuckled. "Ye just got caught up in their magic is all." His brows perked. "A bit of magic, might I remind you, that took place while they were struggling to find their own love. If that same magic first brought ye and Christina together at the Stonehenge, then it stands to reason it might've made it trickier for ye to come together in the usual way MacLomains and Brouns do."

"Aye, that's sound reasoning, my friend," Adlin said as he and Milly entered followed by Christina and Lindsay. "'Tis also more and more likely someone else is involved in all this too."

Graham was never so glad to lay eyes on Christina again. Though he knew very well she was with Lindsay last night and even with Graham in his dreams, he still worried. Wondered. Would she somehow end up in Robert's tent of her own device? More so, Bryce's?"

A soft smile flitted across her face as their eyes met then vanished as Adlin elaborated more on the dream Graham and Christina had just experienced together.

"I think there is little doubt at this point that Jessie is involved with these warlocks." Adlin's troubled eyes went to Graham. "Christina shared everything with me including, with Bryce's permission, how she saw his twin sister when she dreamt about Jessie in the woods by the river."

She had seen his twin sister? That must have been part of the reason she wanted to speak to Bryce alone yesterday.

"What's this?" Grant's brows bunched together in confusion. "Ainsley?"

Adlin nodded. "'Tis interesting, aye?"

"Aye," Grant said softly as he mulled it over.

"Do you think 'tis relevant to why Christina's gem matches Bryce's eyes?" Graham couldn't keep hope from his voice. "Could Ainsley somehow be influencing or even manipulating things from the afterlife?" This made more and more sense. "Because were her eyes not the verra shade of her brother's?"

"We cannae rule out the possibility that she played a part in this," Grant conceded. "But we cannae assume 'tis definite either."

"Aye," Adlin agreed, even as he remained optimistic. "Though the connection betwixt dragon twins *is* known to be verra strong, even if one dies in infancy. And we *did* feel the magic that ignited between Christina and Bryce was of MacLomain origin." He nodded as the idea clearly grew on him. "So as you implied, Grant, there *is* always the possibility…"

"Which could mean one of several things," Grant murmured. "Either Ainsley is, in fact, assisting somehow from the afterlife or mayhap even influenced things when we created the rings." He shook his head. "Or there is always the possibility, as Christina's dream implied, that Ainsley's in contact with Jessie, who through her affiliation with the warlocks did the same."

Christina frowned. "Isn't Jessie being part of creating the rings kind of a leap?"

"'Tis verra hard to know," Grant said softly. "It would depend on the extent of her affiliation with the warlocks…and of course, how much magic she possesses."

"And what of Ainsley?" Graham asked. "Are you saying that if she was part of the creation of the rings and now influenced a ring in Bryce's favor, that it could have ignited what happened between him and Christina?"

"If she did it with the intention of protecting him, most certainly." Adlin nodded, more chipper by the moment. "If Christina's gem harnessed Ainsley's essence, it would have bonded her to Bryce almost as powerfully as the MacLomain, Broun true love connection."

Graham had never felt more hopeful as his eyes met Christina's. Could it be she wasn't meant for Bryce after all? That she and Graham still had a chance?

Speaking of his cousin, Bryce had just ducked in but froze halfway when a piercing war cry rent the air.

Everyone leapt to their feet but not before Sven joined them and frowned. "The Scottish encampment is under attack."

That, regrettably, was the last thing anyone wanted to hear.

After all, that meant history was more off-track now than ever.

Chapter Seventeen

CHRISTINA COULD ONLY thank the Lord Almighty that not only Robert had spoken about current events but then Lindsay and Conall had spent the dwindling hours of the evening before educating her on the Battle of Bannockburn. If they hadn't, she might not understand—outside of being under attack—why everyone was in a complete uproar right now.

Robert had been amiable and overly attentive as they strolled together the previous evening. While he had most certainly been wooing her, he was also very much wrapped up in what would come about today. While he was pleased with his current victory, he remained worried about the Welsh archers the Earl of Pembrokeshire had amassed on behalf of Edward II.

Though Robert had ordered hundreds of yew longbows to be crafted, it seemed he could only find five hundred men with the skills, and inclination, to wield them. That, he explained, was not nearly enough to suit him against what they faced.

"Well, you've got Bryce on your side now," she had said. "And from what I've seen, he's pretty amazing with a bow and arrow."

He gave her an interested look. "More so, with ye around, aye, lass?"

She stated the obvious. "So you saw Bryce, and I fight together."

"I didnae, but some of my men did," he replied. "And though many run superstitious 'twas in a good way knowing ye two will be fighting alongside us on the morrow."

Though he had invited her into his tent, Lindsay intercepted and requested that Christina spend the night with her. It was the decent thing to do, which Robert couldn't argue with.

Despite the disappointment in his eyes, he pulled her close for a kiss she should have seen coming. Though it was nice enough, it couldn't nearly touch Graham's kisses. Lindsay called her on it too as they sat by the fire later.

"Do you love him then, Christina?" she asked softly.

"Love who?"

"You know who," Lindsay replied. "Graham."

Though tempted to shake her head and say no, nothing came out. Not at first anyway. It had felt like the ground dropped out from beneath her when he declared his love for her earlier. She couldn't remember a man ever doing that.

Not the way he had.

Not with that look in his eyes.

More so, she couldn't remember ever feeling the way she had when he did.

"Well?" Lindsay prompted, her voice still soft. "Do you?"

"Honey, outside of Granny, you, Mils, and Jessie, I'm not sure I know what love is," she replied honestly. "Do I like Graham much better than any other man I've ever met? Heck, *yeah*."

Lindsay only gave her a whimsical knowing look before Conall joined them and she learned more about the infamous Battle of Bannockburn. Most especially the second day of the battle.

Today.

And being attacked by the English first thing in the morning was *way* off.

It was supposed to be the other way around. The Scots were supposed to eat breakfast then advance on the English.

Nonetheless, she was ready to fight, so she took the weapons given to her. Men were racing in every direction as they exited the tent. Graham and Bryce stuck close to her with Sven not that far behind.

Then she just let her gift take over and engaged the first English warrior that came at her. Still in the heart of the Scots' encampment, she fought for all she was worth. Thrusting, spinning, dodging, jumping, it became an amazing, exhilarating dance just like it had before.

She didn't think about those she killed but about protecting her friends and Graham.

And, most certainly, Scotland's history.

Her heart raced, and her adrenaline rushed. It was fast and crazy, but not in a way that looked like it was going to have a good outcome. More Englishmen seemed to be standing than Scotsmen as she, Graham and Bryce fought their way toward the outside of the encampment. As she assured Robert, Bryce did an excellent job shooting off arrows, but sadly enough, he was outnumbered as were Robert's prized archers.

This had been an ambush.

A well-planned one at that.

"*Just focus on fighting, lass*," Graham said into her mind. "*Nothing else. Just fighting.*"

He was trying to warn her against looking around too much, but it couldn't be helped.

Too many were falling.

The Scottish were losing.

This made no sense. How could this be happening when day one of the battle went as it should have? What had changed? She didn't suppose it mattered at this point. The damage was done, and everything was going very, very wrong.

The Scots were being slaughtered, and history was about to change for the worst.

"*Dinnae fight to the death*," Grant's words floated through her mind, and she suspected everyone else's. "*If we cannae save this battle, there is the slightest chance that we can save the next.*"

Christina knew that wasn't true. Grant was speaking out of fear for his immediate kin, and she didn't blame him. Every couple needed to come together properly. The rings' magic needed to be ignited. She never understood that better than she did now as so much Scottish blood spilled.

It was as if she could feel the very essence of the country bleeding away.

Fading.

If they lost here today, Scotland's ultimate ruin would be set in motion. She didn't doubt it for a moment. This was it. The beginning of the end.

Angry that it had come to this despite how hard Grant and his family had tried to save their beloved country, she fought with a whole new ferociousness. One that had her slashing men down before they ever saw her coming. One that had her roaring in denial.

Where was her warlock?

Where was the cause of all this?

She wanted its blood more than she had ever wanted anything. She wanted to chase it down and wrestle the God forsaken evil right out of it. Slay it so thoroughly that even hell wouldn't exist for it. Wipe its scummy residue from the Earth.

Almost as if her prayers were answered, she could have sworn she saw it just ahead through the forest. The same slippery shadow she and Graham had seen in their dream. Eyes narrowed, thinking only of Scotland and even Jessie now, she raced after it. When she did, she kept utilizing her gift and sprinted with all the power she had.

"*Och, lass, slow down!*" Graham and Bryce roared into her mind, but she didn't listen. She was out for vengeance, and *nothing* was going to stop her. She would kill it for what it was doing to this country and her friends. More than that, she would kill it because of what had happened to Kenna. Because, one way or another, if it weren't for these evil warlocks, her friend would still be alive.

Clearly startled that she could move so fast and was gaining ground, the warlock spun back and confronted her. Seeing nothing but its tall, slimy darkness, she roared again and thrust hard.

Only for Graham's blade to intercept hers.

Somehow, he had caught up and managed to stop her. But why?

"What are you *doing?*" she seethed, wide-eyed and furious, only to find the warlock clutching none other than Jessie in front of him.

Dear Lord, she had nearly run a sword through her friend.

"Kill me, Christina," Jessie said, her face without expression and her voice level as her eyes held Christina's. "Graham, step away and let Christina do what she needs to do. It's the *only* way."

"Yes, kill her," the warlock rasped, his eyes trained on Christina. "Run that sword through her, *warrioress.*"

Bryce and Sven skidded to a stop, their eyes taking in the tense situation.

"Absolutely not." Christina shook her head as she lowered her blade and narrowed her eyes at the warlock. "Release my friend."

"Kill me," Jessie said calmly, her eyes steady. "Or he will kill you, Christina."

Something about the way her friend was looking at her made everything else fall away. Almost as if she could sense her in a whole new way. The steady throb of her heart. The utter lack of fear someone facing imminent death should feel.

Jessie was trying to tell her something with that look.

She was letting her know it was okay to let go.

That this was meant to be.

As if caught in the same thought process, she felt Graham's mind skirt alongside Jessie's. They mutually agreed. It was as though they saw something only Jessie could show them. Something they barely understood but trusted. They trusted the feeling so much that they ended up doing the unthinkable.

Christina and Graham plunged their blades into Jessie at the same time.

Or so they thought.

At the last moment, evidently sensing what they were going to do, the warlock thrust Jessie aside and took the blade for her.

Then everything happened very quickly.

The warlock shuddered, his saddened eyes firmly locked on Jessie as he wailed mournfully, decomposed rapidly then burst into a cloud of dust. Meanwhile, Jessie's eyes narrowed on Sven and Bryce whose eyes narrowed right back.

"Death comes to those who fly," she whispered, repeating the same words Rona had said back in New Hampshire. "Death comes to Scotland."

Then she bolted into the woods.

Half a second later, Sven and Bryce bolted after her.

Though she should probably race after them, she was too stunned and needed a moment to process everything. Jessie would be okay. Two dragons had her back.

"What the *hell* just happened," Christina murmured, dumbfounded as her eyes fell to the pile of ashes. All that was left of the warlock. "Did we just kill..." her eyes floated to Graham. "Did we just kill our warlock? Was it *that* easy?"

"Based on your gem," he said softly, his eyes on her ring, "I'd say we did."

"Well, I'll be damned," she whispered as she stared at it. "Am I seeing things or is my gem a beautiful shade of deep dark brown?"

"I'd say mayhap 'tis," he murmured, smiling as his eyes met hers. Gorgeous eyes the same exact shade as her gem. "I'm fairly certain we just ignited our MacLomain, Broun magic." He shook his head. "I never should have been able to move fast enough to stop your blade from hurting Jessie." Awe lit his eyes. "And I've never seen you glow as brightly as you did when we destroyed the warlock." His smile widened in what some might call triumph. "Not even when you and Bryce fought together."

She barely breathed, and her heart hammered in anticipation as she looked from him to the ring several times before she whispered, "Does this mean what I hope it means?"

He took her hand and reeled her closer. "What do you hope it means, lass?"

"I think you know."

"I'd rather hear you say it."

"I bet you would."

He grinned. "So?"

She met his grin. "I guess I hope it might mean you're my one true love."

He perked his brows, pulling her closer still. "You guess you hope it *might* mean? 'Tis bloody vague, lass." His eyes stayed with hers. "What do you want, Christina?"

She didn't have to think twice.

"Well, *you*, handsome." She winked and kept grinning. "Who else?"

Before she could get another word out, she was firmly against him, and his lips were on hers. Nothing had ever tasted so sweet or curled her toes with desire while still standing up. Their tongues tasted and sampled and the kiss deepened but not for long.

"I dinnae mean to disturb ye but 'tis time to battle and I thought ye might like to watch if nothing else," Robert the Bruce's voice interrupted.

Surprised, Christina and Graham pulled apart, only to find themselves standing in front of a fire outside of Robert's tent. It was still morning, and all the signs of warfare and slaughter had vanished. Instead, it appeared all were marching off to a battle that had yet to take place.

"Yes," she whispered and nodded, more than a little confused.

"It seems the second day of battle is about to begin," Grant informed as he, Adlin, Milly, Conall, and Lindsay joined them. His pleased eyes went to Christina and Graham. "We Scots are getting ready to march on the Sassenach."

"We did it then," she whispered, her eyes drifting to Graham's. "We fixed history?"

"Aye," he murmured, with nothing but adoration in his eyes. "So it seems."

"Och, I look forward to my wife looking at me like that again," Robert muttered. "But first we've got to win this battle then take back Stirling Castle."

His *wife*? He remembered her? Better yet, she existed once more? That's when she noticed that Robert no longer gazed at her with desire. If anything, he looked at her with simple fondness.

Adlin and Grant smiled at her and nodded, evidently having followed everything that just happened. All was exactly as it should be now. Or should she say so far? She wasn't foolish enough to think things couldn't go wrong still. Not when it came to magic. And not considering how darn easy it was to kill their warlock. Nevertheless, everyone was certainly more optimistic as they joined Robert and headed for a battle none would soon forget.

"Unless we are needed, we will sit this one out," Adlin informed Robert. "We shouldnae risk being remembered in history if possible and this battle is fairly well documented."

"Aye, of course." Robert nodded, a pleased and emboldened look in his eyes as they met Adlin's. "That tells me victory will be ours."

Adlin only shrugged and grinned, but it was more than enough. Who knows? It might have been the final push of confidence Robert the Bruce needed to win today's battle.

A battle, thankfully, that Graham explained to Christina in better detail as the events unfolded. Events they made sure to stay far away from this time so they wouldn't inadvertently end up in the midst of battle again.

The Scots advanced out of Balquhidderock Wood to face the enemy as the morning sun crested the horizon. Abbot Bernard of Arbroath carried the Scots' ancient lucky talisman, the Breccbennach—or Monymusk Relquary—which held the relics of St. Columba.

"Wow," Christina whispered, in awe of the sight.

Robert made an impressive, rallying speech invoking the power of St. Andrew, John the Baptist and Thomas Beckett. His men roared their approval, their eyes eager and full of battle lust. Shortly after that, horns resounded, and war standards flew in the cool morning wind.

"What's happening now?" she murmured as the Scots grew quiet and respectful.

"That is Abbot Maurice of Inchaffrey," Graham explained as a robed man walked out in front of the army. "He will lead mass now."

As he did, the Scots knelt in prayer.

As it turned out, the tactic was more than just spiritual.

"That will allow Robert's captains a few extra crucial minutes to form the battle lines," Graham said. "Where across the Carse, King Edward, and his army thinks we Scots are surrendering."

As she nodded, Graham continued, explaining how Edward reputedly said, "*Yon folk are kneeling to ask mercy.*"

Then Sir Ingram de Umfraville, a Balliol supporter fighting for Edward, replied, "*They ask for mercy, but not from you. They ask God for mercy for their sins. I'll tell you something for a fact, that yon men will win all or die. None will flee for fear of death.*"

"*So be it,*" Edward retorted.

Bunch of dumb asses, Christina thought. But thank God for downright stupidity and arrogance.

"That whole stretch is the Bannockburn," Graham informed, pointing out the long, snaking waterway for which the battle was named. "'Twill most certainly prove King Edward's nemesis."

"Then it's good the battle ended up where it's supposed to," she remarked.

"Aye," Graham agreed, keeping her hand in his the entire time. She got the sense based on their excitement that he and his cousins would have loved to battle here.

An archery duel soon followed, but the Scots *schiltrom* rapidly took the offensive to avoid its inevitable outcome. Robert's brother, Edward's schiltrom advanced on the English vanguard and took down the Earl of Gloucester and Sir Robert Clifford, while Randolph's schiltrom closed in on their left.

"Rumor has it, just before this happened an argument broke out between King Edward and the Earl of Gloucester," Graham commented.

"It seems he complained that the Sassenach forces needed rest after spending a sleepless eve in the marshland getting eaten alive by

Scottish midges last night." He smiled and continued. "When the King accused the earl of cowardice in front of the men, Gloucester did what you just witnessed. He jumped on his horse and charged the Scots." He gestured at the battlefield. "And that's how he ended up. Carved up in full view of both sides." He nodded, pleased. "Another morale dampener to be sure."

"It does my heart bloody good to see Robert Clifford finally fall as well," Conall muttered to Lindsay. "He'll never have the pleasure of being enchanted by you again, lass."

Lindsay had enchanted Robert Clifford when she and Conall were on their adventure. In doing so, she had saved a band of Scots from being slaughtered on a hillside outside Happrew. Instead, as she continued to enchant Robert, an ambush was set up, and the English were killed. All but Robert who they allowed to escape so he could someday be a part of history.

More importantly, so he would die today.

"Now see what's happening," Graham said to Christina, impressed as they watched. "The Sassenach knights are caught in between the Scots schiltroms and the mass of their own army and cannae bring many archers to bear."

He pointed to show her what was happening. "Some are trying to break out on the Scots flank to down them with arrows." He shook his head. "But 'tis too late. They're already being dispersed by Sir Robert Keith's Scots cavalry." He chuckled. "The rest were badly deployed. Now their arrows fall into the backs of their own army!"

In the center of the field, a ferocious, deadly hand to hand combat between knights and spearmen ensued as it almost seemed the battle hung in the balance.

"See what the Bruce does now." Graham pointed in another direction. "'Tis a crucial moment and he acts wisely committing his own schiltrom." He smiled, pleased. "They include Gaelic warriors from the Highlands and Isles."

Her eyes widened as the English seemed to be losing ground under the onslaught. Meanwhile, the Scots warriors cried, "On them! On them! They fail!", as they drove the English back into the burn.

"Och, the bloody cowards," Graham seethed as he scanned the battlefield then narrowed his eyes on a retreating retinue. "Now that the battle's momentum is obvious, they're escorting King Edward away." He shrugged. "I might not like it but 'tis as it needs to be."

He shot her a crooked grin, excited. "Because just watch what happens next."

As Edward's royal standard departed, panic set in.

The English knew they were in trouble.

The Scots schiltroms hacked their way into the disintegrating English army. Those fleeing caused chaos in the massed infantry behind them. In the rout that followed hundreds of men and horses were drowned in the burn desperately trying to escape.

It was nothing short of incredible watching everything unfold first-hand.

Though somewhat overwhelmed by the large-scale loss of life, she wasn't as horrified as she figured she should be. Perhaps because of her gift igniting? Or perhaps because of the men she had so recently killed. Whatever the cause, something had changed inside her and made seeing all of this easier to cope with.

Even so, she was glad when the battle eventually came to an end.

Scotland had won.

"Sassenach casualties are heavy," Graham reported, relish in his eyes as he peered down at the remnants of the battle. "Thousands of infantry, at least one hundred knights and one earl lays dead on the field."

According to Conall and Lindsay the night before, some escaped the confusion including the Earl of Pembroke and his Welsh infantry. They made it safely to Carlisle, but many more, including several knights and the Earl of Hereford, were captured as they fled through the south of Scotland. Edward II with five hundred knights was pursued by Sir James "the Black" Douglas until they reached Dunbar and the safety of a ship to take them home.

The capture of Edward would have meant instant English recognition of the Scots demands. As it was, the British could absorb such a defeat and continue the war. Nevertheless, for the Scots, it was still a resounding victory. Robert was left in total military control of Scotland, which would enable him to transfer his campaign to the north of England.

"Politically, he just won Scotland's defacto independence and consolidated his kingship as former supporters of Balliol will quickly change sides," Graham said. "In exchange for Bruce's noble captives, Edward will be forced to release Bruce's wife, daughter and the formidable Bishop Wishart, who's been held in English captivity since thirteen hundred and six."

For the Scots soldiers, there was the wealth of booty left in the English baggage train and the exhilaration of victory. It wasn't long before word spread that Stirling Castle's gates had opened and the English within surrendered.

"Do ye wish to head that way and see the castle without…"

"Nope, I'm good," Christina replied before Graham had a chance to finish. "I think I've seen all I want of Stirling Castle for one lifetime."

"Then let's head back to the encampment." He grinned, a twinkle in his eyes. "'Tis bound to be a night of celebration."

She grinned back, well aware of what he meant. Yet, she worried.

"What do you think happened to Jessie?" She shook her head. "And Bryce and Sven?"

"'Tis hard to know," Grant said sometime later as they sat around a fire outside. "But I suspect we'll find out soon enough." A wise look entered his eyes. "I would say Bryce has begun his adventure. It can be no other way now that 'tis clear Christina is not meant for him."

Milly frowned. "So he's on his adventure with Sven along?"

"Aye, it seems verra likely," Adlin said. "But he's a good ally to have and verra likely part of all this somehow."

"As is Aðísla," Lindsay murmured. "Someone we've barely seen this time around."

"Someone Sven is in pursuit of," Conall added as he kept an arm around Lindsay.

Adlin shrugged. "I dinnae doubt he will catch up with her in the end."

"I suppose I always figured she would return to her people after we corrected Scotland's history." Graham frowned. "So I dinnae ken why Sven is here at all."

"Nor do any of us," Adlin said. "But I'm sure we will before all is said and done."

Grant's eyes went between Christina and Graham as his voice grew soft. "You should know that Sven sent Adlin and me one last telepathic message before he vanished. It seems Kenna *did* confide in him about why she thought you two coming together was going to make all the difference for this country."

A respectful silence fell as he continued.

"She dreamt about you racing through the woods this morning determined to end the warlock...determined if nothing else to avenge her death." He looked back and forth between them. "Both of you. Together. As a team fighting with the unmistakable passion of two people who had fallen in love and would do anything to protect Scotland. Anything to ensure a brighter future for her country."

"Why not tell us this sooner?" Graham murmured, pain in his eyes.

"Because she didnae want to risk disturbing your destiny, lad. Or Chistina's. She wanted you both to have the happiness you deserve and of course save her country in the process." Dampness glittered in his eyes. "May she be at peace with God now. For she was the best sort of person, indeed. One with a great deal of courage in a situation where most would lack it. She was an admiral Scotswoman and a true hero."

All murmured a prayer as Graham squeezed Christina's hand. Though this might not be easy, as their eyes met, they couldn't be more grateful. Certainly not that they'd lost Kenna, but that they had found each other in a way they never expected. They would never forget her. What she had done for them and most certainly what she had sacrificed for Scotland.

After that, the conversation revolved around fond childhood memories of Kenna as everyone bid her goodbye. As the night wore on, however, they began focusing on what was going to happen next. Were Bryce and Jessie already on their adventure together?

"Jessie had no wound that I could see when we faced off with the warlock," Graham pointed out, clearly having been giving it some thought based on his almost hopeful expression. "So mayhap 'twas not her that I hit with my dagger in the forest."

"No wound that you could see," Christina said softly. "Things were pretty intense and happening fast. Not a lot of time to look her over. She could have very well had a wound bandaged up and hidden beneath clothing."

"Aye," Graham agreed. "True."

"What concerns me more is the obvious connection she shared with that warlock." Christina fought a shiver. "What are we supposed to make of the fact our warlock sacrificed its existence to save Jessie?" She frowned, saddened. "It seems pretty clear she's wrapped up in dark magic somehow…maybe even in control of it."

"Aye, mayhap," Grant said, his tone soft and contemplative. "Yet 'tis also clear she's trying to destroy it."

Milly frowned and shook her head. "I find it hard to believe she's capable of being part of something so dark, to begin with."

"I second that," Lindsay said.

"Well, 'tis not to worry over this eve." Adlin offered an infectious grin no doubt intended to lighten the mood. "Let us enjoy this victory before we face yet another battle, aye?"

Everyone nodded and continued to enjoy one another's company. They would spend one more night here in case Jessie, Bryce and Sven returned then leave in the morning.

As to be expected, Robert the Bruce, as well as his brother and nephew, were in excellent spirits. Though Robert spent little time with them, he expressed his gratefulness to all for being there. For making right history though he didn't have the first clue how they did so. It seemed he had no memory of dreaming of Christina all those years ago and certainly no recollection of wanting to marry her. He didn't even remember kissing her the night before.

"*He kissed you then?*" Graham said into her mind, grinning though she didn't miss the jealousy in his eyes. "*And here I thought you were tucked safely away with Lindsay.*"

"*A kiss can happen awful quick,*" she teased. "*And be forgotten just as quickly.*"

"*Aye.*" He eyed her with the sort of promise that made her squeeze her thighs together. "*I'll most certainly see to that, lass.*"

"I must admit though," Robert interrupted their internal conversation as his warm eyes turned her way. "I feel an unexplainable connection to ye, lass. One of friendship though we dinnae know each other all that well."

She smiled and nodded. "You'll always have my friendship, Robert."

When Christina and Graham finally stood sometime later, long past ready to be alone, everybody grinned. Most especially Conall and Lindsay.

"'Tis verra good things worked out for you two," Adlin said, his smile widening.

"Aye." Grant nodded, smiling as well though his expression grew a little more serious. "You have our apologies for, well, thinking things might have had to go in a different direction."

A different *direction*? Though tempted to scowl at them, all she was capable of now was a wide smile as she winked. "All's well that ends well, right?"

Then it was just plain old fun as she and Graham acted like a couple of high school kids just falling in love. Though they knew they bypassed friendship and shot right to something more in a heartbeat, it didn't matter. Especially considering how awful it had felt to have everything forced to a halt yesterday.

A mere twenty-four hours ago that felt more like months.

They skipped the small talk and pretty much tripped over themselves getting into their tent. Between stealing kisses, laughing and ripping their clothes off, they barely made it to the cot. Once they did though, everything faded away. The merry pipes in the distance and the partying.

All that existed was them.

This.

What they had found.

Their kisses intensified as his touch became more tender, and their bodies brushed along one another's. She might be a warrior at heart, but she suspected he would always have a way of making her feel soft and feminine.

His touch was light at first as he left her mouth, nibbled down her neck then swooped lower. He tasted every inch of her, starting with her breasts before he worked his way down. She thought her heart had been thundering before, but it couldn't touch what he invoked as he explored.

Her senses came alive in a way they never had before.

Her magic.

She could hear his heartbeat racing along with hers, then synchronizing, before every sensation grew even stronger. His spicy scent magnified and wrapped around her. The heated texture of his skin. The feel of his rock-solid body so close to hers.

He seemed to swirl around every part of her from the inside out. It blew her mind and his too based on his groan of appreciation as he moved lower. Once his talented mouth was between her legs any awareness of magic vanished altogether.

All she knew was how he made her feel.

Alive. Wonderful. Without end.

When she climaxed, things became even fuzzier but more amazing. Colors zig-zagged every which way as she cried out. Then he was over her again and spreading her thighs even wider.

"*Graham,*" she whispered into his mind, so far gone she wasn't sure if he heard her. More than that, she didn't know what she was asking.

It seemed he did though because he didn't thrust quite yet. Instead, he waited, peppering kisses here and there before his eyes met hers and he waited a little longer for her to come down.

Because that's what she needed.

She was so wrapped up in the intensity of her magic and what he had made her feel that she was afraid she might miss something. That when they came together, she might be too far gone to enjoy it.

Yet when he finally thrust, slow and easy, she was more than ready.

Their eyes never left one another's as he moved. As their passion built. Sex with a man had never been like this. Without frenzy.

Calm and precious yet still wild somehow.

There was no rush to find completion. No endless energy she needed to exhaust. Everything she felt now was the real deal. Genuine, wonderful and normal. Well, as sizzling hot normal as it could be between a witch and wizard she supposed.

Trembling, she dug her nails into his back, wrapped her legs around his waist, and enjoyed the feeling. The lust and love. The excitement of being with him.

Never once did she take control.

Never once did she want to.

Rather, she basked in the pleasure he offered. The poignant feelings rolling through her like waves. Swells that grew stronger and stronger the more he thrust. The more he built her up. When the next climax hit, it came hard and fast, and she cried out.

Seconds later, he did the same.

So far gone again she couldn't speak or think straight, her eyes slid shut. Sated, content, little registered after that and she drifted off to sleep.

Until a very clear voice woke her up.

"Death comes to those who fly," Jessie murmured. "Death comes to Scotland."

When Christina opened her eyes, she was in the last place she ever could have imagined.

Chapter Eighteen

GRAHAM COULD HAVE imagined a hundred different ways to wake up next to Christina after what they experienced but nothing like this. Not after finding each other like they did. After loving one another so well.

Now, far from the cot they had just enjoyed, they turned and stared at each other just like they had when they first met...in a dream, that is.

At Mystery Hill in the twenty-first century.

It seemed she was just as confused as he was when she shook her head, patted her body and said, "Am I real?" She cocked her head. "Are you?"

Graham did the same and nodded. "Aye, lass. We're real." He looked around, frowning. "This is real."

Unlike the dream, however, they weren't dressed.

"But..." Her voice trailed off as she narrowed her eyes and scanned the area. "Do you think there's a warlock around here?"

"I dinnae know, lass." Graham scanned the area as well before he spied two piles of clothes. One for him and one for her. "It looks like someone's expecting us."

Christina grimaced as he handed her clothes. "They expected us to arrive naked?"

"So it seems," he said as he pulled on a tunic and wrapped the MacLomain plaid around his waist. "Friend not foe I'd say based on the clothing."

"Someone who seems to prefer me in medieval pants," she added as she pulled on her own clothes then eyed him with appreciation. "You look good in a skirt, darlin'."

"'Tis a tartan," he muttered but met her grin and winked. "I think you'll appreciate its design."

Taking his meaning, she kept smiling. "I bet I will."

As they pulled on their boots, she considered the stone dwelling. "So why do you think we ended up here again?"

He had been feeling out the place with magic since they arrived and was surprised by what he discovered. "I think we've just been through the magical time flux Conall and Lindsay inadvertently created. Or should I say we've finally been released from it altogether. When we were, it put us back where we began." He kept concentrating and scouted out the area. "I sense something else too, but I cannae quite figure out what it is. Can you?"

When Christina went very still, he knew she was utilizing her gift.

"I can," she whispered. "Jessie was here...as was another." She visibly shivered as her eyes went to his. "I didn't sense him when we first arrived but definitely a warlock." She shook her head. "But I think he's long gone now."

"Aye then," he murmured, fully intending to remain vigilant regardless. "It seems, mayhap, our dream about Jessie and a warlock being here had some truth to it after all."

She frowned. "So do you think us being here has more to do with Conall and Lindsay's magic or Jessie and the warlock's?"

"I dinnae know," he replied. "Mayhap a bit of both."

"Why here though?" she asked again. "This isn't where we began. Technically, you and I met at the house." She frowned as she wrapped a fur cloak around her shoulders. "In the flesh anyway."

"Aye, in the flesh but this is where we first connected." His eyes met hers. "So mayhap we're back where we were meant to be all along, and you're with the one you're supposed to be with."

A soft smile curled her lips. "I thought we'd already come to that conclusion."

"Aye." He gave her a look. "But as I recall, at one point in this verra dwelling you were of the mind that Robert the Bruce might be the one for you."

"True." She shook her head. "Hard to imagine now."

He couldn't agree more. But then he never imagined her with the Bruce. Or should he say he never *wanted* her to be with him.

"So assuming Conall and Lindsay's magic was at play," she said as he took her hand and they exited, "what do you think finally freed us from their time flux?"

"Likely lying together for the first time after igniting the ring's magic," he replied. "'Tis known to be a verra powerful coupling."

"To say the least," she murmured, renewed appreciation in her eyes as they met his. "I've never felt anything like it."

He couldn't agree more, well aware of the difference in her this last time. She lacked the anxiety that had been present in their previous lovemaking. The fear that even though he seemed to keep up with her, she *might* just be too much for him.

"'Twas verra good, lass," he said softly, reeling her closer before he tilted her chin and brushed his lips across hers. "'Twill always be like that. Ye dinnae need to fear anymore."

"Always," she whispered, considering that.

"Aye, *always*," he murmured, ignoring a flash of fear that she might not want such a thing with him in the end. That she might decide to stay here.

Before she could respond, her attention was caught by something through the woods in the direction of the house.

"What is it, lass?" he asked.

"I don't know," she whispered before she started walking. "Remember back when you first arrived and we came out here looking for Jessie? How I felt like it was some kind of decoy?"

"Aye." He nodded and kept stride with her, wishing he had a weapon. "Are you feeling that way again, then?"

"Sort of," she murmured. "It's hard to describe." She started jogging. "It just feels like we should be at the house instead of here. Just like before when Jessie vanished." She shook her head. "Almost like we're going in circles that we're not in control of...like there's something bigger going on that we're not seeing."

When they arrived in the yard, all seemed as it should be.

At first.

"Something is verra wrong," Graham murmured, alarmed. "Off."

"Hell yeah, it is," Jim muttered, appearing at the front door. "One moment you two are standing in front of the fire, the next you're gone. And in the short time you vanished, that old oak's about withered up and died."

"What do you mean?" Christina frowned and shook her head. "We've been in medieval Scotland for days, nearly a week. And it *is* going on winter here, so the tree's probably just hibernating."

Yet it was clear that wasn't the case. Jim was right. The tree was dying quickly.

"You've been gone for a few hours at most, Christina." Jim shrugged. "But I suppose that's not surprising considering how time goes by differently between here and Scotland." He flinched as he eyed the facial bruise she had acquired at Stirling Castle. "That looks painful." He frowned. "Are you okay?"

"Yeah, I'm fine. Just a little scuffle with a medieval Brit." She waved it off. "So we've really only been gone a few hours?"

"Aye, ye havenae been gone long," Blair said, appearing beside him.

"Yet 'tis obvious that isnae the case for ye two," Rona murmured, joining them as well. "How are things in Scotland? Is all well?"

Just when they thought things might be on the right path, it seemed they weren't quite there. Because it was clear Rona had never left. That she had remained here the whole time.

"How did I not notice it before?" Christina whispered, eying the sky as snow began falling. "The storm is here that was on its way when we left." Her eyes met Graham's. "It looks like you're right. Conall and Lindsay's time flux *did* pretty much release us back where we began, give or take a few hours."

Or Jessie and the warlock did, he thought.

"While you were gone, we found some alarming things." Jim urged them to come inside and caught them up. "Things that definitely back up that you've been gone as long as you say you have and not just a few hours."

When they walked inside it was truly as if they had never left except for the delicious scent. It was clear Christina's stew had had time to cook. As Christina headed for Jessie's chair, eying it as though she might find her friend there against the odds, Rona handed Graham a mug.

"Ye look like ye could use a wee dram, Brother," she said, curious as she looked at him. "So what happened to ye two?" Her astute gaze went from Christina to him, a little sparkle in her eyes despite their circumstances. "There is a mighty glow about her ring now that I dinnae recall seeing before."

"Aye," Blair agreed, a wry grin on her face. "And 'tis just the shade ye two claimed it to be."

As Graham began filling them in on everything that had happened, Christina received Jessie's little book from Jim.

"I know it's private, but I figured I better take a peek inside in case she scribbled where she might've gone," Jim said. "Instead, I found a whole lot more than I bargained for."

When Christina began flipping through it and sank onto the sofa, Graham joined her.

"What the heck am I looking at?" she whispered. "Is this what I think it is?"

"Bloody hell," Graham murmured as each picture told a different story.

Christina flipped back to the first page and the people standing outside by the old tree. There was no mistaking who they were. Milly, Christina, Jim, and Jessie.

"This was the first day we arrived," she murmured. "Jessie never leaves her cabin up in Maine and doesn't show emotion, so we were all shocked to find her standing out there looking up at the tree crying."

"She dated when she drew these." She continued flipping through the pages as she shook her head. "She had to have dated them incorrectly."

"Right," Jim said. "Because that first picture was apparently drawn a week before Milly caught wind of this house. Over a month before she actually bought it."

Each page told the tale of not only how Milly and Lindsay came together with their MacLomain's but Christina and Graham's story too.

"So do those pictures accurately depict your adventure together?" Jim asked Graham and Christina. " I only ask because Christina doesn't have a shiner on her face in any of those."

"Aye, 'tis our adventure," Graham acknowledged, dumbfounded.

"How could she have possibly..." Christina whispered as she eyed a drawing of herself swinging a sword. The picture almost seemed to come alive it was depicted so well. As if the viewer could see how impressive Christina was in battle. How magnificent and magical.

"I didn't even know she could draw," Christina continued. "I always thought this was just a journal she wrote in." Her eyes swept over everyone before she looked at Graham. "I might be going out on a limb here, but this almost seems like she foresaw all of our stories before they actually happened." She frowned, baffled as something occurred to her. "That she might've somehow *controlled* it all."

Though that would require a tremendous amount of power, Graham found himself agreeing with Christina's assessment.

"Mayhap," Blair said. "But know this. No one can control Broun, MacLomain connections. 'Tis beyond the scope of a witch or wizard's magic."

Christina's eyes met Blair's. "What about a warlock's?"

"Nay." Rona shook her head. "And if it is then 'tis because of the influence dark magic had over the creation of the rings and nothing more."

"Right," Christina murmured. "Warlocks that might very well be under Jessie's control."

When everyone seemed confused by that statement, Graham continued filling them in on all that had happened. Outside of what was obvious in Jessie's book that is.

"So history is on track again." Blair nodded as she handed Christina a glass of wine. "That's good news!"

"Is it back on track though?" Graham glanced out the window. "That oak is verra much tied into MacLomain and Broun history. What can it mean that it's dying?" He looked at his sister. "What do you make of it, Rona? Did you sense its death coming? What might be connected to it?"

"Nay," she said softly as she clearly read his thoughts. As she caught what he had not shared yet. "But I sensed Fraser's. He *did* die, Graham." Her eyes were moist. "There cannae be any doubt."

He knew how close she and Conall had been with Fraser. That this would prove especially difficult for her. So he filled both her and Blair in on everything they had learned from Kenna.

"Consider it a glimmer of hope, Sister," he said gently. "Where before there was none."

"But I sensed his death," she reiterated.

"Where ye didnae sense the tree's," Graham pointed out. "Mayhap you are being as affected by everything happening as we are. Mayhap 'tis disturbing your magic as well."

"Fraser died years ago," she countered.

"Just like Uncle Darach disappeared years ago," he reminded. "Only to return recently as this curse unravels."

"Is it a curse then, Brother?" she whispered, her eyes drifting to the fire. "But then I suppose it must be to test the lives of so many."

"But at least it's a curse that's *unravelling* rather than only getting worse," Christina said, renewed optimism and determination in her eyes as she set aside the book. "After all, three couples have already found true love, and as you mentioned, your Uncle Darach has returned unharmed."

He liked that she focused on the positive and especially liked her comment about *three* couples finding true love.

"We should eat," she promptly declared, standing. "Unless that is, someone can return us to medieval Scotland, so we can figure out what's going on back there?"

Unfortunately, though none had any issues getting here, going home remained a different story. So they settled in, ate, drank and went over everything they knew about what was happening in case they missed anything.

"This is verra good, lass," Graham complimented Christina, more than impressed with her cooking skills. As was everyone else.

"Thanks." She offered him one of those charming smiles he loved so much. "But it can't touch my southern cooking."

"You'll have to make me southern cooking then," he replied.

"Not so sure if you've got the proper ingredients back home." She shrugged and kept smiling. "But I'll give it my best shot."

"So ye'll be returning home with us then?" Rona asked, pleased based on her expression.

Christina chuckled. "Well, I've gotta be there to keep kickin' the bad guys' asses, right?"

"Sorry about the cursing, Granny," she murmured in her mind then winked at Graham because she knew he heard her.

"Who knew you were such a fighter? And so strong!" Jim grinned, impressed. "And here you were bitchin' about carrying a few boxes when Milly moved in."

She snorted. "Hey, I might be strong, but that doesn't mean I like moving stuff."

Graham didn't miss the way Blair eyed Jim and Christina with what *might* just be jealousy. Though tempted to pull Christina onto his lap after they were done eating to dispel that jealousy, he wanted a few moments alone with his sister, Rona. So he joined her when she returned to the fire and Jessie's little book.

"How fare ye, Sister?" he murmured. "We've had no time to speak since Conall and Lindsay's adventure."

"I'm better than I was," she assured, grateful it seemed that he had joined her. "Just wary of my gift faltering."

"Aye, that cannae be easy," he agreed, eying her. "But mayhap in some ways not entirely unwelcome?"

Though it was hard to imagine his own magic faltering, hers had oftentimes been more of a burden than anything. Knowing when life and death were coming. Having that kind of intense foresight. Especially in their day and age when death came far more often than life.

Rather than comment on his statement, she rested her hand on his arm and met his eyes. "I'm so verra sorry about Kenna. She was a good friend to us all." She swallowed. "'Twas kind of ye to be there for her after Fraser died."

He could tell by the look in her eyes that she had known about him and Kenna for some time. "I'm sorry I didnae tell ye…or anyone for that matter."

"There is no need to be sorry." She shook her head. "And 'twas not like I was around all that much for ye to confide in, aye?"

"I dinnae think any of us have been around all that much in general since Fraser died," he said softly. "One way or another, we've all been running. Coping in our own way."

"Aye," she murmured. "But 'tis time for that to end. To be there not just for our country but our kin."

"Aye, Sister." He wrapped his arm around her shoulders and pulled her to his side. "Hopefully, if we get this worked out, time will reset itself, and ye'll soon have a nice reunion with Ma and Da." He grinned. "Or at least 'tis soon on the horizon."

"Aye?" She smiled. "That is good to hear. I miss them."

"And they miss ye," he assured.

"*'Tis odd that Blair hasnae commented on Fraser, aye?*" he continued within her mind so their cousin would not hear. "*'Tis as if she is pretending she didnae hear it.*"

"*Like all of us, she is a changed creature since he left,*" she reminded. "*She hears but refuses to believe. 'Twould be too difficult to hope only to have those hopes dashed.*" Her eyes met his. "*What of ye, Brother? Do ye truly believe he might be alive somewhere out there?"*

"*I do,*" he stated and meant it. "*Mostly because Kenna seemed so sure of it...and Christina.*"

"*'Tis clear ye put a lot of faith in Christina.*"

"*Aye, all of it.*"

A small smile ghosted her face. "*She makes ye verra happy.*"

"*She does,*" he agreed. "*Despite all we're going through.*"

"*'Tis good. I like her. More than that, I like the way she looks at ye and makes ye feel,*" she said. "*May I someday find the same sort of love.*"

"*Ye will,*" he replied. "*And he will be verra lucky indeed.*"

"*Aye, he will,*" she agreed, grinning as she continued to leaf through Jessie's book, commenting aloud absently. "Ye've all had interesting adventures thus far. 'Tis hard to imagine what lies ahead for Bryce..."

When she trailed off, stunned, he grew alarmed. "What is it?"

Yet he already knew as she stopped on the last picture. One that had not been there before.

A map of what was now known as The United Kingdom.

"'Tis gone," he whispered, pained. "Scotland is gone."

"'Tis," she whispered, just as heartbroken. "'Tis all England now."

Chapter Nineteen

"IT'S JUST A drawing," Christina assured, trying to sound confident.

"One in a book full of drawings that have *actually* come to pass," Blair reminded, scowling.

"True." Christina pointed at her shiner. "But it's not one hundred percent accurate, or this would've been on my face in quite a few of those pictures."

"Scotland still exists." Jim pointed it out on his cell phone. "I just Googled it. Scotland is alive and well according to this."

Everyone frowned at the phone as Christina snagged it from him, nodding as she scrolled and pulled up recent images and articles to show them. "See. It's still here so I wouldn't trust that book. It could be another warlock playing games." Her eyes went to Graham. "Remember, I *did* see two of them when I dreamt of Jessie."

"Aye." Graham's troubled eyes met Rona's. "Do ye sense anything? Any great loss?"

"Nay." She shook her head, hopeful. "So mayhap 'tis as Christina says."

"It is." Jim nodded and squeezed Blair's shoulder. "Your country's intact. Promise."

Blair clenched her jaw and narrowed her eyes at him before she spat, "Ye shouldnae make promises ye dinnae know if ye can keep," then headed upstairs.

"Damn woman always takes things the wrong way," Jim muttered as he headed after her.

"I think we finally just saw Blair's response to the news about Fraser," Rona murmured to Graham.

Christina sighed, frustrated with Jessie. When had she drawn these pictures? Would this latest one come to pass? If so, what had she done to everyone? To her best friends? To an entire country of innocent people?

"We should get some rest," Graham said softly, obviously sensing her building emotions though she was trying to remain calm. "There is nothing we can do until we've heard from Grant or Adlin."

Rona nodded and embraced him goodnight before she surprised Christina and did the same to her. "Thank ye for the good food, lass. I look forward to tasting more once we are officially sisters."

Before Christina had a chance to respond, Rona continued. "I will sleep down here and tend the fire if that's all right with ye."

"You don't have to do that." She eyed the flames. "Maybe it's time to let it burn out. Maybe it's somehow part of everything Jessie's putting us through, and I've done nothing but help her along by keeping it going all this time."

"'Twas the fire that started us on our journey," Graham reminded. "So mayhap 'tis not all that bad, lass."

"I know," she murmured, just not sure anymore.

"I think it should remain burning." Rona offered Christina a soft smile. "If for no other reason than to keep me warm."

Christina nodded, unable to dispute that logic. "Sure thing then. Thank you, sweetheart."

When Milly had vanished, Christina had taken the room Lindsay had slept in the first night and given Jim Milly's room. Better yet Jim and Blair because she knew Blair ended up there half the time. Or at least she hoped.

As she had been prone to do since staying here, Christina lit a few candles instead of turning on the lights when she and Graham entered. Maybe it was her way of feeling close to Granny again or perhaps foresight that she would ultimately end up someplace that had no electricity.

Her eyes were inevitably drawn to the tree outside. What was happening to it? Because whatever it was, it couldn't be good. She didn't realize she had drifted to the window until Graham came up behind her, wrapped his arms around her stomach and pulled her back against him.

"'Tis not your fault or mine, lass," he murmured. "And 'tis likely not Jessie's either."

"I think we both know that's not true," she whispered and leaned her head back against his chest. "And I think it's past time I stop giving her the benefit of the doubt."

"Nay." Graham turned her and cupped her cheeks, passionate. "That is the last thing you should do, lass." He shook his head. "If we stop having faith in our own then all is lost."

"But is she our own?" She searched his eyes. "Because it doesn't feel like it lately."

"Because you are hurt and confused and can only focus on your pain," he said softly. "You need to focus instead on the fact that 'tis verra likely she's helping us now even if she wasnae before."

"Here's hoping." She bit back emotion and swallowed hard. "But how am I, all of us for that matter, supposed to forgive her if she's been behind everything all along? Darach's disappearance? Kenna's death? Maybe even Fraser's?"

"You cannae look at it like that, lass, and well you know it." He led her to the bed and sat her down. "'Tis time for you to stop dwelling on this. 'Twill do no good."

"But," she started before he interrupted.

"Did you know this room once belonged to my great-grandma in the late eighteenth century?"

"It did?"

"Aye." He nodded and grinned as he pulled her shirt off. "Her name was Coira O'Donnell before she became both a MacLomain and a great wizard."

"Wizard?" She arched her brows, curious. "Not a witch?"

"Nay." He started on her pants. "A wizard. Back during the days of Adlin's prior life when there were light and dark wizards."

"Ohhh, that sounds shady," she teased. "So there were evil MacLomains running around?"

"Och, nay." He chuckled. "The white wizards believed in the new God where the dark wizards believed in the old gods. Neither was evil just varied in their beliefs. Paganism and Christianity."

"I see," she murmured, eying him. "So if you lived back then would you have been a white wizard or a dark wizard?"

"Dark." His eyes never wavered. "I am Pagan, Christina."

"Oh, dear Lord," she whispered. "I didn't see that one coming."

"Is this going to be a problem?"

She wasted no time putting his mind at ease when she saw the flash of worry in his eyes.

"No, we don't have to share the same beliefs. That's not a determining factor in my book." She grinned. "Though Granny's gotta be rollin' in her grave." She chuckled. "She always said I knew how to pick 'em."

A frown settled on his face. Maybe even a little sadness. "I like to think had I the honor of meeting her that she would have liked me."

Oh, she could put her foot in her mouth, couldn't she?

Naturally, he would be worried based on everything she had shared with him. How religious her granny had been.

"I was just teasin', sweetheart." She cupped his cheeks, dropped a kiss on his lips and meant every last word. "Granny would have loved you to pieces and don't you doubt it for a second." She dropped another kiss, surprised when unexpected tears welled as she really thought about it. "In fact, I get the funniest feeling she was lookin' down from Heaven and right there with us on our adventure." She nodded, sure of it, before she dropped another kiss. "I think she supported me every step of the way which meant bringing you and me together." Another kiss. "You're the sort of man she would've been proud to see me with."

"Then I couldnae be more grateful," he said softly, sensual heat gathering in his eyes under her onslaught of kisses.

"Me either," she murmured as he began dropping kisses on her legs as he worked her pants down. "*So* grateful."

"Aye," he murmured. "We're verra lucky."

"*So* lucky," she managed to get out before his nibbling and kissing, and licking became too much, and she fell back on the bed.

When he rested her thighs on his broad shoulders, remnants of their conversation faded away altogether. Her eyes rolled back in her head as he brought her over the edge so fast it made her head spin.

Still, she refused to let him give all the pleasure this time.

"No," she gasped when he started to undress. "Stop."

Unsure, he slowed when she sat up and stopped him before he could pull his shirt off.

"Allow me, darlin'," she murmured seductively as she managed to stand on wobbly legs and help him lift his shirt over his head. She made sure he saw just how much she appreciated his form as she looked him over, trailing her fingers down his neck, collarbone then his hard chest to the chiselled muscles of his abdomen.

"Well, I see what you mean," she whispered, pleased as his tartan fell away with a few quick yanks and his rigid erection made a welcome appearance.

"Actually, it can go up or down," he said hoarsely. "For easy accessibility."

"I've rarely seen it down," she commented as she sank onto the bed again.

"Not that," he managed, chuckling.

"Then what?" she murmured, barely following his explanation and just as hoarse with desire before she began pleasuring him. After that, not much came out of him but groans and grunts and all the sorts of sounds that drove her crazy.

By the time she was finished, his legs were likely as wobbly as hers had been because they fell back on the bed together, laughing yet again. The next thing she knew he was over her and kissing her with the sort of passion most girls would die for.

"I dinnae want ye to come back to Scotland just to fight the enemy," he murmured against her ear as he knelt back and had her straddle him. "I want ye to come back to be with me always."

She offered no response other than a ragged breath as she wrapped her arms around his neck and sank onto him. Their eyes held as he released a similar choppy breath of pleasure and wrapped his arms around her.

Nothing felt as good as being wrapped up in his arms. Held by him as though he never wanted to let her go. And he didn't. She could see it in his eyes, hear it in his voice and feel it in his touch.

He meant every word he had said.

"What gave you the impression I was only going back to fight?" she whispered, never looking away as she began making tiny rolls with her hips. Miniscule but seductive motions that had him clutching her tighter.

"I dinnae know." He shook his head. "All I know is I love everything about ye, lass," he rasped. "I dinnae want this to ever end."

He made that very clear not only with the sweet thoughts churning with hers but by the way he grabbed her butt and took over.

The way he moved, rolling and thrusting his hips, as he set her on fire. Sweat slicked their bodies as their lovemaking intensified.

In and out.

Over and over.

Faster and faster.

Then, as he was so capable of doing, he made her orgasm so hard that things got a bit fuzzy. She felt him roar and tremble against her, so she knew he found fulfilment, but everything else remained hazy as she basked in the afterglow of killer sex.

The next thing she knew she was cuddled beneath the blankets next to him, contented by the steady thrum of his heart. At peace beside him in a way she knew would never change and she certainly would not find with another.

She yawned and cuddled closer to him, inhaling his familiar scent before she drifted off to sleep. This time dreams came and went. Of them together. Happy. Then other images.

Rough seas.

Dark waters.

A man.

He stood on a ship with dark sails, white-knuckling the railing as he glared at her through what quickly became a raging storm. She would never forget those icy pale blue eyes or his remarkably handsome bearded features.

He was a MacLomain.

And he wanted her and his family nowhere near him.

He wanted them gone in a way that bespoke a cold, hardened heart.

"*Dinnae forget yer promised to a Highland Laird*," came his voice from somewhere deep inside her mind. "*'Tis all that can save ye now, lassie.*"

Then her dream with Robert the Bruce flashed through her mind before she was talking to Lindsay again then running straight through Graham for the first time. Unfortunately, the feeling this time was alarming.

Ominous.

Like nothing she had felt before.

It was as though he was melting away. Further and further away until she couldn't see him or feel him anymore. As if everything they had shared simply ceased to exist. She felt the disconnection as if part of her soul had been ripped away.

Then she shot up in bed.

Dim light flooded the room, and there was no sign of Graham.

Terrified, she knew something was wrong and flew to the window.

No snow.

No storm.

It looked just like it had outside the morning she travelled back in time.

She dressed and raced downstairs only to find Jessie in her usual spot in front of the fire with her little book beside her.

"Good morning, Christina," she said, just as she had before. With no expression on her face. "Are you all right?"

"No, actually, I'm not!" She frowned, scooped up the book and shook it at Jessie. "I think it's time for you to start explaining things."

"I'm not sure what you mean," Jessie said in her usual monotone voice.

"Yes, you damn well do," Christina spat as she began leafing through the book. "For starters…"

Where were the pictures? What was she looking at?

"For starters *what*, Christina?" Jessie said. "Were you looking for a specific remedy? Because those are just thoughts and ideas."

"What the heck?" Christina whispered. "There's nothing but recipes in here."

"Is that what's in that?" Jim commented as he came downstairs. "I wondered."

Though tempted to rant and rave like a lunatic, Christina bit her tongue, eyed Jessie and worked to temper her rage. She wanted to throttle her. Tell her friend exactly what she thought of her. More than that, she wanted to punch her square in the face.

But what if this was all some elaborate trick and she was playing right into it?

She needed to remain calm and *focus*. Not give into panic because Graham was no longer here. That it seemed like they had never even met. That by some evil stroke of misfortune, they may never. Not if she was stuck in an ever tightening time loop that made no sense.

Because it felt just like that. A time loop.

No *wonder* she had felt like they were going in circles yesterday. Time was looping back on itself. But why? And who was controlling it? A day being played over that clearly didn't replicate the one before it. Because obviously, she hadn't leafed through Jessie's book first thing in the morning before.

Keeping in mind she was in a time loop, she started to really pay attention.

Her original version of this morning included her getting up early after dreaming about Robert the Bruce. Shaken, out of it, she had researched him then went running only to end up at Mystery Hill where she ran straight through Graham.

"I think I'm going out for a morning jog," she murmured, as she scooped up her sneakers, plunked down on a stool and started pulling them on. Maybe if she recreated the morning, she could find her way back to Graham. Maybe she could figure out what was going on.

"Good day for a run," Jim said, eying his phone before he tossed it on the counter in front of her and started making coffee. "Gonna be stormy later though."

Christina froze as she was lacing up her sneaker. Did she dare look to see if Scotland still existed? Should she? Of course she should. Avoiding things never got anyone anywhere. So she slowly picked up the phone.

"Oh no," she whispered. Her eyes grew moist as she tried to pull up images and information about Scotland.

"What is it?" Blair asked, frowning as she joined them.

"Nothing," Christina managed as she closed the cell phone's online pages, and finished lacing up her other sneaker. She didn't bother warming up but sprinted out the front door. She could not run fast enough. She couldn't get to the Stonehenge fast enough.

Because, as it stood now, Scotland was gone. Officially *gone*. It no longer existed on Google Maps or any other map. Just like the picture in Jessie's book the night before, it was all England now.

Scotland was nothing more than a historical relic.

That must mean that they failed somehow. They had done something wrong. Because the warlocks' ultimate goal was to destroy Scotland's history which would eventually do away with Scotland itself. What had gone wrong though? They had ignited the ring, defeated the warlock and fixed the Battle of Bannockburn. Graham was, without a shred of doubt, her one true love.

So why had everything *still* gone terribly wrong?

When she arrived at Mystery Hill, it was just as it had been that morning. Cool and blustery but refreshing. Lindsay appeared just as she had before and though Christina had every intention of ranting about what was happening, she bit her tongue.

What if this was all some elaborate trick? The second warlock at work? What if by disrupting history she somehow ruined her future with Graham?

More alarming, Scotland's history if there was still hope.

Yes, some might say the time for hope had passed because Scotland no longer existed but she wasn't quite ready to give up. She needed to see Graham again. Run into him. *Feel* him.

Sure as heck, right on time, she was following Lindsay only to run smack into Graham. Or *through* him. Like before, the feeling was extraordinarily profound. Unique. *More*. This time, however, she experienced the feeling with a whole new clarity. Not just love and magic but something more pronounced. Something *additional*.

What *was* this?

He turned and looked at her, caught in this strange place between times. Like her, he seemed in awe, baffled by what he had just experienced.

"Hey, handsome," she murmured, trying to keep her words familiar to perhaps jog his memory. But it didn't matter. Like before he no longer seemed to be able to see her though he still looked for her. Was this the last time she would lay eyes on him? Because it felt that way. It felt like he might be slipping away forever.

"Graham," she whispered, her chest tight as he faded. "Don't forget that I love you, darlin'."

She swallowed hard and squeezed her eyes shut to tears she refused to let fall. What if that was it? What if she was caught in some time limbo and they would never meet again like they were supposed to?

She frowned as she realized how morbid her thoughts were. How she was letting them get the better of her. Frustrated, she shook her head. This was no good. Time to stop being so sappy and take action.

251

So she muttered, "Enough with 'what if's' Christina," and headed back toward the barn just like she had that day. If Fate had rearranged her destiny, she intended to meet it head on, kick its ass then make it her life's mission to find Graham again. To hell with time travel. She would find another way to damn well get it done.

Nothing would stand in her way.

"*Dinnae forget yer promised to a Highland Laird,*" rumbled through her mind again. "*'Tis all that can save ye now, lassie.*"

She never stopped running, pushing her body, until she was back at the barn and leaning against its wall just like before. Fortunately, the tree was alive and well again. That had to mean something good. Yet all she kept focusing on was the guy's words from her dream. Why was he haunting her? Who was he? What did he mean?

"I don't know who I made a promise to," she muttered. "Graham or Robert." She shook her head. "I just don't know."

"Are ye not quite right in the head then, lass?" came a familiar voice. "Talking to yerself like ye are."

Christina couldn't help a smile as Rona appeared right on time just like she had before. Except her greeting was different this go around, wasn't it?

"No, I'm not quite right in the head," she acknowledged. "And maybe you can help me with that."

"Aye?" Rona perked her brows. "How so?"

"Well, I haven't quite figured that out yet, sugar but I'm hoping..."

"Life..." Rona whispered, interrupting her.

Christina frowned. "Excuse me?"

"Life." Rona's eyes glazed then widened before she closed the distance, put her hand on Christina's belly, smiled and met her eyes. "Brand new life."

Chapter Twenty

GRAHAM WOULD NEVER forget the feeling he had when Christina walked through him. How remarkable it was. Yet there was something else as well.

Something unexplainable.

Until that moment—when he turned back and saw the shine of the ring for the first time in this strange in-between place—he didn't know what it was. Yet when their eyes met this time, he finally did. He finally felt the time loop they were caught in. More than that, he, at last, understood the astounding feeling he had. It was the wondrous sensation of not just *two* hearts beating together in synchronization but *three*.

It was the feeling of his family coming together for the very first time.

Him, Christina and their child.

"It was never Robert ye were promised to," he whispered, caught in a dream with her, caught in some strange limbo. "It was our child and me…"

He was certain of it.

Moments later, when everything faded including her, he tried not to panic. Utter darkness surrounded him. As dark as it had been in the cave when they first travelled back to Bannockburn.

Where was she?

Where was he?

Would he ever see her again? His unborn child? Or was he forever caught in the jaws of a closed time loop? Lost in nothingness. Trapped in a curse.

He refused to give into fear though. Instead, he focused on what was most important. Christina and his unborn child. A family he couldn't imagine living without though he had only just met them.

Moments later he swore he saw her ring flicker in the darkness.

Seconds passed before the flicker became brighter and brighter until it was blinding and he had to close his eyes.

"Graham?" Christina whispered.

When his eyes shot open, she was standing in front of him by the barn. Rona was there, but all he could see was Christina.

"Graham?" Unsure, she looked at him. "Is that you? *Really* you?" She shook her head, hope mixed with fear in her eyes. "Or the past you?"

He had no idea what she meant. Nor did he understand how they had ended up outside the barn when the last thing he remembered they were in bed. But he didn't care. Not one bit.

"Aye, lass, 'tis me." He closed the distance and pulled her into his arms. "It's always been me...us..."

When he cupped her cheeks and kissed her deeply, everything began to swirl around them, and the pressure dropped. They were time traveling again. Thankfully, this time they landed right back where he hoped they would.

In front of the fire in MacLomain Castle's great hall.

They were home.

"Well, it's about damned time!" came a voice that made them smile against each other's lips before they reluctantly pulled apart.

Christina offered his mother a warm smile. "Good to see you again, Nicole."

"I know." Nicole planted her hands on her hips and shook her head. "And I see you're still kissing my son."

Christina cocked her head, grinned and didn't hold back. "Would you have it any other way?"

"I don't suppose it'd matter if I would," his ma muttered, though there was an approving grin in her voice.

"Of course it would." Christina winked. "Or at least I'd tell you as much."

Ma's eyes widened before she chuckled, shook her head and ended up embracing Christina before him. The next thing he knew more and more kin were embracing them. His sister and da, uncles, and aunts. Milly and Adlin. Even Jim and Blair were there.

It was a grand family reunion that didn't make much sense.

"Conall and Lindsay would have been here too but 'twas best they stayed at Hamilton Castle for now," Adlin explained. "Though the countryside isnae as bad as it was, 'tis still verra unstable."

"Aye," Uncle Grant said as he and Aunt Sheila joined the festivities. "But we refused to miss your homecoming."

"You make it sound like we've been gone a while," Christina said.

"A few months," Milly said, shocking them as they sat in front of the fire and were handed whisky. "Caught, it seems, in some residual magic plus darker things."

Graham frowned, pulling Christina down onto his lap. "Darker things?"

"Aye," Adlin said. "By the sounds of it, possibly a second warlock."

"By the sounds of it?" Christina frowned and shook her head. "I barely understand what just happened so how can you?"

Grant tapped his temple and eyed her and Graham then her stomach. "'Twas a lot of magic at work. Good and bad. And kin connects with kin in times such as these." He winked. "No matter how young."

"All the more reason you should be drinking this instead of that," Nicole said, beaming as she switched Christina's whisky for water then ducked away. Graham couldn't remember the last time he had seen his mother so happy outside of having Rona back in her life. His da either for that matter.

He suspected they were thrilled not only about Christina's pregnancy but that he and Christina were finally home. He could tell by the thankful looks his kin were casting them that they had given everyone a good scare being gone so long. Lost in a time loop that not even Adlin or Grant could access.

"We thought it seemed almost too easy when the first warlock was killed," Adlin explained. "So we werenae all that surprised to discover a second one might be at work. A very tricky, well disguised back-up plan if you will."

"God," Christina whispered and shook her head. "Graham and I thought there might be a second warlock too." She frowned. "A back-up plan? As in perhaps Jessie's back-up plan because she certainly seemed to control the first warlock."

"Mayhap," Graham responded before anyone else could. "But if 'twas her, keep in mind she might have been trying to warn us about that one too, lass. Dinnae forget our strange dream when we saw her and the warlock flee the Stonehenge." He arched his brows. "A warlock that you said was long gone when we arrived there." He shrugged. "If she truly meant us harm dinnae you think a warlock would have ambushed us at Mystery Hill the moment we left Robert's encampment and travelled forward in time?"

"Good chance," she murmured, resting her hand on her belly protectively. "So what was the point of a time loop then? My dream and then starting the same day over again?" She swallowed as her eyes flickered over Aunt Cassie and Uncle Logan before they landed on Grant and Adlin. "Because I'm pretty sure I was warned or better yet helped by a...relative of yours beforehand."

When both appeared confused, she described the dream. How the man looked and sounded. What he had said.

"Bloody hell," Rona whispered, tears in her eyes. "That sounds just like Fraser...minus the beard."

His aunt and uncle nodded, hope in their eyes.

"And he was where?" Grant asked, perplexed. "At sea?"

Christina nodded. "Most definitely."

"On a Viking ship?" Adlin said.

"I'm not sure." She shook her head. "I'm sorry." Confusion lit her eyes. "What do you think he meant? Don't forget my promise to a Highland Laird?"

"My guess is your promise was always to protect your unborn child," Grant said softly. "I would also venture to say that someday he will be a chieftain...or a Highland Laird."

"*He?*" Graham smiled broadly at Christina. "We're having a son."

"I know, I heard." She smiled just as broadly, their eyes lingering on one another's before she looked at Grant and Adlin again. "So how does our son tie into it all? When I first ran through Graham, I couldn't have been pregnant." She shook her head. "And when I dreamt of Robert I definitely wasn't."

"Aye, but 'twas all part of the same time loop, was it not?" Adlin reminded. "A time flux or loop in part created by Conall and Lindsay and I'm beginning to think, by Jessie as well. Then, as it turns out, the unforeseeable addition of your wee one. He would have most certainly assisted in helping you two come together."

"Wow," Christina whispered. "That's pretty epic."

When her eyes met Graham's to see what he thought, he only nodded and rested his hand on her stomach. It was hard to believe she was already pregnant. That it had happened that fast. But he could not be happier. "As I believe two wise arch wizards recently said, anything is possible."

"We are quite wise," Grant murmured, amused. "Arenae we?"

"Aye, old friend," Adlin agreed, chuckling.

Meanwhile, Christina's eyes stayed with Graham's. "Anything *is* possible." A soft smile graced her lips as she looked down. "Seeing how I'm on birth control."

Yet she still worried as her eyes went from Grant to Adlin again. "So what about Jessie? Was she really there in the twenty-first century? Was the second warlock truly killed though I never saw it?" She frowned. "And what about Bryce, Sven, and Aðísla? Have they returned?" She shook her head. "And who do you suppose provided our clothes when Graham and I travelled to the future after we..." she cleared her throat, not mentioning the sex. "After the Battle of Bannockburn was set back on track."

"Nay, none have returned, I'm afraid," Grant replied. "As to what you witnessed in the twenty-first century, 'tis hard to know but my guess is you defeated any hold the last warlock might have had on Scotland's history by remaining true to Scotland and those you love."

"I don't understand."

A warm smile came to his lips. "Anyone in your position would have grown verra angry with Jessie. Most in fact. You had your friend *right* in front of you. Someone you thought had caused so much harm. Yet you didnae lash out." He gave her a pointed look. "You wanted to but you didnae. You remained calm and kept the bigger picture firmly in mind. That evil could be at work. Therefore, Graham's or any of our lives could be at risk."

She nodded though a frown tugged at her lips. "I really *did* want to kick her butt and strangle some answers out of her."

"Had you, things might have gone verra differently," Adlin responded. "Keeping that fire burning and not attacking Jessie when you had the opportunity were two verra wise decisions, lass."

"Why the fire?" Graham asked, his interest piqued. "And though I'm glad she didnae attack Jessie, what makes you say that with such conviction?"

"Sven," Grant provided. "He felt fire was verra much connected to Jessie. That she has some sort of control over it." His eyes flickered between them. "Seeing how you often travelled through time together when near a fire, 'tis verra likely she controlled your adventure." He shook his head. "Which means, assuming she had some dark control over the time loop, had you hurt her, the loop might have been destroyed taking you with it."

"Or released from it," Adlin remarked and frowned. "Though 'twould not have been good to test that theory."

"So if we're to ken things correctly," Graham said. "If Jessie controlled our time traveling and adventure, then would it not stand to reason she was trying to bring Christina and me together? Which means she would have been helping Scotland, not hurting it?"

"It seems more probable than not," Grant murmured. "I suppose we will just have to wait and see where your friend really stands in the end, Christina."

"I guess we will," Christina said softly, frowning. "Still, could the last bout of evil really have been that easy of a test?"

"You underestimate just how hard that test would have been for most," Grant said softly. "You showed great restraint and a sound mind. One that's valued among our kind and most welcome in our family, lass."

"Our kind," Christina murmured, grinning a little. "You make me sound pretty important."

"Because you are," Grant said. "A wise warrior with godlike abilities who can find reason and restraint in battle. Within what some might have considered their darkest hour. Yet still, you were a warrior who knew when to fight and when not to. 'Tis a rarity indeed."

Christina kept with that charming grin of hers. "If you say so, sugar."

Yet Graham knew as he held her close and they continued enjoying everyone's company, that Grant's words had meant a great deal. That being accepted so readily into the family meant a lot as well.

"Just one more question and I'm almost afraid to ask," Christina said, her worried eyes flickering over everyone.

"What is it, lass?" Adlin asked, clearly concerned.

"Scotland." She trembled ever-so-slightly. "Does it still exist in the twenty-first century?"

"Aye." Grant nodded. "It does." His eyes grew troubled. "Why do you ask?"

Though they had heard about the picture in Jessie's book thanks to Jim, Blair, and Rona, they were surprised to hear Scotland had vanished on Jim's cell phone the next morning.

"That morning never happened, Christina," Jim said. "Not like that." He shook his head. "You had to have been living your own reality in your time loop because when we woke up the next morning, you and Graham had vanished. Again." He offered her a look of reassurance. "No worries though because Scotland definitely still existed."

Relief lit her eyes. "I can't tell you how happy I am to hear that."

"Aye." Adlin offered a wide smile. "See, you really *did* save Scotland by handling the remainder of your time loop so well. Because as Grant said, had you handled it differently, things might have changed in dire ways indeed."

"Well, I'm just glad it worked out." Her eyes warmed as they met Graham's. "More than you know." She looked at the others again as one more thing occurred to her. "So why do you suppose Jessie's cryptic words kept popping up through our journey? Death to those who fly. Death to Scotland."

"I'm afraid that remains a mystery," Adlin replied. "But I strongly suspect it has more to do with Bryce's adventure and mayhap Sven's. 'Twill be them that gets to the bottom of things once and for all." A renewed smile lit his face as he eyed everyone. "Until then, we will rejoice in the fact that Scotland still exists far into the future and that things, no matter how small, do seem to be improving for the better." He nodded, pleased. "So we *are* making a difference."

Everyone agreed, content enough for now to enjoy the reunion. Graham and Christina visited for a little while but not too long. He could tell she was drained from their traumatic experience and could use some rest. Besides, he wanted to spend some time alone with her.

Before they left, however, Adlin took him aside and put his mind at ease.

"The MacLauchlin clan have heard of Kenna's unfortunate outcome," he said respectfully as he met Graham's eyes. "The remainder of the clan is now safely within our castle walls under orders of protection from ye, Cousin. He who would have been their new chieftain had ye married Kenna."

Graham nodded, grateful. "Thank ye, Adlin, but ye should have told them that 'twas ye that saw to their safety."

"Why?" He clasped Graham's shoulder and shook his head. "When 'twas clearly my first-in-command who has all along."

"Why did you never say anything if you knew?" Graham asked softly.

"Because I didnae feel 'twas my place to interfere. I knew well the dynamics between ye, Kenna and Fraser." He shook his head. "'Twas enough that I became chieftain when 'twas clear ye would have welcomed such a position. Not out of a need for power but because ye truly love our people." His eyes stayed with Graham's. "So I suppose in matters of the heart, I wanted ye to remain in charge." His voice grew softer. "I could only protect Kenna so much against the chieftains she was promised to. She needed a marriage alignment with a powerful clan."

"Which you always knew would be ours one way or another," Graham murmured.

"Aye." Wisdom lit Adlin's eyes. "And we both know ye would not have allowed her to be married off to one of our clansmen. Ye cared about her and Fraser far too much to let that happen."

"Aye," Graham agreed, realizing it could have only ever gone the way it did.

"I should go see to her people. 'Tis the least I can do," Graham began before Adlin shook his head and cut him off. "Ye'll do no such thing. The MacLauchlins are well cared for, and ye can visit with them later. Now go see to yer new lass and wee one, aye?"

Though tempted to argue he recognized the stubborn notch of Adlin's chin. He would not budge on his request. Probably for the best considering Christina was waiting for Graham and she needed rest. Not to mention he was eager to see her again though it had been mere minutes.

"Aye, Cousin." Graham embraced Adlin and was about to head off but paused, wondering. "Did ye ever discover who shot that arrow at my ma then?"

"Nay, but 'twas an interesting thing." A twinkle met Adlin's eyes. "Not long after that the arrow vanished but not before several people claimed it glowed first."

"Glowed?" Graham didn't have to consider that long. "Like mayhap a godly sort of glow?"

"Aye, I would say so." Adlin kept grinning. "If I didnae know better I would say Fionn Mac Cumhaill might have verra well been behind it. A means to push Christina to embrace her gift for all to see."

"And, in effect, fuel the continuation of a journey we needed to see through," he murmured. "Not only with each other but with Kenna."

"That would be my guess," Adlin agreed before he ushered Graham along. "Now go be with yer lass, aye?"

"Aye." Graham grinned before he did just that.

"They never did answer my question about who they thought might've left our clothes at Mystery Hill," Christina remarked as she and Graham made their way upstairs a few minutes later.

"Because 'tis likely they dinnae know," he responded. "Any more than we know who provided clothing for us at the tavern on Conall and Lindsay's adventure. Whilst some speculated it might have been Adlin's sister, Iosbail, from the afterlife, others felt it might have been Jessie."

She frowned. "Why Jessie?"

"Because 'tis strongly suspected she was at the tavern that night caring for Grant when he was wounded," Graham reminded. "Though 'tis truly hard to know."

"It sure is," she agreed softly. "Like Grant said, I suppose we'll just have to wait and see how this mystery unravels. In the end, is our friend our enemy or our enemy our friend?"

Graham offered no response but knew she was right. Either way, he had no intention of discussing it anymore right now. He was happier than he imagined possible that *she* was so happy as he showed her his chambers.

Their chambers hopefully.

"Well, where else am I gonna sleep?" she remarked, reading his thoughts as she grinned at him. "I know we didn't plan the whole pregnancy thing, but I was really hoping…"

That's all he let her get out before he pulled her into his arms and kissed the words right out of her. He kept kissing her long and hard, making sure his actions got through just in case his words didn't.

Yet when he said them, he cupped her cheeks, stared into her eyes and made sure she knew just how much he meant them. "I'd never assume or expect you to stay in medieval Scotland because you're carrying my child, lass. 'Tis your right to do as you please." He tilted his head. "But you should know that nothing would make me happier than you staying."

He remained perfectly honest because she deserved it.

"Though I will be around more often than before 'tis important that I continue to help out surrounding clans." He hoped he didn't drive her away with his words. "'Tis important that I dinnae abandon them and hide behind these castle walls."

"I agree," she said readily. "Don't forget how I passed the majority of my time back home."

"Running for charity," he said.

"Right," she replied. "And I don't intend to stop doing that here. I just have to figure out how to put my gift to good use and continue helping those in need."

"Aye," he agreed, proud. "After the birth."

"I'm not sure I said it quite like that."

"But 'tis surely how you meant it."

"I meant it like I said it, Graham." She frowned. "I want to help."

"And you will," he conceded. "I dinnae doubt it."

"Great." She perked up. "So we understand each other?"

He frowned. "We do?"

"*Ye willnae win this argument son*," his father's amused words floated through his mind. "*I have been there, done that.*"

"*Damn straight he has*," his mother's words echoed, just as amused. "*And he never did win that argument.*"

"We will speak of this later, aye, lass?" he murmured to Christina.

"You bet we will, handsome."

His parent's chuckles echoed away as he scooped her up and at long last, brought her to his bed.

"So you'll be staying," he whispered as he came down over her and their eyes held. "You'll remain with me?"

"Of course I'll stay with you," she whispered back, giving him the one word he had been waiting for. "Always."

After that, they forgot all about talking and moved on to much more pleasurable things.

Things born of friendship and the wonders it could lead to.

The country was still in rough shape, but at least it was on the map again. It existed. Loved ones were lost but wouldn't be forgotten. Wrongs had been righted, and famous battles won.

History was once more on track, and everything was *almost* perfect...

"Did I mention I love you, Graham MacLomain?" she whispered in his ear.

There it was. Now things were perfect.

"Aye?" He met her eyes. "'Tis good that."

"I know." She lifted her brows. "What about you?"

He grinned. "You mean ye?"

She met his grin. "No, I mean you."

They laughed as he flipped her and proceeded to show her all night long how much he loved her, his murmured words making her smile.

"Aye, lass, like I said before and will never stop saying, I love *ye*...and I love *you* too."

The End

Coming Soon

Laird Bryce MacLeod will do anything to see Scotland's history saved. Even if it means chasing down Jessie, a twenty-first century lass who might very well be his enemy. What he discovers when he catches her, however, is someone with deep, dark secrets and unanticipated intentions. Hidden truths so remarkable a whirlwind adventure through time begins.

First, they find themselves in league with Angus Óg MacDomhnaill, Lord of the Isles, a noble Scottish captain rumored in some circles to be a pirate. Danger and intrigue abound as they help the Scots capture three English supply ships and deliver their cargo to the Scottish army. As they do and more mysteries are unveiled, attraction ignites and roars to life.

Caught in the throes of newfound passion, they finally join King Robert the Bruce and face off with the English once more at the Battle of Byland Moor. Yet there's another enemy as well. An evil whose sole purpose is meant to test their hearts in a way neither saw coming. An enemy determined to rip Jessie away from Bryce forever. Will the power of love be strong enough in the end? Or will the curse that threatens Scotland be too much to overcome? Find out in *Avenged by a Highland Laird*, the epic conclusion of The MacLomain Series: A New Beginning.

Previous Releases

~The MacLomain Series- Early Years~

Highland Defiance- Book One
Highland Persuasion- Book Two
Highland Mystic- Book Three

~The MacLomain Series~

The King's Druidess- Prelude
Fate's Monolith- Book One
Destiny's Denial- Book Two
Sylvan Mist- Book Three

~The MacLomain Series- Next Generation~

Mark of the Highlander- Book One
Vow of the Highlander- Book Two
Wrath of the Highlander- Book Three
Faith of the Highlander- Book Four
Plight of the Highlander- Book Five

~The MacLomain Series- Viking Ancestors~

Viking King- Book One
Viking Claim- Book Two
Viking Heart- Book Three

~The MacLomain Series- Later Years~

Quest of a Scottish Warrior- Book One
Yule's Fallen Angel- Spin-off Novella
Honor of a Scottish Warrior- Book Two

~Promised to a Highland Laird~

Oath of a Scottish Warrior- Book Three
Passion of a Scottish Warrior- Book Four

~The MacLomain Series- Viking Ancestors' Kin~

Rise of a Viking- Book One
Vengeance of a Viking- Book Two
A Viking Holiday- Spin-off Novella
Soul of a Viking- Book Three
Fury of a Viking- Book Four
Her Wounded Dragon- Spin-off Novella
Pride of a Viking- Book Five

~The MacLomain Series: A New Beginning~

Sworn to a Highland Laird- Book One
Taken by a Highland Laird- Book Two
Promised to a Highland Laird- Book Three
Avenged by a Highland Laird- Book Four

~Contribution to Pirates of Britannia~

(Kathryn Le Veque & Eliza Knight's Series)

The Seafaring Rogue

~Viking Ancestors: Rise of the Dragon~

Viking King's Vendetta- Book One
Viking's Valor- Book Two
Viking's Intent- Book Three
Viking's Ransom- Book Four
Viking's Conquest- Book Five

~Calum's Curse Series~

The Victorian Lure- Book One
The Georgian Embrace- Book Two
The Tudor Revival- Book Three

~Forsaken Brethren Series~

Darkest Memory- Book One
Heart of Vesuvius- Book Two

~Holiday Tales~

Yule's Fallen Angel
+ Bonus Novelette, Christmas Miracle

About the Author

Sky Purington is the bestselling author of over thirty novels and several novellas. A New Englander born and bred who recently moved to Virginia, Sky was raised hearing stories of folklore, myth, and legend. When combined with a love for nature, romance, and time-travel, elements from the stories of her youth found release in her books.

Purington loves to hear from readers and can be contacted at Sky@SkyPurington. Interested in keeping up with Sky's latest news and releases? Either visit Sky's website, www.SkyPurington.com, subscribe to her quarterly newsletter or sign up for personalized text message alerts. Simply text 'skypurington' (no quotes, one word, all lowercase) to 74121 or visit Sky's, Sign-up Page. Texts will ONLY be sent when there is a new book release. Readers can easily opt out at any time.

82526348R00150

Made in the USA
Middletown, DE
03 August 2018